When Life Gives You Gives You
More
Lemons

When Life Gives You *More* Lemons

LORNA BARRETT

POOLBEG

Published 2022 by Poolbeg Press Ltd
123 Grange Hill, Baldoyle
Dublin 13, Ireland
www.poolbeg.com
Email: info@poolbeg.com

A catalogue record for this book is available from the British Library.

ISBN 978178199-487-0

www.poolbeg.com

About the Author

Lorna lives by the sea in West Cork. She finds inspiration in the landscape and the characters there. She lives with her family and her beloved mutt, Lionel.

Acknowledgements

Thank you to Paula Campbell, Gaye Shortland,
David Prendergast and all at Poolbeg

For my beautiful sisters Yvonne and Paula.
Gifts given to me before I was born.

———

Chapter 1

There was a path worn from the big house to Suze's little cottage on the beach in Howth. The tiny house frequently succumbed to WIFI outages due to its position on the edge of the Irish Sea. As a result, she often had to go to Seán's house at the top of the garden to get coverage. Seán made his millions from some internet company he founded. Luckily he had been in Silicon Valley and not in the cottage at the end of his garden when he was working on his start-up.

This time it was Seán who had made the short trek. Suze had invited him for dinner.

"Something smells good," he said when he stepped into the little cottage.

"It's only the barbecue coals so far. I got steaks in the new butcher's. Hope you're hungry."

"I am. Here you go. I brought wine and dessert. I popped down to O'Connors' and got some of their brownies. I know you can't resist." He handed the bottle and paper bag to Suze.

"I really should resist though. I'd say there's thousands of calories in them. Anyway, who cares? They're delicious. Thank you!" She handed him back the bottle. "The opener's in the drawer."

She admired him as he went about uncorking the wine. He looked right at home in her little kitchen even though his bulky frame made the kitchen feel even smaller when he was in it. She mused that he had grown into his looks over the years. His haircut was stylish and while wearing glasses as a teenager made him the butt of many jibes from the other kids, he now looked sophisticated and undoubtedly handsome.

Once he poured them both a glass of wine, he asked what else he could do.

"You can set the table. It's still warm enough to eat outside, I think."

She headed out to the barbecue with the seasoned meat.

Seán got busy taking dishes out of the press and cutlery out of the drawer. He loved these meals with Suze. He wasn't a good cook and would live on takeaway food or boxes of cereal if it wasn't for her frequent dinner invitations.

It was a picture of domestic bliss, Suze thought. Anyone looking in from the outside would assume they were a couple. They weren't and she didn't know if they ever would be. But she liked it when Seán called. She liked the company. It was easy to be with him.

When the steaks were cooked, they both sat at the patio table that sat on a patch of green between Sue's house and the Irish Sea. The waves lapped gently on the shore just a few metres away from them as they ate.

"I was thinking of taking a holiday. Somewhere hot. Before the winter sets in," Seán announced between mouthfuls of steak.

"Oh yeah? That sounds great. Any particular place in mind?"

"South Africa. I've always wanted to go on a safari. We could combine a relaxing holiday with a bit of big game spotting," replied Seán.

Suze stiffened when she heard the 'we'. She saw that Seán noticed.

"I was thinking that maybe you'd come too. You know I'd love it if you were with me."

"Ah, I can't. I'm up to my eyes in work. I've been given a lot more editorial duties lately. Before, I could just take my laptop and answer the 'Dear Suze' letters, but I've to go to London this week for an editorial content meeting. And there's talk of another meeting the following week."

She would have loved a trip to South Africa. She had never been. It was one of the places on her list of must-visit destinations. But she loved her new job more. Especially now that Penny, the editor and founder of Gorge.com, had broadened her brief. She had asked Suze to do a monthly feature on a famous personality. Penny didn't specify who the interviewees would be. That was up to Suze. The readers

3

would want somebody inspiring. Someone who had overcome adversity and made it to the top. Olympic athletes, business leaders, ordinary people with extraordinary stories to tell. Suze was already making up a shortlist in her head.

"Pity. I looked up some hotels around Table Mountain and they look amazing. Some other time, then," he said, disappointment in his voice.

Suze felt bad. Seán was a good man. They had a wonderful time in Venice after attending Joe and Paolo's commitment ceremony in Rome. Seán was a wonderful travelling companion. He had swatted up on all things Italian so was able to point out every landmark and artefact in the city. He spared no expense when it came to their hotel, though of course they had separate rooms for the trip, having just been reacquainted after almost thirty years. They had an *awkward.com* moment one night when after a lot of Bellini cocktails they thought it might be a good idea to have a snog. It wasn't. Suze didn't think that Seán was unattractive, but she wasn't ready for a new relationship. She wasn't sure that she ever would be.

"So can I take it that you're never going to sleep with me?" Seán said without warning.

Suze nearly choked on a forkful of meat. He had always been persistent but never this blunt.

"Seán! I never made any promises. I was always up-front with you. You know I can't move on until Peter does. It's not fair to him."

"What about me? Is it fair to me to keep me hanging on?"

"I'm not. At least not on purpose. I've never made any demands of you. You're a free agent. Go to South Africa. Go wherever you have to go. I can't be what you want me to be right now."

Suze was suddenly mad with him. Why did he have to do this? Why did he have to push things to the limit?

"I'm sorry, Suze, I don't know why I'm being like this. It's just that it's frustrating seeing you every day, wanting to be with you. Do you know how ... Oh God. I'm sorry. Please. Forget I said anything."

But he had ruined things. The silence between them was suffocating. They both played with their food, their appetites deserting them.

Suze wished things were different. She wished she wasn't the cause of Seán's misery. She didn't mind him getting things off his chest. In fact, due to her own history she quite liked it when people did. It beat the hell out of keeping everything inside, waiting for the inevitable explosion to happen someday.

"Seán. I like you. I really do. Maybe someday we will be more than friends but now is not the time." She reached out and squeezed his hand across the table.

She noticed that his smile didn't reach his eyes.

He helped her clean up after dinner. The conversation was stilted and strained. They both knew that a line had been crossed and that their companionable dinners had come to an end. They would both miss them. He said goodnight to her and walked back up the path to his big empty house.

Chapter 2

Suze couldn't shake the feelings of guilt about Seán, even though she had done nothing wrong. She had often wondered if there was a future for them. They had known each other when they were kids and they still got on great together. On paper, they were probably as well suited as many couples out there. Suze worried that she had messed up. Seán couldn't be expected to wait around for her forever. Her phone rang and interrupted her thoughts.

"Mam!"

It was Emma.

"Hello, love. Are you OK?"

"Dad's on the internet."

Why did Emma sound so alarmed, thought Suze? She was glad that Peter was online more. He could barely send an email when Suze lived with him and she had tried to encourage him to get to be more tech-savvy.

"That's good. Isn't it?" she said.

"No. He's *on the internet*. As in, *dating*. Internet *dating*. God, this is mortifying!"

Suze could hear that Emma was almost in tears. Internet dating? *Wow*. This was exactly what she wanted though, wasn't it? She wanted Peter to move on, to hopefully meet somebody new. Then maybe someday she could do the same.

"How do you know? Did he tell you?"

"No, I saw it on his computer. I saw his profile. He has that nice picture of himself up. You know, the one you took of him in Lanzarote a few years ago. He was tanned and he had that white T-shirt on. His hair is all blond and, oh well, you know the one. I wouldn't mind but he looks much different now. Totally different. Some poor woman is going to get the fright of her life when she sees the actual him. It's like fraud."

"Emma! He's not that bad. Or old for that matter."

"And another thing. He's got a MacBook. I mean, I've only got my crappy college laptop and he has a Mac. Where is the justice in that?"

"Your dad has been working for almost thirty years. I think he deserves to buy himself whatever type of laptop he wants." She heard Emma grunt at the other end of the phone. "And he obviously trusts you very much. There aren't many dads I know who would show their daughters their dating profile."

"What? No. He didn't. I was just having a look at his computer when I saw the icon for *beginagain.com*. What a stupid name. I suppose it could be worse. He could be on Tinder."

"You mean he doesn't have a password? You were able to click on it and get in? You'll have to teach your dad how to protect his privacy. He's naïve when it comes to the internet, love." Peter was a latecomer to modern technology and it would take him a while to get to grips with all the pitfalls.

"He had a password. I got it after a couple of goes. PAULEMMA7. People always use their kids' names as their password. Everybody knows that. I reckoned there had to be a number so I put in Eric Cantona's shirt number. God, he's so predictable!"

"You mean you hacked your dad's computer? I can't believe you would do something like that. If he found out, he'd go mad. And I wouldn't blame him. Jesus, Emma."

"Mam. You're giving out to me for guessing a password that a four-year-old could probably guess with the basic amount of information. I thought you'd be outraged that he's on the internet flaunting himself. *Do you not care? I can't believe you're not going ballistic!*" Emma sounded almost apoplectic.

"Emma, your dad is a big boy. He can make his own choices."

"Well, excuse me for caring. I thought you would too. I was obviously wrong."

"Of course I care. I want him to be happy. He deserves it after everything I put him through."

Suze talked the talk but she couldn't get rid of the nagging feeling that she wasn't exactly over the moon that Peter was looking for love with somebody else. She'd need to write this in her notebook and ask her therapist about it at her next appointment.

Emma was still ranting in her ear.

"But what if anybody I know sees him? *What if he ends up dating one of my friends?*" she wailed.

"I know that photograph of him is good but it's not that good. He's a middle-aged man, for goodness sake! I doubt very much if any of your friends are on the lookout for the likes of your dad, so relax. Let him get on with it. And if he does get a date and you happen to be around, make sure he doesn't go out looking like Justin Bieber."

Suze and Emma laughed at the memory of Peter getting dressed up for a work night out, wearing a pair of Paul's jeans that barely buttoned on him. The back pockets were halfway down his legs. Peter had found them in the hot press and mistakenly thought they were his.

"Seriously, Em, let him be happy. And don't log on to his computer again. It's morally wrong. How would you like it if your dad hacked into yours?"

She heard Emma's sharp intake of breath as she said goodbye.

Suze went to her computer and changed her years-old password from PaulEmma74 to something less hackable.

Chapter 3

"Hello." It sounded like someone taking their last breath.

"Sarah?" asked Diane. "It's four o'clock in the afternoon. Are you in bed?"

"I was just having a catnap. I have to sleep when Rosa does."

"You need to hire a nanny," said Diane. She was worried about her friend who had a baby to look after and a busy coffee shop to run.

"What I need is to get a decent night's sleep. At the moment I get three hours if I'm lucky. It's like a form of torture. No wonder the Japanese used sleep deprivation as punishment during the war."

"Well, you were far too old to be having a baby in the first place. You've nobody to blame but yourself."

Sarah had heard how Diane felt about her getting pregnant at their age a hundred times. In principle, she actually agreed with Diane. But now that Rosa was here she wouldn't change her for the world.

"You don't know what it's like. Sometimes it's hard. Like really fucking hard. But most of the time it's great. Ah, forget it. You never liked Rosa in the first place."

"That's unfair. It's not that I don't like Rosa. I don't like babies, period. It's nothing personal. It mystifies me why so many women feel the need to reproduce. Vanity is the only conclusion I can come to. Or idiocy as it was in your case."

"*Ouch!* Don't hold back there whatever you do."

"The truth hurts."

Sarah knew her friend would have a fit if she could see her right now. Sprawled on the couch wearing her pyjama bottoms and a T-shirt covered in spat-up breast milk. But no matter how much Diane couldn't understand Sarah's life, she loved to hear from her. It reminded Sarah that there was a life out there, outside her little cocoon. It reminded her that someday she might maybe even live in that world again.

"Also. Where the hell is Doctor. Tom?" said Diane. "Surely he should be sharing some of the burden with you? He is half responsible for the child."

"We had a fight."

"Again? Oh, for fuck's sake! How you two managed to get it together at all is a mystery. What happened this time?" It blew Diane's mind that a doctor could have unprotected sex and not realise the consequences. The least he could bloody do was show up and do his fair share of the parenting.

"I told him that Joe and Paolo offered to come over for

as long as I need them and take care of Rosa. He hit the roof. He said I was giving them status in Rosa's life that they don't deserve. I mean, I jumped at the chance of having a pair of babysitters I can trust. I've been neglecting everything lately. The house is like Paddy's Market. I couldn't tell you what the turnover in The Bakery has been for the last few months. I was told but I forget now. My head is like mush."

"Tom needs to stop thinking about himself and consider what you need for a change."

"Then he accused me of trying to trivialise his role in Rosa's life."

Diane was about to respond but realised that Sarah wasn't finished.

"He brought up the fact that Paolo was in the labour ward when Rosa was born, *blah blah blah*. That's when I lost it. I told him to get out. Except I didn't say it that nicely. I used the f-word liberally and I threw in a few bastards and bollockses while I was at it. I feel terrible now."

Diane heard Sarah start to cry at the other end of the phone. She could kill Tom. How dare he make Sarah feel bad when she was already at her wits' end!

———

Suze had just opened her laptop to watch *Money Heist*. She cursed when her phone rang but changed her tune when she saw it was Diane calling.

"Hey! How are you?" Suze missed her friend. Things hadn't been the same for the four friends since Diane moved to Marbella and Laurie to LA.

"I'm fine. Which is more than I can say for Sarah. She's a basket case. I'm tempted to hire a couple of guys to take Doctor Tom down a dark alley and give him a good hiding."

"I'll go halves on whatever that costs you," said Suze. "I called to her the other day. She looks a wreck. She was sitting in her chair, breastfeeding Rosa. I was chatting away to her and next thing I knew she was fast asleep."

"We have to do something. Get her some help."

"She doesn't think she needs any. After she fell asleep the other day, I took Rosa, winded her and walked her around the garden for ages to get her to sleep. When Sarah woke up she got all pissed off with me. As if it was my fault that she nodded off."

"She needs a holiday. Away from Rosa and the whole shebang. How about we all go away somewhere? We'll pick some place warm and exotic. Laurie can join us too."

"Oh, that sounds brilliant! Do you think we could actually do it? You know, I'm pretty sure I could take a week off at the end of next month. I'll call Laurie to see if she's free. I don't know about Sarah though. Do you think she'd leave Rosa? She is still breastfeeding."

"She needs to get her off the boob and onto the bottle. We'll give her a month's notice and tell her we're going. Joe and Paolo offered to come over and look after Rosa so she hasn't really got an excuse. God, Suze, imagine if we manage to pull this off? It would be great to be together again. I can see us drinking cocktails poolside in some fabulous resort. We'll be waited on hand and foot and have all of our whims indulged. I can't wait. We have to make it happen!"

Chapter 4

"We're hoping to get away together for a week's holidays. The last week in September. Do you think you can make it?" Suze asked Laurie.

"I'm looking for ideas for a sitcom at the moment. The four of us on a week away will surely supply me with lots of new material. I'm in."

Laurie was excited at the thought of spending a week with her best friends in the world.

"Diane suggested Miami. She's thinking of somewhere that we'll all have to travel the same distance. It's not fair to ask you to fly all the way to Europe from LA."

"Don't worry. Distance doesn't bother me as long as we're all together." Laurie meant it. She loved LA but she missed Suze, Sarah and Diane like crazy. "But Miami does sound wonderful. I could do with getting out of LA for a while."

"Why? Is everything OK? Is Kevin behaving himself?" Suze would strangle Kevin if he was acting the maggot.

"Kevin is treating me just fine. It just feels that life is so fake here sometimes. It feels like I'm living in a dream."

"So you're sure you can tear yourself away for a week?"

"I will make it happen. I can't wait to be with you guys and laugh about things without worrying if I'm going to get cancelled or if what I'm saying is politically correct or not. And let's face it, with Diane it's usually not. And I'll be with people who will stay out past ten o'clock. Jesus, I can't wait."

"Are the people really that boring? To me they just look bloody perfect," said Suze.

"They look perfect but they're mostly dull as shit. I don't think I've had a good belly laugh since I left home. I mean Kevin is funny and all but even he can't make up for all the people who definitely are not."

Laurie found it difficult to describe their LA lifestyle to anyone living outside the bubble. When she talked to her friends she tended to dial down the experience. Kevin was A List. And as a result, Laurie was too. Their lives were a whirlwind of premières, parties and red-carpet events.

The Hollywood experience reinforced the idea that when you've got it all, you get a whole lot more. She still remembered being on the hamster wheel where she wrote columns to get money which barely paid their rent in Dublin. Kevin got small parts and sometimes worked for nothing in the hope of getting a lucky break. Those days were light years away to them now.

16

Kevin had appeared on the *Tonight Show*, the *Morning Show* and every other talk show in America. He was being tipped for awards and everybody wanted him at their parties. Much to Laurie's delight and surprise, he took it all in his stride. When he came home from a day filming, it was just like he was coming home to their old apartment in Malahide. Only their home nowadays was about ten times bigger than they had in Dublin.

They didn't need all of that space, of course. They had it simply because they could afford it. More was most definitely more in Hollywood. There were some of the rooms in the house that Laurie hadn't seen since taking a tour with the realtor. Who needed that seventh bedroom anyhow? They had a pool and a pool house. They could have easily lived in the pool house and still have all the room they needed to live comfortably.

Being Kevin's wife opened doors that Laurie would have thought firmly shut and double-locked to her when she lived in Dublin. He introduced her to a group of writers and next thing Laurie knew she was sitting in a room with some of the most talented writing crop in Hollywood, working on what the studio hoped would be the next big thing. She still felt besieged by imposter syndrome and was constantly trying to prove herself in front of her new peers.

The only blot on the landscape was the difficulty she was experiencing in becoming pregnant. The trying was not the difficult part. The trying was great.

They'd got an appointment with the best gynaecologist

in LA where Laurie had undergone a series of tests. She had sonographs, hystero-sonographs and laparoscopies among other things. The most recent ones she had undertaken were to see if her body was recognising Kevin's sperm as something foreign and was attacking them. She couldn't bear it if that was the case. She couldn't imagine any part of her rejecting and killing any part of Kevin.

The results were inconclusive. Kevin and Laurie fell into the twenty per cent of couples who have unexplained infertility. The doctor had suggested IVF as an option to explore. Laurie and Kevin were still contemplating whether to go for it or not. Kevin wanted a baby just as badly as she did. Laurie knew that he tried to downplay his own disappointment so as not to upset her. He had given her so much and she wanted to give him this one thing that millions of women were able to give their partners without any difficulty whatsoever.

They had so much love to give a child. Kevin would be a great dad. She knew it with one-hundred-per-cent certainty. He would be hands-on. He would change dirty nappies and get up for the night feeds. Kevin would be all in from day one.

Laurie had wanted to tell Suze how miserable she was that she wasn't pregnant but she couldn't say it. She was living the dream and she knew she would sound like a spoiled wagon. She was young, just thirty-four. Her biological clock wasn't on its last legs quite yet. Look at Sarah. She was over forty and she got pregnant. Laurie had a few years to go before that.

Chapter 5

"Diane! What the hell are you doing in Ireland?" Sarah was shocked to see her friend when she answered her front door a few days later.

"You need help and I'm here to give it," said Diane. She gave Sarah a good look up and down.

"I know!" Sarah said. "You don't have to say it. I look like something the cat dragged in."

"I suppose you're busy," Diane said, trying to excuse the state of her best friend. Except that no amount of busy could excuse looking like you haven't washed your hair in a month, but she held her tongue.

"Will you hold her for a minute? I'll go and clean myself up a bit," said Sarah, handing the baby to Diane.

Diane held Rosa at arm's length. As far away from her as she could. The child was dribbling water from her mouth and green globs from her nose. Jesus Christ, she should have come sooner. Surely this wasn't Sarah and Tom's baby. They were both good-looking people. The mixing of their DNA couldn't have resulted in this. Rosa looked more like the offspring of Shrek and Princess Fiona. Diane wondered if there was a possibility their baby was switched at birth.

"She's teething. I know she looks a mess now but she's really gorgeous underneath all that gunk. And her cheeks aren't normally that red either."

Diane couldn't imagine this child ever being gorgeous.

"No, she's *em*, grand," she lied. "You have to take her though. She'll ruin my jacket. I'll tell you what. You hold the baby and I'll tidy up."

Sarah took Rosa. "The place looks bad. I just can't get to the tidying. Rosa won't settle. I can't put her down. She wants to be up in my arms all the time."

Diane wondered again why Sarah kept falling out with Doctor Tom. She needed him to help her look after Rosa. Rosa with the weeping nose and mouth and god knew what else. She was again thankful for not having a maternal bone in her body.

Diane was glad to see baby's bottles on the counter. At least Sarah was attempting to wean Rosa. Maybe there was hope for her friend after all.

"Go upstairs and see if you can get her down. And then get some sleep yourself. You need it. You look like a banshee."

"Fucking hell! Thanks a million."

"I didn't come all this way to bullshit you. I came to try to help you sort yourself out."

"Hey, what about your fugitive status? Won't the police be after you if they find out you're back in the country?" asked Sarah, suddenly freaked out that Diane could be taken away in handcuffs and thrown in prison at any moment.

"James called me last week. He came clean to the police. He told the guards that he forged my signature on the mortgage deeds. Of course there's a chance that he'll face charges for that and for manipulating the bank's share price. He might even go to jail."

"I'm glad he did the decent thing in the end!"

"James was never a bad man. He was in a desperate situation and he reacted by taking desperate measures. I think he's sadder about it than anything he's ever done."

"That's a bit of a turnaround. You couldn't say his name without your blood pressure going through the roof. I'm glad that everything's worked out though. It means you can come home more often and that's a really good thing. I miss you."

Diane missed her friends too but now wasn't the time to get mushy.

"I see I've got a lot of work to do," she said, looking around the chaotic kitchen.

"I know it looks bad but it's mostly surface stuff. It's been a particularly bad week."

Diane could see that Sarah was embarrassed about the state of herself and the house. "It's fine. Five minutes and it'll be shining again which is more than I can say for you. Now go and get some rest. You and Rosa."

"But May will be in from school soon. She'll need something to eat."

"It's not a suggestion, it's an order. May is eighteen. She can make her own food. Now go to bed."

Sarah took Rosa and went upstairs.

Diane could still hear Rosa crying several minutes later. How Sarah wasn't gone off her rocker or at the very least downing a bottle of vodka a day was beyond her. Sarah wanted to do it all. She wanted to be Rosa's food source, May's mum and be the boss at The Bakery. She would have to learn that nobody could do it all, not even the superwoman that she was.

A while later Diane heard the key in the door and then a heavy bag dropped in the hall. May was home.

"Auntie Di! What are you doing here? Wow! The place is so clean." May looked around the kitchen at the gleaming surfaces and clutter-free room. "Where's Mum?"

"Your mum is upstairs. I sent her to lie down but by the sounds of it the, eh, baby is still awake."

"She isn't always this cranky. She's teething. She's normally smiley and happy. You've just seen her at her worst."

Diane didn't look convinced.

"Mum said you don't like Rosa."

"For goodness' sake! It's not that I don't like Rosa. I don't like babies in general. They're like … just … there. They've nothing to say. Nothing to add to anything. But I'm sure I will be as crazy about her as I am about you when she's your age."

May laughed at Diane's staunch defence of her stance on the infant population.

"I'm glad you're here. Mum isn't coping well. She'd, like, totally kill me for saying it, but she does need help. She won't let me do anything because she says that Rosa's not my problem. I don't see Rosa as a problem at all and I don't think it's fair on my little sister to be thought of as a problem either. Mum keeps fighting with Tom even though he's only trying to help. She insists on doing everything herself. We had an au pair but Mum got rid of her."

"Yes, what happened there?"

"She used to cry every night."

"But that's normal for a baby, I believe?"

"No, not the baby –"

"Oh, you mean Sarah! Well, with the baby not settling, I don't blame her."

"No! The au pair. She was homesick and she used to cry so much she'd end up throwing up. Eventually Mum had enough. She booked her a flight back to Madrid and drove her to the airport the next day. She said she doesn't have time to mother another human being right now."

"Poor Sarah. Well, I'm here now so things are going to change. She needs to start taking care of herself."

Chapter 6

Sarah was grateful for Diane's presence. She was grateful for anybody who tried to make her life easier, though she might not always show her gratitude because she was too busy being annoyed with herself for not being able to manage her own domestic situation.

The truth was that it was hard. She hadn't imagined she would have another child. The emotional toll it took on her was almost as much as the physical one. How could she bring a child into the world when the planet was going to hell in a handcart? She had been lucky, no blessed, with May. May was smart and streetwise. Smarter than herself sometimes. A lot of times. She found herself fretting about mad stuff lately. Like would Rosa be bullied in school because her mother was older than all the other mums?

She was worried about her business too. She had taken her eye off the ball. Only for May the whole show would have come crashing down around their ears months ago. Then, in turn, she rewarded May for her hard work by being a terrible mother and even worse boss.

Tom was another subject that Sarah tried to avoid thinking about. He said he wanted to help but it seemed that his "help" always came with conditions attached. As far as Sarah was concerned, he only called to the house to see Rosa and criticise Sarah. There was no doubt that he loved Rosa. He was beyond besotted with his little girl. He was less so with Sarah. He was no longer interested in her as a woman. Who could blame him? Some days it took all she had in her to get dressed and have a shower.

Physically, Tom of course was unaffected by the birth of his child, while she had stitches from her fanny to her arse and she doubted she would ever want to have sex again. Her body was thicker and she feared she would never get back to her pre-pregnancy shape. Tom would find a younger, fitter woman to love and she would remain unlovable and unrideable forever.

Rosa continued to fuss and Sarah rooted in her cot for a stray soother. She was relieved to find it in her blanket. She put it in her own mouth to remove the blanket hairs and then placed it in Rosa's. So much for sterilisers, she thought, as the soother had the desired effect on her daughter. Rosa was a little fighter. She fought sleep at every turn. Thankfully though, sleep was getting the better of her little body now. Sarah felt her relax in her arms and waited a couple more minutes before putting her down in her cot.

She tucked her blanket around her and felt an enormous rush of love for her. She was beautiful when she was asleep. She had her moments when she was awake but her baby's sleeping form always caught Sarah's emotions unaware.

She felt that she should go back downstairs but she knew that Diane would have a fit. She forced herself to get into bed. At first she just lay on the covers but then she got undressed and got in under the quilt. Diane was in her house. Everything was under control.

Diane shooed May off to her room to allow her to finish cleaning the downstairs. She shuddered to think what upstairs was like but at least if anybody called the areas they saw would be shining like a new pin. She felt bad for calling Sarah a banshee and for not wanting to hold the baby but she and Sarah went back a long way. Sarah knew it wasn't personal.

It had felt good to fly into Dublin airport earlier. Diane hated to admit it but she missed being at home. She was making an effort to live like a local in Marbella but the thing she missed most was her friends. OK, they had FaceTime but it wasn't the same. She had decades of shared history with Suze and Sarah and a few years with Laurie.

Things weren't the same, of course. Sarah had taken herself off to another planet and Laurie likewise. Suze was on the mend and forging a career for herself with *Gorge.com*.

Even if Diane was in Dublin, the friends weren't available to each other as they once were.

Then there was Serge to consider. There was no way that he would want to move to Ireland and leave his beloved football team and his other business interests. Diane reckoned the Irish weather would be as much a deterrent as anything else. She was extremely fond of him. She was fully aware that she didn't love him. But she wasn't a falling-in-love kind of gal. She liked him and she liked shagging him. That was enough for Diane.

Diane started to entertain thoughts about bi-locating. Now that the threat of being arrested the minute she got off a plane had dissipated, her imagination ran wild. What if she opened another shop in Dublin? It could be done. She would have to find the right location, of course. A small town or village with an affluent population. Somewhere not a million miles from where she stood now.

Chapter 7

Peter was in his bedroom taking shirts out of his wardrobe and putting them back in again. He wished that Suze was here to tell him what to put on but, then again, if she was here, he wouldn't be trying to figure out what to wear for his date with another woman. A date which was due to take place in a few hours. The blue shirt with the dark-blue tie? Or the red tie? Or no tie at all?

Who knew that getting dressed was so complicated? He had got too thin for his clothes and nothing looked right on him. He was never a dedicated follower of fashion but, even to his untrained eye, he looked terrible. He got into his car and went into town. He'd seen Arnott's bags around the house and imagined Suze had bought him stuff there in the past.

He looked at his watch. It was almost four o'clock. He had time. Not much but enough, he hoped. He parked in the Ilac car park and walked the short distance to Henry Street.

He found the men's department and had a wander around. It seemed to be broken up into different shops. He wasn't expecting that. And so much stuff. Holy Jaysus, he'd never be able to pick out something with all the choice on offer. He didn't even know what size he was.

He almost accosted a sales assistant who was walking by, totally ignoring his presence.

"How'rya! I want to buy some clothes."

The assistant looked around. "Well, you're in the right place." She was about to walk away.

"I don't know what to buy," he said, sounding like a saddo.

"What's the occasion?" she asked disinterestedly.

Peter didn't want to say it was a first date. He knew how pathetic it would sound to a beautiful young girl like her, coming from a middle-aged man.

"Ah, ya know. Just for goin' out for a few pints with the lads," he said. "See, I lost a bit of weight."

She looked at him pathetically anyway.

"Yeah, me wife died." He didn't know why he said that. He wasn't normally a liar but he needed her to help him. He needed her to be completely invested in his quest for better style. He was desperate for her expertise.

To his great surprise, the lie worked. Her attitude switched from total apathy to deepest sympathy, followed by the desired degree of enthusiasm.

"Well, that's far too young for you, no offence," she said, pointing to the logo'd T-shirt that he'd had since he went to an AC/DC concert twenty years before. "You need something more sophisticated at your age. You want your clothes to reflect your personality and your place in life."

Peter hadn't a clue what she was on about but he followed her around as she picked up stuff and held it up to him to check if it was OK.

"What happened to her?" the shop assistant asked kindly.

"Who?" asked Peter.

"Your wife." The *duh* was silent.

"Oh my wife, yeah. She eh, fell off the side of a ship. Yeah, we were on a cruise and she fell overboard. She'd had a few too many bevvies, you know. It was terrible. Terrible."

Peter was crap at lying, he realised. He'd never been on a ship in his life.

"Oh! Was it in the papers?" asked the young girl

"Not here much, but in the Mediterranean it was in all the papers. I don't really like to talk about it though, it brings it all back."

What was wrong with him? Was he crazy? The papers in the Mediterranean? Jesus wept. Why didn't he just say a car crash? Or savaged to death by a rabid dog? Or why didn't he just keep his big mouth shut. But he had to admit it was working. The girl couldn't do enough for him.

He had about a dozen items of clothes in the bags when he left the shop. She had shown him how to mix and match and had told him that the denim blue matched his eyes and that if he was ever ready to date again someday, that he should definitely wear that shirt. *Bingo*. The blue shirt it was.

It was his mates who'd urged him to go online. At first he refused it out of hand. Sure, you only meet weirdos on those websites, he argued. Everyone was doing it, they argued back. The fact that Peter had difficulty finding the "on" switch for a computer was another barrier to meeting his perfect match.

It turned out that his pal Jimmy was doing it. The fact that Jimmy was married to Marie and they had four kids didn't seem to stand in the way of his online activity. Jimmy gave Peter a few tips on how to create a profile and even helped him choose a picture to put up.

He found it in a photo album that Suze had in the sitting room. Jimmy took a photograph of the photograph with his phone and emailed it to Peter's computer. He'd even set up Peter's email account. There was no way that Peter was ever going to be able to do any of that himself.

He felt like he was doing something wrong even though he was a free agent but, to be honest, he wouldn't say no to a ride. But here he was now, after getting a date, and all he wanted to do was to put on his jeans and T-shirt and go down the pub and have a few pints with his mates.

Because that would be easier. He could pretend that Suze hadn't left him and that he wasn't alone. He could banter with the lads about the footie and the endlessly fascinating antics on *Love Island*. But something in his brain told him to go for it. It told him that he had put it all in motion for a reason.

He wasn't suited to the single life. He wasn't made for going it alone. He looked in the mirror again and tried to pick out the positives. He had a full head of hair. And the young one in the shop said he'd nice eyes. That was about it. He hoped that the woman he was meeting, Natasha, wouldn't feel duped when she saw him. His hair was blond in his profile photo but it was greyer now. For all he knew, she could've put up a picture that wasn't anything like she was now too. He hoped not. She looked lovely in her profile.

———————

Peter stood at the bar facing the door. He was nervous but he wanted to wait to get a drink until his date arrived. If she arrived. His palms were sweaty and he felt like throwing up. He turned around and looked at the clock behind the bar for the tenth time since he got there. Five to eight.

She probably would wait until after eight to arrive. She wouldn't want to seem too eager. He wanted to go to the jacks, but he was afraid to leave his spot. What if she came in and he was gone for a slash and she left thinking he hadn't bothered to show up?

He really should've gone out with his mates, he thought. His head wouldn't be wrecked like this if he was with the lads. Even a night in on his own would be preferable to this torture.

Then the pub door opened and she was there. He recognised her from her photo. That was a good start. She gave him a little wave. She recognised him too. Deadly, he thought. That photo was taken four years ago. His confidence started to return by the time he walked towards her and said hello.

"Hi. Peter? I'm Natasha. It's nice to meet you." She smiled and held out her hand to him.

Peter was already on his way in for a kiss on the cheek and he kind of stuttered mid-head-bend and shook her hand too. Awkward!

"It's nice to meet you too. I thought you wouldn't show up and all. Here, let's sit down here. Can I get you a drink?" He hoped his frayed nerves didn't show too much.

"Thanks, I'll have a glass of white wine, please. Sauvignon blanc if they have it."

What? Sovingnone something. Hopefully the bartender would know. She looked nice. She was younger than him, he thought, having a quick sneaky peek back at her. She was also having a sneaky peek at him and they smiled at each other. She had a nice smile. Nice teeth. Her hair was nice. Long and wavy. He sucked in his stomach while he waited for the bartender to serve him. She'd be checking him out. He didn't mind. His new jeans fitted him great around the backside. Well, the young one in the shop said so.

He ordered and the young lad behind the bar knew at once what he wanted when he said Sovingnone white wine. Thank God for that.

As he waited for the drinks he was hoping that, when he turned around, she wouldn't have run off. She was lovely. He couldn't believe it. He had dreams, nightmares really, about going on a first date. They never ended well. He usually woke up drenched in sweat, having dreamed up all sorts of scenarios, the worst being his date turned out to be a bloke. He shivered at the thought of it. No, whatever happened, Natasha was all woman.

But she was still there when he turned around. He couldn't wipe the grin off his face as he carried the wine and a pint of Guinness back to the table.

He sat down and they clinked their glasses.

"I hate these things," said Natasha. "First dates."

"This is my first first date but I get where you're coming from. To be honest, I thought you wouldn't show up. In a way, I hoped you wouldn't and I'd just go home and forget about it."

"Wow! Thanks a million!"

"Ah, no. No. That's not what I meant. I'm delighted you did. I meant that it's easy to stay in your own bubble. Ya know? Never leave your comfort zone. Just go to the pub with your mates. I didn't mean … I …"

"It's OK. I know what you mean."

She had a lovely smile. It was kind of contagious and it made Peter smile too. She took a sip of her drink and asked him what he did for a living.

"I'm an electrician by trade but I started doin' a bit of buildin' contractin' a few years ago. I have a few fellas workin' for me. Mostly house extensions." He had survived the hard years of the recessions and kept his lads on the payroll. He was proud of himself for that. "What about yourself? What do you do?"

"I work for an IT firm."

Oh, that was a problem, Peter thought. There was no-one less IT than himself. He veered off the subject of jobs and began to talk about his family. He knew he was rabbiting on nervously, but she was a good listener and seemed to be genuinely interested when he talked about Paul and Emma like the doting dad that he was.

"Would you like to have another drink or will we head to the restaurant?" he asked.

"We should go. The reservation is for nine, you said?"

They left the pub and went to the restaurant where Peter had made a reservation. They ended up ordering the same things for starter and main course. Natasha insisted that they order different desserts so that they could try a bit of each.

When Natasha held out her fork with a lump of double-chocolate fudge cake on it, he was unsure what to do. Suze never liked sharing her food and said it was unhygienic to use the same fork. Natasha's fork had been hanging in the air for a couple of seconds so Peter had to go for it.

He was totally overthinking it. He imagined his saliva mixing with hers in a way that was far too intimate for so early on, and he went a bit red. To try to overcome his awkwardness and to push the thought of her saliva from his mind, he made a big moaning noise in appreciation of how delicious the chocolate fudge cake really was. A few heads at other tables looked around, making him blush even more.

He looked over and Natasha was laughing at him.

"It's good, but I didn't think it was that good," she said.

"*Aw*, I'm a divil for chocolate," he said, his face returning to its normal colour.

They chatted easily over coffee and suddenly the waiter was dropping the bill and the night had come to an end.

They went outside onto Wicklow Street.

"Would you like to go somewhere else?" He badly hoped that she would say yes.

"Sorry, I can't. I've got to be up really early in the morning. I have a conference call with the Dubai team so I have to be in the office by seven." Standing on her tiptoes, she planted a small kiss on his cheek. Then, looking in his eyes, she said, "I had a lovely night, thank you."

"Me too," he said. "Oh, here's a taxi. You take that. I'll get the next one."

He watched her taxi pull away and decided that he'd walk for a while. His head was buzzing with the possibility that he might see her again.

Chapter 8

The next day at work Peter couldn't stop thinking about Natasha. He didn't want to tell any of his crew that he'd been on a date but all he wanted to do was to talk about her. He wanted to shout it from the rooftops that he had dinner with a beautiful woman. He felt like a teenager all over again.

He kept thinking about the little things they said to each other. She laughed at all of his jokes, which he took as an encouraging sign. Suze had stopped laughing at the things he said a long time ago. She had probably heard it all before. He had probably said it all before too. It was nice to have a new somebody to say stuff to.

She was bleedin' gorgeous. He was still stunned that she hadn't made some excuse during the night to leg it. She had a great figure and her hair and make-up were lovely too. She was like one of those posh birds you see on the television. He was hit by a barrage of doubts then. Why would a smart, well-groomed, good-looking woman be bothered with him? Was she just being polite when she laughed at his jokes? Was she just being polite staying out long after would have been acceptable for a first date? Was she just being polite when she kissed him on the cheek before she got into the taxi and looked into his eyes and told him she had a really lovely night?

Jaysus, this was torture. He was better off when he was on his own, not havin' to wreck his head with all this dating stuff. He had got over the pain of Suze leaving him and he was used to being on his own. Why didn't he just stick to being by himself instead of opening himself up to rejection and ridicule and all this self-doubt?

God, but imagine if she turned out to be worth it? Imagine if she was "The One". He needed to go for it even if it scared the life out of him. He took out his phone and decided to send her a text.

"Hiya. Thanks for a great night last night. Hope we can do it again sometime soon. Peter."

He wondered about putting in a smiley face or some other emoji. Or an 'x'. Nah, he decided against it. He was too old for that carry-on. That was only for the young ones, so it was. *Send.* He stared at the phone, willing it to vibrate.

Natasha's phone beeped on the desk in front of her. A text alert. It was from Peter. She was surprised at how glad it made her. She replied immediately. **"Yes, would love to. Call me."** *Send.* She hoped it didn't sound too dismissive, like: 'Call me. Sometime. I'm not too bothered.' She was bothered. She wanted to see him again. She had thought about him while she was getting ready for bed last night and would have liked nothing more than if he had been in it.

She liked him. She had been out on a few dates since she joined *beginagain.com* and Peter was the first 'non-creepy' man she'd met. The first few were a disaster and she had decided before the date that if Peter turned out to be as bad, then she'd give the whole online-dating thing a wide berth in future.

Her life was great as it was but she missed having that special somebody. A special someone would be the icing on an already pretty amazing cake. The men she had relationships with hadn't made any lasting impressions on her. The sex was fine but she never seemed to want to see any of them outside the bedroom. She didn't want them hanging around reading the papers on a Sunday morning or holding hands with her strolling through Stephen's Green.

The thought of growing old on her own depressed her. Her career wasn't going to keep her warm at night forever. What she hadn't told Peter was that she was Vice President of Operations for Europe and the Middle East for iBuy, one of the biggest electronic payments companies in the world. Men were sometimes put off by successful women. No, that wasn't exactly correct. All the men she had met were either turned off or were threatened by her success.

In the business world, she was usually more successful than they were. She decided that she didn't want to scare Peter away. He was sweet and had a really lovely, honest quality about him. She could sense a vulnerability about him too. He reminded her of her brothers. Down to earth, good craic, honest-to-god fellas. She had met all sorts of men over the years but she found that she couldn't make that connection with them. Their backgrounds were so very different to her own. She was flying so high in her career that she felt she needed an anchor. Someone to keep her connected to her true self. Even after meeting him only once, she felt that Peter might be that someone.

Her girlfriends were married with kids and they lived totally different lives. She loved her friends but found she had very little in common with them nowadays. Their lives were filled with orthodontist appointments, football practice and ballet classes. They found it hard to empathise with Natasha.

To them, she had it all. She wondered if her friends thought that it served her right that she didn't have a man in her life because she seemed to have so much else. She had her own house in Dublin and an apartment in Dubai where iBuy's Middle East office was. She travelled first class to meetings and to fabulous holiday destinations around the world.

She spent on shoes what her friends spent on their mortgages. She had a wardrobe that would put Kate Middleton to shame. When they looked at her, they couldn't hide their envy for the things she had. To top it all, she didn't even go to the gym. She managed to maintain her slim figure thanks to her hectic schedule. That was probably the thing that annoyed them the most.

Yet they all still made an effort to keep the friendships they had since childhood alive. She visited them and listened to how stressful their lives were and how shattered they were all the time, trying to juggle work and family life.

Their husbands floated in and out, completely unmarred and unscarred by having kids. They didn't have to take big tranches of time off work or sabotage their careers when the babies came along. They didn't have to beat themselves up because their bodies were never going to be the same again. Sometimes Natasha felt she was more male than female. A male with great boobs and a great ass, but a male nonetheless.

Her phone rang then.

It was him. He didn't mess around, she thought as she picked up the phone.

———

Peter could hardly believe she had answered.

"Hi, it's me. How are you?" he asked.

"I'm good, thanks. You?"

"Brill." He hesitated, then went for it. "I was putting on a roof this mornin' but I couldn't concentrate on it. I got one of the young lads to take over. In case I fell off."

41

"Sounds dangerous. Why can't you concentrate?"

He could hear the smile in her voice. She was teasing him.

"Because I keep thinking about you. Your eyes. You've got lovely eyes. I wanted to tell you that."

"Thank you, Peter. You have too. The shirt you were wearing last night really picked up on the colour blue."

He felt totally vindicated for telling the shop assistant that his wife fell off a ship. It was the best lie he had ever told.

"How about another night out? Dinner? The pictures? The theatre even?" He hoped she didn't want to go to see a play, he'd be bored out of his bin. But if it was something she wanted to do, he'd suffer through it for her.

"You know, a movie sounds great. It's a long time since I've seen one. In a cinema, I mean. I'm not free until Saturday. How is that for you?"

"That's great. You pick the film. Even if it's one of those chick-flick things, I won't mind. I'll try not to start cryin' if it's a sob story!" he said, laughing.

She was laughing too. "Great. I'll pick an action movie, just to be sure there's no tears. See you Saturday."

"Saturday," he said and hung up the phone.

"*Yes!*" he said out loud as he put his phone back in his pocket.

The lads looked at him.

"Wha? Get back to work."

Chapter 9

"We're going to West Cork." Suze was in charge of telling Diane about the change of plan for their holiday. "Instead of Miami."

"I'm sorry! I mustn't have heard you properly. I thought you said we were going to West Cork instead of Miami," said Diane.

"I did. We are. Sarah doesn't want to go abroad in case there's any kind of emergency," said Suze, somewhat relieved that they were on FaceTime and not in the same room.

Diane rolled her eyes. Jesus, her dislike of tiny humans was increasing at an alarming rate. "What kind of emergency do you think is going to arise, Sarah? There are going to be three grown men looking after Rosa. And one of them happens to be her father. So because you don't trust three adults to take your place, you're proposing we spend our precious week together in the back of the beyond?"

Sarah looked like she was going to cry but Diane thought it was time for some tough love. Sarah, her friend, had disappeared someplace and Diane wanted her back.

"That's a bit harsh. She just doesn't feel comfortable not being in the same country as her baby at the moment," said Suze, trying to calm the situation.

"Can you not talk for yourself now?" asked Diane, looking at Sarah who was almost cowering behind Suze's back.

"I asked Suze to tell you because I was afraid of what you'd say. And I was right, by the way. I knew you'd go ape. You've no idea what it's like to have a baby so don't stand in judgement. I'm trying to be the best mother I can. I'll tell you what. You guys go to Miami or Havana or wherever. I won't go. I didn't even want to go in the first place. I only agreed because you bullied me into it."

"Oh no, you bloody well don't! You don't get out of a girl's week away just like that. You are going, miss. And what's more you are going to bloody well enjoy it."

"Oh yeah, cos it sounds like it's going to be so much fun," said Sarah sarcastically.

Diane rarely looked at things from other people's perspectives but she tried to think about Sarah's feelings. She started to back down.

"I suppose there must be a five-star hotel down there where we can stay. Somewhere with a spa."

Sarah made a face at Suze, willing her to tell Diane just what their plans for somewhere to stay were.

"There are no five-star hotels. Not where we're going

44

anyway. Only a handful of AirB&Bs. Anyhow, we're going to stay in Joe's mother's home place. Her brother died and didn't make a will, so it was left to her. She doesn't want it and asked for it to be put up for sale. Sarah would like to see it before it's gone out of the family for good."

Suze knew Diane wouldn't like that plan at all.

"I beg your pardon? My ears are definitely playing up. I thought you said we were staying in a house that your mother-in-law lived in a hundred years ago."

"She's only seventy-eight," answered Sarah.

"Are you both trying to wind me up? What about Laurie? She'll have to travel thousands of miles to slum it in some rundown house in the middle of nowhere!"

Diane was sure that playing the 'Laurie the Hollywood wife' card would make them see sense. What started out as a heavenly break away with turquoise seas and white sand was turning into a nightmare.

"Laurie is fine with where we're going. She doesn't care where we go as long as we're together," said Sarah defiantly.

"Laurie knows? What? Did you call her on the sly and get her on board, knowing then that I couldn't say no without sounding like a complete cow?"

"Something like that," said Sarah.

"*Fuckers*," said Diane, repacking her bags in her head. She could forget about the flip flops and bikinis she had packed. She could forget about sarongs and big floppy sunhats. She could forget about the fabulous sundress that she had just got into stock and was flying out the door in her boutique in Marbella. It looked like she was going shopping for wellies and a wax jacket.

"I'm sorry, Diane. I know I've hijacked your week. I promise that next time I'll go anywhere you choose on the planet. I'm sure that nothing will happen to Rosa but I'm worried about Tom being in Joe's and Paolo's company. I'm not sure how they're all going to get along."

Sarah had to allow all three men look after Rosa in her absence. Tom was dead set against leaving Rosa with Joe and Paolo as he felt that his position was being diminished by giving Joe and Paolo responsibility for her. Sarah's head was melted with all the goings-on so she told them all to come and mind Rosa.

Tom would be staying in the spare room in Sarah's house and Joe and Paolo would stay with Joe's mother. Joe and Paolo would mind Rosa while Tom was at work. Tom had reluctantly agreed to share the duties when it was obvious to him that Sarah wasn't for turning on her decision.

She had weaned Rosa by now and the pain in her boobs was getting less and less. She was no longer oozing milk and she'd even lost a couple of pounds in the last few weeks. The past year had been tough on her mind and even tougher on her body.

When she had May it didn't knock a feather out of her. Nearly seventeen years later at the grand old age of forty-three, it knocked the stuffing out of her completely. It came like a juggernaut and kept rolling. Sometimes reversing over her and driving off again.

How women *chose* to have babies at this age baffled her completely. She couldn't wait for Rosa to be May's age. And the poor little mite wasn't even one yet. There was a lot of living to happen between now and then. For both of them.

"You owe me big time," said Diane. "Both of you. What the hell are we going to do with ourselves in Ballygobackwards?"

"We can go for walks. We can read books. I don't know the last time I actually finished a book," said Suze excitedly.

"Read a book? Oh, how thrilling! Well, I can tell you this for nothing – I didn't take a week out of my hectic schedule to read a fucking book!" fumed Diane.

"Oh relax, Di. It'll be just the four of us. It's going to be fun. Now stop giving out about it and slap on a bloody smile for everybody's sake," ordered Suze.

"It's all my fault. I mean it. My life is just one big disaster. You should all go without me. I'll probably be so wrecked that I won't be any fun," said Sarah, tears filling her eyes.

"That never stopped you going anywhere before," said Diane.

"Hey, you two. Give it up. That's just mean, Diane. And, Sarah, your life is not a disaster. You've got two beautiful daughters and lots of support from the people in your life who love you. So stop feeling sorry for yourself. Let people help. Let them figure it out."

"Fair play, Suze. No wonder that column of yours is famous," said Diane.

Sarah was sobbing now. Jesus Christ, would someone please give us back the real Sarah, thought Diane. The funny,

47

ditzy Sarah who used big words in the wrong context. The Sarah who saw the fun in every situation. The Sarah whose kindness oozed from every part of her.

"Thanks, Suze. Thanks, Diane. I promise I won't cry while we're on holidays. I'll get my shit together, I really will. You've no idea what spending time with you all means to me!" And she started to cry all over again.

Chapter 10

The stretch limo rolled up to the arrivals at Dublin Airport. Diane had organised the car and a driver for their trip. There was no way she was travelling on public transport or squashing herself into a hire car for four bloody hours with Suze at the wheel. She was still trying to get over the fact that their holiday destination was West Cork instead of Miami. She'd brought a case of champagne to ease her disappointment and their journey.

First stop was Dublin Airport. Laurie's flight had touched down and they hopped out of the limo and into the arrivals hall to wait for their friend.

"We should be in the departures lounge right now, you know," Diane said under her breath to Suze.

"Zip it," warned Suze, running her fingers across her mouth. "We've been over this a hundred times. Look at Sarah, she's relaxed and happy. Don't set her off again."

Diane looked over at Sarah standing expectantly at the rail, waiting for the first sighting of Laurie. She did look good. Her hair was still in need of some kind of proper cut, but she looked a lot better than a few weeks ago. Anyway, nobody would be looking at them where they were going. Diane couldn't even manage to find Ballygra on a map. Sarah's squeals brought her out of her thoughts.

"*Laurie! Laurie! Over here!*"

They all strained their necks to see their beautiful friend coming through the doors.

"Oh my God, she looks amazing!" said Sarah.

"Even more gorgeous than before," said Suze.

"Fuck me," said Diane. How the hell did she always look so perfect?

"Is that chap bothering her?" said Sarah.

There was a guy leaning into Laurie, almost in her face. He was wearing a hoodie with the hood up and the string tied tightly so his face couldn't be seen fully. He looked like a scanger and Sarah was worried that he was trying to rob her.

Sarah looked at Suze and Diane and they seemed worried too. Surely the security guards at the airport should be on the alert for this sort of thing. Laurie had flown in first class so she should get first-class treatment all the way through the airport.

Sarah looked around to see if there was anybody who could help her or else she was going to jump the barrier herself and run to her pal's aid.

Then Laurie was standing in front of them. The guy was actually linking her arm with his.

Sarah tried to hug Laurie but it was difficult to do with another person hanging off her. "Do you know there's a guy attached to your arm?" she said, ignoring the guy and kissing Laurie.

"And he's crying," said Suze.

They had no idea what the hell was going on. Laurie did have a habit of picking up waifs and strays. She was talking about moving out of LA, buying a ranch and rescuing abandoned animals. That was mad, but this was ridiculous.

"Yes. He's been crying since we left LAX. He did fall asleep for a few minutes somewhere over the Atlantic. Look, I'll explain later. It's so great to see you. I missed you all so much. I can't wait to spend the week catching up and hearing all the gossip."

"I'm sorry but I just can't ignore the fact that there's a grown man crying on your arm. What's going on and where are you going to put him?" said Diane in her usual direct manner.

"*It's Jesus Martinez,*" said Laurie in a whisper, using the correct Spanish pronunciation of his name: *Heysoos.*

Suze and Diane gaped at her.

"Let's go – hurry," said Suze.

A number of paparazzi had noticed Laurie in the airport and were trying to get a picture of her. Laurie didn't care if they got a photograph of her but she certainly didn't want them to recognise Jesus, who was one of Hollywood's newest stars. He'd already starred in a couple of movies and had all the credentials to be a real superstar.

51

"Right, we're parked right outside the door," said Diane, rushing them all back to the waiting car.

"What are we going to do with him?" asked Suze. Jesus was still crying and she could see snot on the shoulder of Laurie's soft leather jacket.

"Could you drop him to your mother's?" asked Diane.

"Diane, I can't leave this piece of emotional wreckage with my poor mum," said Laurie, disregarding the fact he could hear her. "I'm sorry but we're going to have to take him with us."

They all looked at the snivelling man-child still holding on to Laurie for dear life.

"Jesus Christ. You could've brought Rosa after all. What's another crying baby between friends?" said Diane to Sarah.

"Are you kidding? No way! The only thing I have to do for the next week is have as much fun and drink as much champagne as I can," said Sarah, holding up one of the glasses provided, waiting for someone to pour.

"Good grief!" said Diane. This was definitely not the start to the week she had imagined.

The driver pulled out of the line of traffic and onto the motorway.

"Here. Hold my glass too, Sarah. I knew I'd need a drink but I didn't think I'd need one before we got outside the bloody airport."

"Am I missing something, Laurie?" asked Suze. "What are you doing with Jesus Martinez? Or, rather, what is he doing with you? Forget the fact that he's crying like a baby.

Why is he here at all?" She knew of Jesus Martinez through her work on *Gorge.com*. He was featured in one of their Hot/Not articles and he was unsurprisingly top of the Hot list.

"He was in a movie with Kevin a few months back and they're like best buds now. He calls over to the house and they just hang out playing video games. They're like a pair of kids. Anyway, Jesus called Kevin the night before last in floods of tears. We thought that somebody had died, he was so distraught. Kevin couldn't get any sense out of him on the phone so he went over to his house. When he got there, the house was in flames and the fire department had just arrived. Jesus had no idea what was going on so Kevin took him home to ours."

"Oh my God. What did happen?" said Suze.

"His girlfriend broke it off with him," said Laurie. "That's all we know. He went out and got shitfaced. He came home and next thing he knows his bedroom is on fire."

He was wailing now. By this time, Laurie had almost forgotten he was there, despite the fact that he had her arm in a death-grip. More snot left his nose and rested on her shoulder. She would ditch that jacket as soon as she got to their destination but for now it was the only thing between his bodily fluids and her bare skin.

"He must have really loved her," said Sarah, feeling sad for the poor guy.

This set him off again, so they tried to change the subject.

"So, how is Kevin?" asked Diane.

"Kevin's good," said Laurie simply.

Her friends knew that he was more than good. He was one of the coolest guys on the planet and he was married to their friend.

"You know, you don't have to underplay things," said Diane. "We're your friends."

"Yeah, we're already totally jealous of you – so feel free to bring us to the point of thinking our lives are completely shit by comparison," said Suze.

"Tell us what it's like to be married to man who's more fabulous than Brad Pitt," said Sarah.

Laurie laughed but she knew it was true. At least the three women were honest enough to admit it. Others were jealous of her. Some people she had considered her friends had completely cut off all communication with her because they just couldn't stand the fact that she had it all.

"OK, it's pretty fucking amazing," she said as Jesus clung harder to her.

"Do you want to swap places?" offered Suze.

"I'd love to, please," said Laurie trying to extricate herself from Jesus' grasp. He was having none of it and Laurie had to stay put.

Diane put a glass of champagne into her free hand, which made the fact of having a grown man attached to a part of her easier to bear.

The crying stopped all of a sudden and they all held their breath.

He was asleep.

"Thank God for that," said Sarah.

"He's exhausted himself," said Laurie.

"Good, I was going to have to slap him if he didn't stop making that racket," said Diane.

"So now he's asleep, tell us what's going on," urged Suze.

"Well, as I said, Kevin went over and his house was on fire and Jesus was stumbling around the place. He was completely wasted. He'd been at a nightclub and we reckon he did more than drink. Maybe cocaine. Anyway, it turns out that Maria, his childhood sweetheart, the love of his life, called him up from Mexico and told him that it was over. She said she was in love with someone else. The someone else turns out to be Jesus' best friend Raymondo. The poor guy had a complete meltdown. He and Raymondo were like brothers. It was like the biggest betrayal ever. He just lost it."

"So how did his house go on fire?" asked Diane.

"Kevin doesn't know. The fire department were checking the place to find out what started it. It could've been a cigarette or maybe an electrical fault. Jesus was in such a state he'll probably never remember what happened. It was lucky that he didn't pass out and go up in flames with the rest of the house. Anyway, Kevin's away filming and I couldn't leave him at home alone. He's too fragile and I'd be worried sick that he'd do something stupid, if you know what I mean. Or set fire to our house."

The women looked at the now sleeping Jesus and started to feel bad for him. They were less annoyed about his snivelling all over Laurie's jacket.

"I bet she was beautiful. His girlfriend, I mean," said Suze.

"I think he has a photograph of her in his pocket. He kept taking it out on the flight and kissing it," said Laurie, gently fumbling in his pocket, trying very hard not to wake him in case he started up again.

"Here it is," she said.

They all leaned in to see what kind of beauty had captivated Jesus. They all stared at the picture.

"Is that a moustache?" asked Diane after studying the photograph for a few moments.

"No, it must be the light. She looks quite dark-haired anyway," said Suze. She rummaged in her bag for her glasses.

"Here, Sarah. You've got good eyesight. Have a look at this."

Sarah, who was normally so kind and considerate of other people's feelings, had drunk a glass of champagne and it had gone straight to her head.

"*Yikes*, that's one hairy upper lip alright! She looks like one of those East German shot-putters in the Olympics years ago."

They all stifled nervous laughs as Laurie tried to put the photo back in Jesus' pocket. The gorgeous man under the hoodie had been crying like a baby over an ugly girl with facial hair.

Chapter 11

The journey wasn't as awful as Diane had anticipated, thanks in no small part to her idea of hiring the luxury car. Having a Hollywood movie star with them only served to make it more interesting. They left the motorway and the driver was forced to slow down. They passed little towns and villages which they *oohed* and *aahed* over, out their darkened windows.

"When was the last time you were here?" Suze asked Sarah.

"Me? I was never here. Granny O'Hara hated the place. She couldn't bear the countryside and the darkness. She never brought Joe to visit and he never brought us."

"You mean we're all going on a holiday to a place that you've never actually been to?" Diane could feel herself getting annoyed all over again. She ordered herself to be calm and think only happy thoughts.

"I never said I'd been here. I only suggested it because I

could kill two birds with the one stone. I'd have had to go and see the house at some other stage if not now. *Aw*, Diane, don't get mad again. We'll have a great time. Ballygra means 'town of love', you know.

"You don't mean to say!" Diane growled.

"*Down to Lovetown*," sang Sarah, trying to sound like Barry White but, being a small white woman, didn't quite pull it off.

Diane snorted and Sarah poured more champagne into her glass. This seemed to have the required calming effect.

———

At last, the car pulled to a halt.

"This is it," the driver said, pressing a button and lowering the screen between him and his passengers.

"This is what exactly?" asked Diane.

"This is as far as the car can go. The house is up that lane but it's too narrow for this machine."

Suze decided to interject before Diane throttled him. "That's fine. We'll get our things and walk the rest of the way. It's not that far, I'm sure."

Suze looked at Sarah. Sarah shrugged her shoulders. She actually had no idea how far it was. The narrow lane was tree-lined with grass growing up the middle.

"For Christ's sake," muttered Diane.

The driver handed them their bags out of the boot. Diane regretted bringing the third bag. She only had two arms to wheel the first two. The bloody driver wasn't much help. He didn't offer to help them with any of their luggage and she was buggered if she was going to ask him. His non-offer would be reflected in his tip.

Laurie had only one bag with her. That girl knew how to pack. She had flown from LA with just one suitcase and a hold-all bag. Diane would have to ask her how she did it.

The driver took out the remnants of the case of champagne and left it beside them at the end of the lane. He could fuck right off, thought Diane. There now would be no tip at all.

The pathetic mess that was Jesus was looking around like a lost child and Diane felt a huge urge to slap him. In fact, she took a step towards him but luckily Suze was taking charge of the situation.

"Hey, Jesus! Why don't you take some of the bags like a good man?" She indicated the bags strewn around the lane.

"Where are we?" he asked Laurie.

"*Em* … we are … well ... Where are we exactly, Sarah?"

"We're in Ballygra. On Ireland's most southerly tip. Apart from that I haven't a feckin' clue."

Jesus picked up as much as he could and started to walk up the lane. He was their little mule and he had even managed to carry the case of champagne. He was a strapping lad and the beauty of his muscular frame wasn't lost on the women who admired him as they followed him.

"That goddamn driver," grumbled Diane as they rounded another bend with no house in sight. "I did pay him to take us to our destination and he only bloody well brought us halfway."

"There's no way he could've got it up."

"That's what he said last night!" said Sarah who was still giddy from the champagne.

"Yeah, *haha*, very juvenile," said Suze, laughing despite herself.

She loved being with her friends. She hoped that Jesus being with them wouldn't ruin their fun. In fairness, the guy had said hardly a word and maybe he would spend the week in silence. He was very pleasing on the eye, tall and dark with smouldering green eyes. Suze supposed it wouldn't be any great hardship to look at him for seven days.

They plodded on up the lane. Just as it got too dark for them to see Jesus' outline, they were at the house. A fine sizeable house. No rundown cottage at all.

Sarah fumbled in her bag for the keys. She eventually emptied out the contents of her handbag onto the front steps and they all used the torches on their phones to try to find them. There was a soother, baby wipes, tissues, old dried-out make-up, teething gel, condoms (too late) and no keys.

"Well, there ye are! Welcome to the O'Neill residence," said an old woman who suddenly appeared at the door.

"Oh hello. Yes, here we are. Who are you?" said Sarah, standing up and leaving the debris from her handbag on the ground.

Suze groped around in the dim light and stuffed everything back into Sarah's handbag along with a few little stones from the gravel driveway.

"I'm Mrs. Celia Murphy and I'm pleased to meet you. I worked here with the late Mr. O'Neill, may he rest in God's Holy Peace," the woman said, blessing herself at the same time. "I heard ye were coming and I wanted to make sure the house was ready for ye. Oh, there's a man too. I thought it was just four ladies." She peered at the wreck that was Jesus. "Is he alright?"

"Oh yes, he's fine. Jet lag is all that's the matter with him. He was a last-minute surprise addition," said Sarah, not wanting to go into it with Mrs. Murphy as she really didn't know what he was doing there herself.

"Well, come on in out of it, will ye?" Mrs. Murphy stood aside and let them all in. "What were ye doin' comin' up that oul' boreen? Everybody uses the driveway around the back."

"Driveway?" said Suze. "Oh. We didn't know there was one."

Diane cursed the driver again under her breath. Her designer luggage was in rag order after coming up that lane. The tiny Louis Vuitton wheels were made for gliding over highly polished marble not being horsed up a bumpy lane with grass growing up the middle of it.

"Oh, it's lovely," said Sarah, sobering up slightly. "I was expecting some place cold and unlived-in but this is really gorgeous."

The others agreed. The hallway was wide and long with rooms off either side. The antique furniture was in keeping with the Georgian era of the house. It reminded them of a boutique hotel.

"There's a fire lit in the drawing room there for ye now. Sit down and I'll bring you all in a nice cup of tea."

Mrs. Murphy bustled out.

"Is she staying to look after us?" said Diane. "I'd like her to. It'd be nice to have somebody to wait on us hand and foot. It would take the sting out of being on holidays in the wilds of West Cork."

"I don't think so. Granny O'Hara did say that the house would be all ready for us when we arrived but she didn't say anything about anyone staying on."

"Pity. I wonder if we could pay her to stay?" asked Diane.

"I think we'll manage to look after ourselves, Diane. Some of us actually do it all year round," said Suze.

"I think we're going to be really happy here," said Laurie. "I can feel it. There's something special about this place."

After supplying tea and countless rounds of what she called *hang-sangwiches*, Mrs. Murphy showed them all to their rooms. There was no room for Jesus so it was decided that he would sleep on the couch downstairs. He was like a baby in a man's body and Laurie was able to lie him down on the couch and throw a quilt over him. He was totally compliant and did as he was told like any good little boy would do.

They said goodnight to Mrs. Murphy and they all made their way up the stairs to bed. The catch-up would start in earnest tomorrow.

Chapter 12

"Mrs. Murphy! Have you been here all night?" asked Diane, padding into the kitchen in her bare feet. She'd thought she was the only one awake and was going to make tea and wake up the girls with a cuppa in bed.

"Sure I said I'd come over early and make sure you had everything you need. I have the rashers on. You'll have a bit of pudding with that, will you?"

Diane had thought that Mrs. Murphy was asking her, but she was addressing the almost naked Jesus who was already at the kitchen table and nodding in response, though he couldn't possibly have understood what he was agreeing to.

"Jesus here was up and about when I arrived," said Mrs. Murphy pronouncing his name in the more traditional Catholic fashion instead of the Spanish pronunciation. "I couldn't catch a bit of what he was saying so I asked him to write his name down."

"*Heysoos*," said Diane.

"Ah sure, he doesn't mind a bit what I call him."

Jesus got up and walked back into the sitting room where he had slept.

"Why is he only wearing a towel?" asked Diane, a bit discombobulated by the sight of the dark muscly Hollywood actor. He looked like somebody had drawn him. Christ, those pecs! How was Mrs. Murphy able to concentrate on rashers with him in the kitchen?

"His clothes are in the washing machine. The poor laddeen said he didn't have time to pack anything. 'Tis a pity that someone wouldn't let the boy put some clothes in a bag. I'll go into town later and get him some things. I don't know if the menswear shop will have anything as fancy as they have in America but I'm sure I'll be able to get him something anyway." She turned the rashers and black pudding in the pan.

"Maybe you shouldn't get him any clothes. He looks fine without them," said Diane, winking at Mrs. Murphy.

"You're not wearing much yourself," the old woman said disapprovingly. She looked at Diane who was wearing tiny cotton shorts and a tinier T-shirt.

What did the old woman expect her to wear to bed? A long flannelette nightie?

The smell of Mrs. Murphy's breakfast cooking on the old range must have wafted upstairs because Suze, Sarah and Laurie arrived into the kitchen within minutes. Jesus also reappeared. There was a lovely, homely feeling in the room and Mrs. Murphy stayed at the frying pan and continued to cook rashers, sausages, black pudding and eggs until everyone was fit to burst.

She fussed over Jesus as if he were a little boy and too helpless to do anything for himself. She just stopped short of cutting up his food and spoon-feeding him. At least Laurie was able to relax, knowing that somebody else was looking after her charge.

"There was some reporter fella down in the village last night on the lookout for himself," said Mrs. Murphy, pointing at Jesus with a greasy spatula.

"But how did they know? You're the only person we met since we got here," said Sarah, hoping Mrs. Murphy didn't think she was accusing her of ratting them out.

"They knew all about Mrs. Flynn and Jesus appearing at the airport yesterday," said Mrs. Murphy, making it sound like some religious episode. "I don't know how they knew about it. We don't get too many famous people here at all, at all."

"The driver! It's because I didn't tip him. The bloody snake!" said Diane.

The others agreed that it probably was indeed the driver as nobody else in the world, including themselves, knew that Jesus was coming to Ireland in the first place.

"There's a great bit of excitement around but don't worry – we'll throw them off the scent."

"We'd appreciate that, Mrs. Murphy," said Laurie. "He's in a kind of delicate state. The last thing he needs is a load of paparazzi following him around."

Jesus had been catapulted from obscurity to world fame and Laurie was certain he wasn't the most emotionally stable person on the planet right now.

"They're just as interested in you, Mrs. Flynn," warned Mrs. Murphy.

"I can look after myself, so don't worry about me. And it's Laurie, by the way."

Sarah stayed back with Mrs. Murphy to help her clean up after breakfast.

"You don't have to do this. We'll be able to look after ourselves. I feel bad that you're making us breakfast and cleaning up as well."

"*Ara*, sure I've been looking after Mr. O'Neill here and, to be honest, I miss it. I miss having somebody to fuss over. Even though he hated when I fussed too much."

"I'm sorry that we didn't ever come to visit him. My mother-in-law didn't like the country very much, I'm afraid. It's odd but she hardly ever mentioned Eddie. Strange because he was her only sibling, her only family left really."

"Well, he was a hard man to like and that's for sure. And he wasn't kind to Sheila at all, at all," said Mrs. Murphy, calling Granny O'Hara by her first name.

Sarah thought it was odd hearing her mother-in-law being referred to as Sheila, like she was actually a person in her own right.

"He was as odd as two left feet. I was probably the only poor eejit who'd put up with him and his ways. I thought he'd marry me, you see. I thought he was going to ask me any day so I kept coming to clean his house and cook his meals. By the time I realised he had no intention of marrying me, it was too late. I was an old maid by then." Mrs. Murphy wiped her eyes with the corner of her tea towel. "Would you listen to me going on like that. Take no notice of me."

"At least you know you're capable of loving someone," said Sarah, trying to comfort the old woman. "I think it would be worse to be like Eddie and never know what it's like to love at all."

"I'm being a silly old woman, that's what I am – ignore me and my foolish carry-on," said Mrs. Murphy, now blowing her nose into the tea towel.

Sarah made a mental note not to drink out of anything dried by Mrs. Murphy.

"Tell me how is that husband of yours? Little Joe, isn't it?" said Mrs. Murphy, changing the subject.

"*Em*, he's fine. Good. Thanks for asking."

Sarah wasn't at all sure that Mrs. Murphy was ready to hear about her and Joe being separated due to Joe being gay. She wasn't sure if she was able for such a bombshell. But then again, Mrs. Murphy had just revealed that she spent her life loving a man who didn't feel the same way about her.

"Joe is gay actually. He left me a while ago. He met someone else. Paolo. He's lovely. They're a lovely couple really."

Mrs. Murphy didn't appear at all shocked.

"I'm very happy for him," said Sarah. "Now, that is. I wasn't too thrilled at first."

"That was nearly as bad for you as me loving a man who was never going to love me back, isn't it?"

And it hit Sarah that it was. Almost as bad. Or was it worse to have loved and built your life and your whole being on something that turned out to be a lie? What a pair they were!

Diane and Suze came back into the kitchen.

"This place is fabulous," said Suze. "It's huge. You get a better feel for it from the outside. Go out and have a look!"

"And you were worried we were coming to a rundown cottage with no roof," Sarah said to Diane.

"Well, you needn't have worried a bit," said Mrs. Murphy. "Big farmers they were, the O'Neills. Eddie inherited the farm and the house when old Mr. O'Neill died."

"What about Granny O'Hara?" asked Diane.

"Ah sure, the girls didn't get anything in those days. The boys were all that mattered. Anyway the parents weren't cold in the grave when things came to a head between Sheila and Eddie. He held the all the power and there was nothing for it but for Sheila to go."

"What an asshole! Sorry, pardon me," said Diane.

"Don't be sorry, girleen. He was a bit of an asshole alright."

"Did he actually throw her out? Was he a complete monster?" asked Sarah.

"*Ara*, sure it's not my place to say anything. I don't like to gossip. Now what will we be havin' for the dinner tonight?"

No wonder Granny O'Hara never returned to the place she was born, thought Sarah. Her brother sounded like a pig. She couldn't shake the image of Granny O'Hara being forced out of her own house by her bully of a brother. She wondered what on earth had come between her and Eddie.

Her mother-in-law had often pointed out an old building on Gardiner Street which used to be a boarding house. She told Sarah she stayed there when she came to Dublin first at the age of seventeen. Sarah thought about it now. Seventeen! A little younger than May was now.

Sarah would love to talk to Granny about it. Really talk. Talk about how she felt that first night in a strange bed, a strange city, alone and afraid. Was she excited too maybe? Excited to be free to do whatever she wanted to do? Why did she pick Dublin, such a big city, over a town closer to home?

Sarah made a promise to herself to spend more time with Granny when they got back. She was always asking Sarah to bring Rosa to visit her but Sarah didn't visit as often as she should. She was great at making excuses about being too busy. She now felt ashamed and couldn't wait to make amends to her mother-in-law.

Chapter 13

When Joe and Paolo prepared to go to bed on the first night of their trip to mind Rosa, Joe's mother made it obvious that she didn't quite understand what the whole commitment ceremony in Rome had been about.

"Where are you going, son? Sure that's Paolo's room. You stay in your old room. What would the pair of you be doing in that small bed?"

Joe wasn't about to explain the ins and outs of their sexual relationship so he threw his eyes up skywards, said goodnight to Paolo and went into his old bedroom. He wasn't surprised by his mother's reaction and her naivety, whether it was real or put on. She made all the right noises and took part wholeheartedly in the ceremony in Rome but she didn't actually want hard evidence that Joe was gay.

Joe looked around his old room with the posters of George Michael still hanging on the wall. He looked at the young George and wondered if they all weren't in denial about his own sexuality all along.

"We need to stay here," Joe said to Tom the following morning while Tom was giving Rosa her breakfast.

"But the arrangement is that you stay with your mother and I stay with the girls," said Tom, not willing to go off-piste from the arrangements that Sarah had made for them.

"Well, what can I say? We need to change it. May said she'll go stay with my mother. It's quieter and she'll be better able to study there. We'll still be looking after Rosa while you're at work."

Tom didn't want to do anything to aggravate Sarah. Their relationship was strained as it was, and disobeying her orders would only make matters worse.

"We're great cooks, especially Paolo. There'll be the best Italian food for dinner every night."

Oh God! Italian food! Tom was a sucker for pasta and home-made tomato sauces. The fact that the food would be made by someone else and handed up to him when he got in from a hard day's work was too much temptation, no matter how much of a fit Sarah might throw.

Whatever Tom did or said these days, Sarah got annoyed with him. If he called before he went to work, then he was calling too early and messing up Rosa's sleep pattern. If he called on his way home from work, it was the same thing. If he called her during the day, Sarah would give out to him because the phone ringing had interrupted her nap.

But that didn't matter now. He was here with his baby daughter and he was feeding her some disgusting-looking, mashed-up, organic cereal and she was kicking her legs in delight. She continuously slapped her plastic spoon off her plastic tray and half of the contents of her bowl was on his shirt. But he didn't care. He was here with her, feeding her. Taking care of her. He didn't want to be anywhere else.

He couldn't believe it when Sarah called him to ask him to move in and look after Rosa. She never asked for his help and wanted to do everything herself. She was the same way at home as she was in The Bakery: she was rubbish at delegating. Thankfully her friends had insisted she go on this holiday and bullied her into submission. He wasn't crazy about Joe and Paolo being a part of the deal but he could put up with that too.

"Alright. But if Sarah goes mad, I'm going to say that you forced me to let you stay. OK?"

"Good man. You won't be sorry when you taste Paolo's linguine with crabmeat," said Joe, going out to the car to fetch Paolo and their luggage.

Tom hoped he wasn't making a mistake by letting them stay. But he really did love Italian food. He loved all things Italian really. OK, the surprise trip to Amalfi that Sarah so lovingly organised had back-fired spectacularly. How was she to know that Tom and his late wife went there on honeymoon? He used to love the place – now he wished he'd never been. Sarah had envisioned a romantic weekend in Priano and Positano but what she got instead was a night sitting in the hotel bar on her lonesome. Things had never recovered for them since then.

"OK, but I'm in charge. What I say goes," said Tom.

"We know. You're the daddy," said Joe.

Chapter 14

The four women spent the day walking on the beach and through the quaint little village. By the evening of their first full day in Ballygra, they were all sitting around yawning.

"Right. Put the knitting needles down, ladies. We're going out," said Diane.

"But it's so nice here by the fire. Can we not just stay in?" said Suze.

"No, we can't bloody well stay in. We're on holidays. We're not eighty. Let's go out and have some fun."

"Out where? I only saw one pub in the village," said Suze.

"Well, one pub is all we need. There has to be something going on around here. Or else the whole population would have died from boredom already."

"I think it's nice here with the fire lit," said Sarah. "And it sounds really windy outside."

"Sarah O'Hara, get up out of that chair right now. You owe me. Remember?"

Sarah could see that Diane meant business. And she did owe her. Diane was being a good sport. They should be in Miami sunbathing and downing cocktails. It wouldn't kill them all to go and have a few drinks in the local pub.

Mrs. Murphy had insisted on staying on to cook and clean for them and as a result they had nothing to do but relax. She mightn't look like much but she cooked like Nigella. They had all eaten far more than they normally would.

Especially Jesus. He was able to put away a lot of food, thought Sarah. Mrs. Murphy loved that. She kept shovelling food onto his plate as soon as he cleared one lot of lamb chops and potatoes. "You love the shpuds," she kept saying to him. Poor Jesus had no idea what "shpuds" were, but he kept eating the potatoes, nodding his head and smiling anyway. Jesus was like her pet project. She had brought him two pairs of jeans from the menswear store in town and some T-shirts that were surprisingly up to date.

"Should we ask Jesus to come with us?" asked Sarah.

"I don't think he should," said Laurie. "Somebody's bound to spot him. I think he should lay low for a while."

They said goodnight to Jesus and walked into town.

When the door opened every head in the pub turned to look at them. The old men nearly fell off their high stools when they saw the four glamorous females floating in the door. It was off season for tourists so they weren't expecting anybody bar the locals. Laurie was the first to the bar and she ordered a bottle of champagne. She rarely drank anything else these days.

"Sorry, miss, we used the last bottle for Nora Collin's engagement party," said the bartender.

Laurie wondered if she should know who Nora Collins was but she decided she probably shouldn't.

"*Eh*, OK. What kind of wine do you have?" she asked hopefully.

"Red or white," said the bartender flatly.

At least Laurie wouldn't have to concern herself about choosing grape varieties. "I'll take a bottle of chilled white wine, please."

"Chilled is not a problem. It'd freeze the balls off a brass monkey out in the storeroom. I'll just go get a bottle."

Laurie waited for the bartender to return with the wine.

"You're not from around here," said the old man on the barstool next to her.

"No. We're staying in the old O'Neill house. My friend's mother-in-law is from here."

"Go away out of that! They were a grand family. Apart from that aul bollox, Eddie. He was an awful prick if ever there was one. Pardon my language."

"Pardoned," said Laurie. It seemed like Eddie O'Neill had no fans in Ballygra.

"The girl had her eye on me, you know. Mad about me,

76

she was. She was a lovely looking lassie, that Sheila. We could've got married if she hadn't hightailed it for the big shmoke," the old man said wistfully.

Laurie couldn't help but think that Sheila had a lucky escape. The man had a serious body-odour issue and had only managed to hold on to two of his teeth as far as she could tell. One on the top jaw and one on the bottom. She imagined that Granny O'Hara's fascination with him was most probably in his head along with the two teeth.

The bartender was back with a bottle of white wine.

"Chardonnay. Is that OK for ya?"

Laurie wasn't normally a fan but she felt the bottle. It was freezing. "Yes, thanks. It'll do grand."

The bartender accompanied her to the table, carrying the glasses that Laurie couldn't manage, obviously happy to have the distraction of the tourists in the form of attractive women though they were a bit old for him. He put the glasses on the table. He opened the bottle and was about to pour for them but Laurie relieved him of that duty.

"When was the last time we were in a pub?" asked Suze. "I mean a proper pub with a pool table. Wow! It has a poker machine and a jukebox too. I might never leave here."

They used to go to a small pub in town before they were legally allowed to drink. It reminded Suze of those times when their whole lives were in front of them and every little thing was a huge big deal. They shared their thoughts, dreams, fears and occasionally their boyfriends, in those days. They knew each other inside out. Suze knew that they couldn't have stayed that way forever, but she wished that they could have a little bit of that old fun back. She could tell that the others felt it too.

"Yeah, do you remember drinking pints of Harp? Or half-pints of Harp with lime for you, Sarah. You were always a lightweight," said Diane, laughing at the memories of them all as sixteen-year-old girls.

"So the next round is four pints of lager?" said Suze.

"Yes, why not?" said Diane. "For old times' sake."

"Make mine a pint this time," said Sarah.

Suze brought the pints to the table and they knocked them back. Lots more pints were ordered and drunk. Sarah saw the juke box and got some change from the bartender. He regretted handing over the twenty-cent coins as soon as Sarah started to sing.

Laurie and Diane started to play pool. They didn't realise it, but they were very drunk. They were loud, obnoxious and totally out of control. The bartender asked them to turn the noise levels down on several occasions and in the end he refused to serve them any more drink.

Diane was about to give him an earful of abuse but she felt a hand on her arm gently tugging her away from the angry bartender. She let the arm lead her back towards her friends but, when she saw Sarah was belting out some song at the top of her lungs, she wanted to dance. She grabbed the man who had led her away from the bar and started to dance around the tiny space in the pub. She put her arms around him and dragged him, stunned and trepidatious, around the floor.

When the music finished he brought her back over to her friends and sat her down on the seat. She wouldn't let him go and pulled him down beside her and insisted on talking the ears off him. She remembered shouting something at him as they were leaving but she couldn't remember what it was.

They left the pub noisily and walked back up the hill to the O'Neill house. They linked arms and laughed so loudly that the lace curtains were twitching behind windows in the street with the locals wondering who was making such a racket at two o'clock in the morning.

They were still laughing when Sarah asked where Suze was. Diane looked to her side where Suze had been but was now absent. The women looked around and heard a whimper coming from back down the street. They tottered back down the hill in their ridiculously high-heeled shoes and found Suze in a heap in the road.

She had caught her heel in a drain grid and the others hadn't even noticed. She had been laughing so much she couldn't even cry out for help but her ankle hurt and she was now crying with the pain. The others helped her up and staggered on home again.

They fell in the door of the house and woke up the sleeping Baby Jesus.

"Are you drunk?" he asked incredulously.

"As skunks," replied Laurie.

"Rot-orsed," said Diane

"You're such a posh drunk," said Sarah.

Suze didn't say anything because she was still crying. Her ankle was really hurting and she couldn't put any weight on it. She hoped that the amounts of alcohol she had consumed would mean that she would sleep through the pain, as she soldiered on up to bed.

"Good night, Jesus," the others chorused as they pounded up the stairs like a herd of elephants.

"Good night, John Boy," Diane called when they were all in bed.

"Good night, Mary Ellen," answered Suze, giggling in spite of the pain.

"Good night, Jimbob," said Sarah.

"Good night, Elizabeth," said Laurie and the house went quiet.

Chapter 15

Suze woke in the middle of the night in agony. She keenly felt the excruciating pain that was emanating from her eye sockets, but there was some other as yet unidentified source. Then she remembered the fall she took earlier on in the street and was able to locate the pain to her right ankle.

She cursed the stupid high heels and the copious amounts of lager she drank. There was a packet of paracetamol in her handbag. But her handbag was in the kitchen. Downstairs. There was nothing for it but to go get it.

She tried not to make noise as she hopped down each stair slowly, though the others probably wouldn't have woken up if there was a brass band playing on the landing. She regretted big-time suggesting they relive their teenage years.

But they had a laugh. They laughed like it was going out of fashion and, no matter how annoyed Suze was with herself for falling over, she still had to giggle at the night's antics. Sarah had sung Beyoncé's "All the Single Ladies" at the top of her voice along with the juke box and practically cleared the pub of what few other customers were left. It was akin to cats wailing being accompanied by more cats on violins. Even the others didn't join in, only watched and listened in stunned silence. They all knew that Sarah didn't have a note in her head but they had no idea that she was that bad. Suze hoped that she never tried to sing Rosa to sleep. The poor baby didn't deserve that.

"Let me help you," said a velvet voice at the bottom of the stairs.

Jesus! Crap. Suze had forgotten about him. Had they woken him when they got in? Probably. In fact there was no *probably* about it. There had been quieter riots in Brixton in the eighties. Suze looked down and she was dressed only in her bra and knickers. In her drunken state she was only able to remove her clothes. It would have required coordination she didn't have to put on her pyjamas so she had just fallen into bed. She put her hands to her bra then her knickers and he smiled at her.

"It's OK. I have seen a woman in her underwear before."

Well, he hadn't seen *her* in her underwear and Suze wanted to run back up the stairs. But running was out of the question. The pain that had been coming out of her eye was now trying to escape from every part of her head. Everything hurt. She held on to the balustrade and wobbled slightly.

Jesus caught her and helped her back up the stairs.

"I need some painkillers from my bag," she said as he led her back to her bedroom and she realised that she had come back upstairs without them. "Downstairs." She made for the door again.

"Please. No. I will get them for you."

"I think it's in the kitchen."

She lay there in bed thinking that she had just told Jesus Martinez to go downstairs and rummage through the contents of her handbag. Wait until she told Emma! Girls Emma's age were mad about Jesus. He had starred in some vampire trilogy that was all the rage. She should probably leave out the bits about the binge-drinking and falling in the street, though.

He was being very kind, but Suze couldn't forget the first impression of him crying for hours on the car journey down here. She heard him come back up the stairs and she pulled the quilt up to her chin. She had exposed enough of herself for one night.

Bless him, he had even brought her a glass of water. Suze wanted to be cured of her hangover more than anything else in the world. She knew she was in trouble with her ankle but the hangover was all-encompassing and her main worry for now. Jesus flipped the tablets out of their plastic case and handed her two. He gave her the glass of water to swallow them down. It was an odd intimate moment and she looked at him gratefully.

"I will stay here in case there is anything else you need

83

during the night," he said, motioning to the old armchair in the corner of the room.

He sat down on the chair. Suze wasn't comfortable with the proposal at all.

"No, you're grand. I'll be fine."

"If you need to go to the bathroom, I can take you," he said.

Suze thought that would top the list of her worst nightmares. Would he wait and hear her peeing? Would he sit her on the throne and then leave? God, there was no way in hell either scenario was going to happen.

"I'll manage. Anyway it's not fair for you to have to sleep on a chair. You'll have cramp in the morning."

It was all too surreal for Suze and her head was beginning to spin. Or was the room spinning? She couldn't really tell. She had to concentrate on not throwing up. She put her good leg out of the bed and put it on the floor to stop the room moving. She was too ill to argue whether Jesus stayed or left.

She closed her eyes and prayed that she'd fall asleep. *Don't get sick in front of Jesus Martinez. Don't get sick in front of Jesus Martinez. Don't get sick*, she ordered herself over and over until eventually she nodded off.

———

"Tell me. What is it?"

Suze tried to sit up in the bed. It took her a few seconds to realise that the person gently rubbing her head was Jesus.

"What are you doing?"

"You were crying."

Suze was in agony. No wonder she was crying in her sleep. Her ankle and her head hurt like hell. But something worse was happening. She felt a wave of nausea rise up inside her. *Fuck!* She felt Jesus pull her body over the side of the bed. She threw up. He was holding a basin and she was pretty sure that some of her puke had splashed his arm and hand. She felt hot, then cold and she knew she was about to be sick again. Jesus remained beside her like an emergency medic. The mortification of it all was too much to bear.

Suze remembered the last time she got sick. The airport. The hotel. The night she tried to end her life. The waves of regret and shame rolled over her as she continued to throw up. She was amazed that the others didn't hear her. She heaved until there was nothing left inside her. She lay back on her pillow as Jesus disappeared from the room, taking the basin of sick with him. She wanted the ground to open up and swallow her. She never wanted to see him again.

She would make her excuses the next morning. She would tell the others that she'd been summoned to London for a meeting. They would give out, especially Diane. But she didn't care. Staying was no longer an option. She groaned when she heard the door open and Jesus come back into the room.

"Please. Can you go? I'm so embarrassed, I can't bear it."

He patted a damp sponge to her forehead. She wanted

to bat his hand away but the cold felt good. He was gentle and kind. She let him soothe her with his gentle touch and his soft Spanish words. She opened her eyes and looked at him. She had to make sure she wasn't dreaming. She wasn't. A gorgeous man was pressing a sponge against her forehead alright.

"I'm fine, Jesus. You can go now. Honestly."

"I want to stay. Now go to sleep. You will feel better."

Suze woke with a start. She saw him asleep in the chair. She threw a pillow at him. "Wake up, Jesus! You need to go back to your room. Quick. Go!" She was obviously still dreaming. She was throwing Jesus Martinez out of her room after he cleaned up her vomit the night before.

"Are you feeling better?" he asked.

She was. Apart from an awful pain in her ankle, she felt surprisingly OK.

"Thank you for last night. You were very kind. I hate vomit. I couldn't even clean it up when my kids were sick. I used to get my ex to do it."

"*De nada.*"

But it wasn't nothing. Jesus had risen in Suze's estimation. Kindness wasn't a trait that every man possessed.

"Can I …? Can I kiss you?" he asked.

She must still be dreaming, she thought.

Jesus was sitting on the side of her bed. The pain in her ankle was immense. It was no dream.

"*Eh*. No. I … *eh* … I … Anyway I'd have to brush my teeth."

"Do you need me to help?"

"*Huh?*"

"Do you need help to go to the bathroom?"

"*Eh*. No. I'll … Are you serious? About wanting to kiss me?"

"*Si*."

Suze got out of bed and hobbled to the bathroom. The clock on the landing showed the time. It was six fifteen. The house was in silence. They had only been in bed a few hours. Nobody would be up for ages. She scrubbed her teeth and slapped her face a few times to bring some colour to her cheeks. She stared at herself in the mirror. She looked odd. Not herself. *Fucking hell*. Jesus Martinez wanted to kiss her. Had he really said that? Her stomach was doing somersaults and she hoped to God that she wasn't going to be sick again.

He was outside the bathroom door. He took her by her elbow and led her back to her room. She got back into bed and pulled the sheet around her. Of course he wasn't going to kiss her. She must have taken him up wrong.

He sat on the side of her bed for the second time. He put his fingers under her chin and she felt his mouth on hers. His kiss was soft and sure. The next kiss was surer, deeper. She felt his hands on her bare skin. She wanted it. Him. She just couldn't figure out why he wanted her.

"I don't … We should stop," she said.

"Why?" he said, kissing her again.

"I … *eh* … I'm too old for you."

"You are a beautiful woman," he muttered.

She wasn't. She knew it. The others were beautiful. She wasn't like them. She was the ordinary one. She always had been.

"I don't …"

"*Shhhh …*"

She did shush. Then she let him slide into bed beside her. She let him do things to her that she thought she would never allow a man do to her again. And she enjoyed it. She allowed herself to believe him when he said she was beautiful. She allowed herself to feel beautiful.

———

She stirred when she heard the toilet flush in the bathroom on the landing. They had fallen asleep in each other's arms.

"Jesus! Wake up. You have to go. Somebody's up."

He stretched himself out and yawned.

Fucking hell, he needed to hurry up.

"Seriously, Jesus, I need you to go," she said as she tried to push him out of the bed. He protested but she pushed harder. When she saw his taut ass bending over to put on his shorts, she had to pinch herself.

"*Ouch!*" she said as she pinched a little harder than she meant to.

"Your ankle is very sore, no?" he asked, sounding so young and lovely and concerned.

"*Em*. Yeah. I'm fine though. Thanks for the painkillers. And ... well, you know ..."

Good God. It was all real. She was pulling a sheet to cover her nakedness and he was putting his pants back on. She had spent years being ashamed of her naked body but she had just spent a few hours romping around with a Hollywood heartthrob. He winked at her as he left her room and closed the door as quietly behind him as he could.

Sex was life-affirming. Bloody fucking hell.

Chapter 16

The others were already having breakfast in the 'good' dining room when Suze got downstairs. Jesus got to his feet immediately, held a chair out and helped her sit down. She looked around at the faces at the table to see if anyone suspected anything. But nobody looked like they knew what she and Jesus had got up to. She was met by misery in each of the faces around the table.

Jesus was scoffing a huge plate of bacon and eggs. He was dipping his bread into the egg yolks. The sight of Jesus and his eggs made Laurie leave the table. Diane and Sarah were mostly silent apart from the odd groan.

"What the hell were we at?" said Diane, holding the top of her head as if it might fall off.

"We were pretending we were sixteen. It was a good idea at the time," said Sarah, almost in tears. "We can forget about doing anything today. Or tomorrow for that matter.

It'll take me the rest of the week to get over this. Tom phoned me this morning and I swear I was still drunk. He thought I'd had a stroke or something, the way I was talking. I had to tell him I took a sleeping tablet and was still groggy."

"It felt like someone was banging a headboard against the wall all night," said Diane.

Suze felt herself go red and she could feel Jesus look at her across the table. She didn't dare return his gaze. If only Diane knew.

"It went on for hours. I thought I had an aneurism," continued Diane.

"You're a wild bunch alright," piped up Mrs. Murphy, carrying in more plates of food.

Laurie had come back in the dining room but almost had to leave again when Mrs. Murphy placed a plate of black pudding in front of her.

"I heard the racket you made in the middle of the night. You nearly woke the whole village."

The women all bent their heads in shame.

"Which one of ye has a laugh like a hyena?"

"*Diane*," they answered.

Diane couldn't stop herself grinning when she remembered that Suze had fallen in the street. Last night it was the funniest thing she had ever seen. Even now it was funny, come to think about it.

"Suze. How is your ankle? Are you alright?" she asked.

"I can't walk properly or put any weight on it. I don't think it's broken though, just sprained."

The others felt sorry for her and offered to do various things for her for the rest of their stay.

"Good morning."

They all turned to the doorway to see who owned the voice.

The women all looked at the man and wondered who the hell he was.

"You invited me for breakfast," he said, looking directly at Diane.

She stared blankly back at him. She mouthed to the others 'What's he doing here?' and they just shrugged.

"*Eh*. Have a seat," Diane said.

"You don't remember me," he said.

It wasn't true. Diane had a vague memory of him from the night before. She remembered his height but no specifics. She wasn't a morning person and wouldn't dream of entertaining anybody before midday.

"And, Beyoncé – how are you feeling this morning?" he asked Sarah who was sitting opposite him at the table.

Oh, for fuck's sake! Singing diva-style came back to Sarah and she turned bright red. Some friends she had. Somebody should have grabbed the microphone out of her hand. Even if she threatened to tear them limb from limb if they touched it. In fact, she sort of remembered saying something like that, come to think of it.

"Oh well, I don't sing very well when I've had a few drinks," said Sarah.

"You don't sing very well, period," added Diane. "You're

the only woman I know who can empty a pub not once, but twice in one night. I think the bartender was about to put a baseball bat through the juke box if you didn't stop."

"Well, my terrible singing isn't news to anyone. Why the hell didn't you guys try to stop me? You're great friends, you are!" Sarah was mortified in front of this handsome stranger who had seen and heard her at her absolute worst.

"Oliver Butler. Well, well, well," said Mrs. Murphy, coming in. "Don't tell me you're responsible for getting these ladies into that state last night. You were always a little terror."

"Not guilty, Mrs. Murphy. I only called in to have a pint before closing time. I didn't realise that there was live entertainment on."

Mrs. Murphy put a full plate of food in front of Oliver. At least Diane knew his name now. She felt it incumbent on herself to make all the necessary introductions even though she barely knew him herself. He didn't bat an eyelid when he was introduced to Jesus and Laurie. Diane reckoned he must live under a rock if he didn't know this pair of celebs.

Suze's phone rang and she excused herself from their company. She hobbled into the sitting room to take the call.

It was Emma.

"I called to Dad yesterday and he was out. Again. You know it'd be nice to be able to go home and have a home-cooked meal sometime," moaned Emma. "There's only so much beans and toast a girl can eat!"

"He's probably busy with work, love. Give him a break."

"Mum, he's dating someone. I told you about the online profile and stuff."

"Oh, yes, of course you did. Well, you're a grown-up now, Emma. Your dad doesn't have to be there at your beck and call every day."

"Dad's out flaunting himself, you're away having fun with your gal pals. I thought that parents are supposed to be at home waiting for their kids to grace them with their presence?"

It always amazed Suze how Emma could revert to child mode at the drop of a hat.

"So, how is … Where are you again?" Emma asked.

"In West Cork and oh, you know, it's fine. Nothing much going on. Just having a quiet relaxing time."

Back at the breakfast table, Diane decided to come clean. "I'm sorry. I have to tell you something. I don't remember inviting you over last night. We were a bit out of it in case you hadn't noticed."

"Oh, I noticed. The whole village noticed, I think," he said as he wiped up the last of the egg with his bread.

Diane felt her stomach heave. She needed to get rid of this guy pronto. She wanted to go out and walk on the beach and let the wind carry her hangover away. She almost groaned out loud when Mrs. Murphy poured him another cup of tea.

Oliver could see that Diane wanted him gone. He on the other hand didn't want to be anywhere else. He remembered holding her in his arms while they danced the night before. Granted she was three sheets to the wind but, even so, he thought she was beautiful. She had talked a lot. Well, shouted mainly to be heard over her friend Sarah's singing. She informed him that she was living in Spain but she was now allowed back in Ireland.

He didn't quite catch why she had been exiled but he didn't think it was for murder or anything sinister. She had a boyfriend who owned a football club. She didn't like football so he took that as encouragement. She had also said that she wasn't in love with him. One thing Oliver learned from working in the hospitality industry was that things that went in sober, usually came out drunk.

"Do you want to go for a walk?" he asked.

That was exactly what she wanted but she had intended to go alone. She was caught now. It would be rude to tell him to leave.

"Sure. I need some fresh air."

He took his dishes to the kitchen where Mrs. Murphy took them from him and plunged them into soapy water.

Diane looked around for her pals. She wanted someone else to go with them so she wouldn't be alone with this guy who she didn't know from Adam. Unfortunately for her everyone had vamoosed.

She and Oliver left the house and walked down the gardens and onto the beach. The strong breeze blew her hair into her face. She tried to tame it and felt his hand on the back of her neck.

"Here, let me help you," he said as he tucked her long hair into the back of her jacket.

The intimate gesture discombobulated an already discomfited Diane.

"Thanks."

"So? Do you and your friends make a habit of going out and, *em*, enjoying yourselves often?"

"Eh, no. Last night was definitely a rare event," she said. "We haven't been together in a long time. We had a lot of catching up to do. That's what this holiday is about."

"Your friend is an excellent singer," he said.

"OK, now you're just lying." Diane looked at him and they both laughed at poor Sarah's singing attempts.

"I thought you liked it when you insisted on dancing with me. 'One Moment in Time' I think it was."

"Sorry! What?"

"You asked me to dance with you. Well, you actually dragged me out to dance with you. Not that I minded by the way."

He heard her murmur something beginning with 'f' under her breath.

"It's grand. It was just a bit of fun."

"Well, it's … I'm … Look, I haven't a clue what happened last night. After a certain point. Or pint. I apologise for anything I did or said."

"You've nothing to be sorry for. It's not every night I'm

accosted … It's not every night a beautiful woman compels me to dance with her. Suffice it to say that I liked holding you in my arms."

What he said hung in the air and even the gusts of wind didn't take the words away. Diane felt like she really was sixteen again. She wanted him to take her back into his arms and dance with her now. Here on the beach.

They walked along in silence past other strollers who were enjoying the greeny-blue ocean.

"I've never been in a place like this before," she suddenly said. "When I was young, my mum and I always went abroad for holidays. Actually, that's not completely true. We went to Wexford one year but it rained solid for the whole week. I think trying to entertain a six-year-old in a hotel room for an entire week traumatised my mother and that was the end of holidaying in Ireland. There's something special about this place though."

Diane surprised herself by saying this. It must be Laurie's influence, she thought.

"Yes, there is. Not that I saw the attraction when I was growing up here. I couldn't wait to finish school and get the hell out. It's hard to grow up in a small village where everybody knows every move you make. No matter how lovely it is. As soon as I could, I went to London. To sow my wild oats as my mother says." He smiled at her.

"Oh? And did you?"

"*Mm*. A few. Maybe a bit more than a few actually," he said, laughing.

Diane looked over at him. He was very handsome. He had dark curly hair and chocolatey brown eyes that danced and sparkled. He glanced at her and Diane felt like she was caught doing something she shouldn't. He smiled at her and he seemed even better looking. His teeth were white and straight except for one incisor which was slightly crooked. Diane liked it. He'd be too perfect without that crooked tooth.

"So you're back now? From London?" She had gone from wanting to get rid of him to having a sudden desire to know every little thing about him in the space of a few minutes.

"Yeah. It's mad, really. Richard Cantwell, he's been my best friend since school. We owned a couple of restaurants over there."

"Richard Cantwell? The celebrity chef?" Diane had seen his cookbooks and his *Cantwell Cooks* TV series.

"The very man. His father died a couple of years ago. Naturally we came home for the funeral. We heard that Ballygra Castle was up for sale. We used to hang out there when we were kids, robbing the orchards and playing games in the woods. We only went to have a look. We had no intention of ever coming back here. But then we fell in love."

"Oh," said Diane, trying her best not to feel devastated. Of course a man like Oliver Butler had a significant other. "And what? You didn't know while you were in London? You needed to come back to Ballygra to realise you're gay?"

"*What?*" He guffawed. "We're not gay. We fell in love

with the Castle. Wait 'til I tell Richard! He's the most alpha male you'll ever meet. He'll get a kick out of that."

Diane couldn't get over her relief. But why was she having these feelings for a complete stranger?

"That's why we're here. We're turning Ballygra Castle into a luxury hotel. We're just putting together all the finishing touches. We hope to be open by Christmas. I'd love to show it to you. If you have the time."

"I'd love to see it." Diane really meant it. Oliver's stock had risen considerably since he walked into the kitchen earlier and the idea of having a reason to meet him again excited her.

"Great. How about I pick you up at five and take you over there?"

"Today? OK. Great. Five it is."

They walked back to the house. At the front door, he got into his SUV, the kind of car the city bankers drove. Diane had seen a fair share of those in her day.

———

Jesus was at Suze's side everywhere she went. She was still feeling giddy about what had happened between them and she found herself grinning from ear to ear. The others had all abandoned her even though she could hardly get from point A to point B without help. Some friends they were!

But Jesus was sticking with her. A little bit too closely, she thought, in fact. She hadn't been intimate with anybody since Peter and even though Seán had tried his best, she hadn't allowed him to do more than kiss her in the dark. It was incredible to her that a guy like Jesus was able to break down the fortress she built around herself.

Despite the fact that her ankle hurt like hell and her movement was limited, inside she was dancing a jig. She could feel a trembling in her lower regions as Jesus gripped her elbow and helped her back up the stairs to her room. At her door, she thanked him and told him that she'd be fine. When she hobbled into the room and turned around he was standing there, on her side of the closed door.

He was looking at her and there was no mistaking what he wanted. She could actually read the lust in his eyes. Suze couldn't make any sense of what was going on, no matter how hard she tried to figure it out in her fuddled head. She had worked with her doctors and therapists after her suicide attempt and she had made great progress.

Not so long ago, she despised herself. She despised her flabby mind and her overweight body. She convinced herself that she was a dummy because she chose to stay at home and raise her kids instead of trying to carve out a career for herself. She told herself that she was ugly and not worthy of anybody's love or touch. Now she was building a career in a successful online magazine and she might be about to shag Jesus Martinez, a twenty-seven-year-old Hollywood actor for the second time in a few hours.

"Jesus, I don't know what you want from me."

"Nothing that you do not want to give to me. Last night

I held you in my arms. When was the last time you let a man make love to you? When was the next time you were ever going to make love? I will tell you. Never. You were afraid. Now you don't have to be afraid anymore."

Chapter 17

Joe and Paolo were enjoying their new roles as Rosa's minders. Being based in Rome, Joe had missed a lot of May growing up and some important milestones. Rosa was not his child but she was his family. He relished every chance he had to spend precious time with her. He found her endlessly fascinating, as he did his own daughter.

May was a wonderful kid and Joe was so proud of her. She took everything in her stride and it seemed that nothing could faze her. She was working hard at school and studying for her exams to get a good place in college, even though all she wanted to do was to work with Sarah in The Bakery.

May had confided in Joe that she felt that Sarah wasn't giving as much attention to The Bakery as she should have been. There was a rumour going around that The Bean Machine, the big international coffee-shop chain, was opening a store in Malahide. Right next door to The Bakery.

May had tried to talk to Sarah about it, but it didn't seem to her that Sarah was taking in the information and its implications for the business. If The Bakery suddenly failed, then May could kiss her dream of one day running one of the best independent bakeries and coffee shops in Dublin goodbye.

Joe felt for his daughter and knew he would do anything for her. Sarah was hard to talk to lately. She was stretched to almost breaking point. Joe didn't know how to approach the subject with her but he knew, if he didn't, that May would be the one to lose out the most.

He and Sarah wouldn't agree to May going to work in The Bakery straight out of school. They both insisted that she do at least a business degree before joining Sarah. She had taken it on the chin and had chosen a course and was doing the necessary study to make sure she got a place. Sarah and Joe even encouraged her to move away for a year, live abroad, look at other options but she had this steely determination that Joe and Sarah could not help but admire.

Joe decided he would speak to Sarah when she came back from the country. The Bean Machine was humungous and already had a lot of shops around Dublin. Over the years lots of coffee shops had opened and closed around her but Sarah managed to grow her own customer base. She was a constant physical presence and she had moved with the times with her online store. The sales of Sarah's quirky kitchenware and furnishings were a significant part of the business.

The problem with The Bean Machine was that it was new to Ireland and it was trendy and customers seemed to flock to it. It sold little baked treats with their coffees and even though they weren't a patch on the ones that Sarah baked, they were perfectly fine and acceptable. He wouldn't say that to Sarah's face, he wasn't that stupid. But if she didn't dedicate some time to coming up with a plan to survive alongside The Bean Machine, then The Bean Machine was in and The Bakery was out.

Paolo came into the room with Rosa in his arms, interrupting Joe's thoughts. Seeing Paolo with the little girl in his big strong arms made Joe love his husband even more.

Then he realised Rosa was noisier than usual and Paolo had a worried look on his face. The baby was crying and going rigid in his arms.

"I think there is something bad going on. She has a pain and she is not focusing on me at all," he said worriedly.

"Let me take her. Maybe she'll calm down if I hold her." Joe took Rosa from him.

"I am telling you. It is no good. There is something wrong. I think we should call Tom."

Joe didn't want to have to call Tom. Tom would like nothing more than to think that the gay daddies couldn't handle a baby with a bad case of wind.

"No, she'll settle. Stop worrying, she'll be fine," he said, giving Paolo a reassuring kiss.

When an hour later she still hadn't stopped crying, Joe thought that indeed it was time to call for help. They had changed her clothes, changed her nappy, tried to feed her and had even given her a bath. Rosa usually loved her bath and splashed around, spraying the room with sudsy water. The minute she hit the bath, she went crazy. They checked the temperature of the water, thinking that maybe it was too hot and they had burned her. But it was only lukewarm, just as she liked it.

"What is that red mark?" asked Paolo, pointing at her little neck as they were dressing her.

"That's not red, it's purple," said Joe, pulling apart the fasteners on her babygro.

The rash was all over her torso and Joe's heart almost stopped. The dread spread to his every fibre and he looked terrified.

"What, Joe? What is it?" asked Paolo, now terrified as well.

"Get me a glass."

"Of what?"

"*Just get a glass. Empty. Quickly.*"

Paolo didn't know what the hell Joe wanted a glass for but he ran to the kitchen and came back with a soda glass and handed it to him.

Joe placed the glass onto the tiny torso and the rash stayed. It was what he hoped against hope wasn't going to happen.

"The hospital. We have to get to A&E," said Joe with more calm than he felt. I think it's serious. "I think it might be meningitis!"

"*Dio mio! Che cosa possiamo fare?*" said Paolo, switching to Italian in his panic. He started running around the place like a headless chicken, picking up blankets and toys and running to the kitchen to get a bottle.

"Paolo, we've no time. We need to get to the hospital. Give me the keys. I'll have to drive because I know the way. You sit in the back with her."

Joe didn't even want to waste time putting her into her car seat. Jesus Christ Almighty! Why didn't he ring Tom earlier? Why was he always trying to get one up on him?

"Call Tom," ordered Joe, handing his phone to Paolo.

Paolo held on to the bundle in his arms and talked to her, trying to calm her all the way to the city centre hospital, all the while trying to get through to Tom. The phone went to voicemail every time.

The traffic was disastrous with closed lanes causing chaos. Joe weaved in and out of lanes and was surprised not to hear sirens behind him. He didn't care if the police tried to pull him over. He wouldn't stop. He wouldn't stop until he got Rosa inside the doors of the A&E.

After what seemed like an eternity, he pulled up outside the hospital steps. There were NO PARKING signs everywhere and Joe duly ignored them. He and Paolo ran up the steps and into reception. They must have made some sight. Two men dressed in their best Italian fashion with a tiny screaming bundle.

Paolo was speaking to the receptionist in Italian. He wasn't thinking straight with the terror he was experiencing. Joe had to push him aside and tell the receptionist and the nurse who had arrived about the purple rash that didn't disappear under the glass.

The medical team took over and prised Rosa from

Paolo's grip. The men stood aside with their arms around each other as they watched her being taken through to an area behind the curtains. The terror was still there but there was also relief that they had made it to the hospital. The doctors would make her better.

Joe dialled Tom's number and once again it went to voicemail.

The receptionist was asking Joe for patient details.

"Which of you is the child's father?" she asked.

"Neither of us is!" cried Joe.

"You're not? So are you the guardians? What is your relationship to the child?"

"Rosa is my ex-wife's child. Her father is actually a doctor here. Tom Harrison. I've been trying to reach him but his phone's going to voicemail. I need to get in touch with him. Is Rosa going to be OK? We should have brought her in earlier!"

A nurse appeared beside them. "When did you notice the rash?" he asked, jotting down notes.

He asked Joe some more questions about Rosa and then disappeared behind the same curtain that Rosa had gone through.

Joe and Paolo sat in the waiting room. They weren't allowed to go to her. Her condition was serious but she was comfortable: that was all they would tell them. Joe had to tell Sarah. She was right not to want to leave Rosa in the first place. He wondered if this would have happened if Sarah had been at home.

He dialled her mobile number and she answered after a few rings.

"Hi, Joe. You were right to send me away. I'm having a great time. It's wonderful to only have myself to think about for a change. So thank you, just in case I forget to say it to you when I get home. Joe? Is something wrong?"

Sarah had sensed from him that something was amiss.

"Oh God, Sarah. It's … it's …"

"*What, Joe? Tell me.*"

"Rosa's in hospital. We're here with her now. I think it might be meningitis. They're doing tests." Joe hated himself for having to say those words. The disease was every parent's worst nightmare. It could cause blindness, paralysis and even death.

"Meningitis? Jesus Christ, Joe. You said you think? What did the doctors say? They haven't actually said it's meningitis?"

"No, they haven't said yet. But she has a purple rash and I did the glass test. It didn't fade under pressure."

Sarah fired questions at him. He answered the ones he could. She was leaving Ballygra and would phone him along the journey.

He and Paolo sat there holding hands, waiting.

From upstairs, Suze heard Sarah shrieking for her. She kicked Jesus out and hobbled downstairs on her gammy ankle to her friend.

Sarah told her what Joe had said.

"So it's not definitely meningitis. Focus on that, Sarah. We don't know for sure. How the hell are we going to get out of here? We don't have a car. OK, don't worry, we'll get a taxi. Get whatever you need and be ready to go."

Sarah was glad that Suze was taking charge. She heard Suze asking Jesus to put her things in a bag, that she was leaving.

Suze went in to Mrs. Murphy and asked her to find a taxi for them.

"To Dublin? A taxi? Are ye mad? It'll cost a fortune," Mrs. Murphy protested.

"We don't care. Sarah's baby is in hospital, we need to get there now. Will you tell Diane and Laurie we had to go and that we'll call them later?"

The taxi arrived and Sarah and Suze got in the car. Jesus was at the front door waving them off, looking stricken, like he was losing his best friend.

"What's going on with Jesus? What's wrong with him?" asked Sarah, looking at Suze.

"Not now. I'll tell you later," she said and took Sarah's hand as she ordered the driver to only hit the road in spots.

Chapter 18

Diane and Laurie wondered if they should leave too and go to the hospital. They called Sarah and she insisted that they stay for the week as planned.

"I can't help thinking we should have gone with them. Poor Sarah will be out of her mind," said Laurie.

"We'd only be in the way and we couldn't help anyway. She'll feel better if we stay put," said Diane.

"I thought you'd run out the first chance you got. I know Ballygra is not exactly your idea of a vacation hotspot. Honestly, if you want to leave, I'll be OK here by myself."

"I wouldn't dream of leaving you here with only Jesus and Mrs. Murphy for company. What kind of friend would I be then? No, I'll stay."

Diane had no intention of going anywhere until she saw Oliver Butler again. She felt terrible for Sarah and knew that she was suffering, but she knew also that there was nothing she could do to help her right now. Another person she felt terrible about was Serge. She was having impure thoughts about another man. Very impure thoughts.

She hadn't stopped thinking about Oliver since the walk on the beach earlier. She couldn't block the realisation that Serge didn't make her heart stop beating in her chest when he looked at her. He didn't make her want to draw a big loveheart with an arrow through it in the sand. Oliver made her want to do that.

"You're a good person, Di. Underneath that hard exterior, there's a softie in there somewhere."

Diane felt really bad now. She was staying for her own reasons and they were not at all altruistic.

"Don't you think there's something really magical about this place?" continued Laurie.

"*Em*, it's nice. The house is not at all what I thought it would be and we did manage to have a lot of fun last night. All in all, it's not too bad, I suppose."

"It's so elemental. The sea, the sky, the ruggedness of the landscape," said Laurie. "I feel so creative. Ideas for the sitcom are flying around my head. There's inspiration everywhere."

"I'm glad you're writing again. I'm glad you're not turning into one of those Hollywood wives, all Botox and silicone implants. If you weren't already my friend, I think I'd hate you. Beautiful, talented, married to Kevin Flynn. Bloody hell, maybe I do hate you."

"Well ..." started Laurie but stopped.

"What? What were you going to say?"

Laurie frowned. "Well … you might think I have it all, but I don't. I'm almost ashamed of myself for not being deliriously happy with everything I do have. But …" She paused. "I'm … I'm desperate for a baby. I want a child more than anything else in the world. Kevin does too. He's as disappointed as I am every time I get my period. I can just about stand my own disappointment. I just can't bear his. You probably think I'm a spoiled, ungrateful cow."

"You can't help wanting a baby. I don't get it, you know that. All the baby stuff. That gene wasn't installed in me at birth, but I can understand wanting something and being frustrated as hell when you're not getting what you want. But you've only been married a short while, give it time."

"We've been trying for a year. You might not think it's a long time, but it is. That's twelve periods that arrive when you're fervently praying they won't. I think I'm infertile."

"Jesus, Laurie. You're such a drama queen. Why do you think you're infertile? Did you go to a doctor?"

"I've gone to loads. I've been to more consultants than a person who's actually sick. The thing is, none of them can tell for sure why it's not happening."

"Was Kevin tested? You know? Did they check his little swimmers? Check that he's not firing blanks?"

"He's fine. It has to be me. It has to be." Laurie's eyes filled with tears.

Diane went to her and held her.

"Now I couldn't help overhearing you there."

Mrs. Murphy appeared beside them.

Probably because you had your ear stuck up against the door, thought Diane. That woman seemed to manage to be everywhere.

"There's a man here, the next parish over. Seamus Sullivan is his name and he has the gift."

"The gift of what?" said Diane rudely. "The gift of butting into things that are none of his business?"

"He's the seventh son of a seventh son," Mrs. Murphy declared as if Diane and Laurie would be suitably impressed.

Neither woman had a clue what she was on about. They looked at her blankly, Laurie with big pools of tears in her eyes.

"So he's from a big family," said Diane. "What does that have to do with what Laurie and I were discussing? In private, by the way."

Mrs. Murphy looked suitably offended. She turned to leave. But on her way out she couldn't resist dropping a little nugget of information she wanted to convey.

"He gives women a rub of his relic. Don't ask me why but the babbies are poppin' out of them nine months later."

"Hold on, Mrs. Murphy. Please!" said Laurie. "You're saying that this seventh son, this man, can help women get pregnant?"

"He's the seventh son *of* a seventh son. That's the important bit. And whatever the gift he has is, he has a stream of women in and out of his house from one end of the year to the other. They come from all over. Foreign and everything!"

Diane wanted to scream. How dare the nosy old cow talk about lines of women popping out babies when Laurie was so obviously distressed.

"So this man sits there while women rub his, *em*, relic as you so quaintly put it," she said. "It sounds like somebody should call the guards. I mean who in their right mind would queue up to rub a guy's so-called *relic*?"

"His relic is a piece of cloth from Padre Pio's robe," said Mrs. Murphy in disgust.

"Oh. Right. Well, maybe you should say that then," said Diane testily. Either way, it was a complete crock of nonsense. "And who the hell's Padre Pio?"

"I want to go see him," said Laurie, her eyes lit up with hope.

Diane gave Mrs. Murphy a filthy look. This eejit with his relic and witchcraft was going to make Laurie's situation worse. They would be sending her back to LA like a basket case.

"I feel that it's right, Diane. I feel like I'm here for a reason. I told you there's something special about this place. I need to go. I can't ignore it if there's a chance it could work."

"So where is this guy with the relic?" said Diane.

"I told you. He's in the next parish over. Dooneybeg. And you can't just go and see him. He has to be expecting you. You need an appointment. I tell you what, I'll put in a good word for you. You're a very nice woman." She looked pointedly at Laurie, making sure Diane knew she didn't think the same about her.

Bloody wagon, thought Diane.

Oliver called at five o'clock as he said he would. His vehicle was parked out front and was very different from his earlier mode of transport.

"What the hell? What is that?" said Diane, completely bemused.

"It's a tractor."

"Yes, I can see it's a tractor. I just don't know why it's here."

"We're going to see the castle in it."

"You might be, but I'm not," said Diane adamantly.

"Look, the main road is closed for upgrading and honestly I don't want to write off my car. Come on, hop up!"

Diane looked at him like he had two heads.

"There's no room for a passenger," said Diane, peering into the cab of the tractor.

"It'll be tight, but I won't complain. Come on," he said and held out his hand to help her up.

She reached out her hand to his, against her better judgement. He pulled her up and gave her the choice of sitting on his knee or standing behind the seat. She wanted to sit on his knee, she really did, but she huffily told him she would stand.

"It's not too far but the roads are full of potholes. I'll try not to make it too uncomfortable for you," he said as the big wheels rolled down the gravel driveway.

They drove down roads that Diane imagined only cows were driven before. She could see his point about driving his expensive car along them and she almost had sympathy for the limo driver as well. But then she remembered her Louis Vuitton suitcase with the wheels barely attached and her sympathy went out the window.

True to his word, it wasn't far. Oliver turned on his indicator and turned into a tree-lined avenue. They rounded the last bend and there it was in all its splendour.

Ballygra Castle.

Diane understood how both men fell in love with it that day.

"*Wow!*" she said, stuck for words to describe the beautiful building.

"I know. You get it now? This place is amazing."

"Oh my God, it's stunning," Diane said.

"I know! When we were kids, an American family owned it. We were so busy playing in the woods that we barely paid any attention to the house itself. As I told you, it was only when we came back for Richard's dad's funeral that we appreciated its beauty. I hope you like it. It's going to be incredible when it's finished."

Diane thought it was incredible already.

Oliver drove around a circular flower bed and stopped the tractor. He helped Diane down and they both stood in front of the house and took it all in.

Then they mounted the steps. He pushed open the big

castle door and she caught her first sight of the magnificent foyer. She could imagine a grand piano underneath a crystal chandelier.

Ballygra was going to have a five-star hotel after all.

Chapter 19

"It's because I didn't want her at the very beginning," said Sarah, repeating her fears to Suze.

The taxi driver was driving at the 120 kilometre per hour speed limit and they were over halfway to Dublin as far as they could make out.

"Stop saying that, Sarah," said Suze soothingly. "You're a great mother. Anyone of us would have been freaked out to find out we were pregnant at our age. Don't beat yourself up about it."

"Tom didn't want her. What if this is punishment for our terrible reactions?" Where the hell was Tom when Rosa was developing this potentially life-threatening rash? Surely having a daddy who was a doctor should have worked in Rosa's favour. It all fed into Sarah's notion that she was going to continue to be punished for not loving Rosa from the first moment she found out she was in her womb.

"You're going to have to let this go. You're not being punished. And no, Tom isn't being punished either. You got pregnant and it was a shock. You weren't even together for very long." Suze needed to stop Sarah going on another self-loathing rant. "Your thoughts would be better concentrated on Rosa getting through this, not on stuff that's water under the bridge and of no use to anybody."

Suze didn't mean to be cruel to Sarah. She was in a very delicate state but she had been over this many times with her.

"I didn't want to leave her. I only went because all of you –"

"Enough. No more. You may not have wanted to leave her, but you did. Rosa might have got the rash whether you stayed or whether you were with us, having fun. We'll never know." Suze took Sarah's hand and squeezed it.

Sarah put her head on Suze's shoulder, closed her eyes and tried to think good thoughts.

Paolo was holding Joe's hand in the waiting room in the hospital. Tom had spoken to them and Joe felt Tom's anger radiating from him when he asked them to run through Rosa's every movement that day. She had been cranky. There was nothing unusual in that. Sarah had her spoiled and picked her up every time she whimpered. They had taken her out to the village for a walk. She was crying a lot in the pram. The men thought that they had done something

119

wrong, like putting her nappy on back to front. Or they'd put on a vest that was too small. They knew that something was definitely making the poor baby uncomfortable.

Joe was scared of rashes in babies. When May was born, he and Sarah knew absolutely nothing about babies and wondered how the hell a hospital would allow them to take a human being home without having any experience whatsoever.

There was an outbreak of meningitis when May was still tiny. Joe remembered being terrified that May would develop the evil rash and die and that it would be all their fault because they hadn't the first clue how to look after a new-born baby in the first instance. All those scary feelings had come back to him right now.

Rosa had looked so helpless when the nurses had taken her to the emergency room. Tom had been so matter of fact. So ... so not like a dad, Joe thought. How could he not be beside himself with worry? How could he not show any emotion – apart from his anger at them? All he wanted was the facts. The cold hard facts. Well, fuck him, thought Joe. I'll worry like her dad should. I'll worry enough for all of us.

He sent off another text to Sarah's phone which was going in and out of coverage on the motorway. Trying to talk to her was proving too frustrating. He had nothing new to tell her but he knew that she'd even want to know that. She'd want to know there was nothing to know.

Chapter 20

"I can't stop thinking about Rosa. And Sarah," said Laurie when Diane came back.

"Is there any word? I tried calling Sarah and Suze but I just got *the customer you are calling may have their phone powered off*. I'm pretty sure they don't."

"Same. I sent a text so hopefully one of them will respond."

"It's shit. Poor Sarah. Maybe we should have gone back with them."

"No. You were right earlier. There's nothing we can do. Just send out the positive vibes and hope for a good outcome."

Diane felt terrible. She had hardly given little Rosa a thought while she was in Oliver's company.

"Oh! The castle. What was it like?" Laurie asked.

"God, Laurie, you have to see it. It's amazing. It's down

a tree-lined avenue and so well hidden you'd hardly know it was there. I don't know a thing about the hotel business but I have a feeling those two are on to a winner. It must have cost them an arm and a leg in the process but I can see people flocking to it. It's exactly the kind of place you Hollywood types love. You know, elegantly understated and immensely private."

"Well, this Hollywood type is glad you're back. Jesus and Mrs. Murphy aren't exactly a bag of laughs. Do you want to do something nice tonight? I was thinking we could get a taxi into town and go somewhere for dinner?"

"I'm sorry, Laurie. I'd love to, but Oliver is picking me up at eight. He wants to pick my brain about interiors. I told him I know a thing or two about decorating."

Diane could see the disappointment on Laurie's face and she felt really bad. But she didn't want to cancel on Oliver.

"Oh. That's fine. I'm sure I saw a box of Scrabble in the sitting room. Hopefully Jesus' English is good enough to give me a decent game."

Scrabble? Oh, for fuck's sake! She would have to cancel.

"You can't sit in playing Scrabble. You're on your bloody holidays. Come with me. Or else I won't go – I'm sure Oliver can find somebody else to pump for interior design tips."

"No. Go. I'll be fine. I can work some more on my scripts. No really, it's OK. I'm sure Oliver wouldn't want me tagging along like a big fat gooseberry anyway."

"You wouldn't be a gooseberry. It's just a business dinner, no big deal."

"If it was just business you wouldn't look as excited as a schoolgirl. I think you like this Oliver guy."

"Don't be ridiculous. I'm going to dinner to give him a few ideas for fabrics. That's all. I have a boyfriend and I'm not looking for another one."

"You could have fooled me. I saw it in the pub when you were dancing with him. Even Sarah wailing like a banshee didn't stop you looking into his eyes and melting into his arms."

"I was drunk."

"Well, that obviously didn't put him off. He still came for breakfast this morning. And you went for a walk on the beach. And you went to see his castle. And now you're going for dinner with him …"

"Stop trying to make it into something it isn't. You've been living in LA too long. You want to turn everything into a fairy tale."

"Jesus, Diane! Just fucking admit it, would you? You've fallen for the guy. There's no shame in falling in love. It happens to the best of us."

"I only met him yesterday for fuck's sake. Anyway I don't believe in love."

"How can you say you don't believe in love? What do you think Kevin and I are doing together if we're not in love? And millions of couples like us? Don't tell me that what they have isn't love. Really, Diane, you should be open to it."

"Hello! I'm not a character in one of your scripts. This is the real world. He's a good-looking guy and, to be honest,

I wouldn't kick him out of bed for eating crisps. I've got a bad case of the hots, which I will just have to ignore because I have a perfectly nice boyfriend waiting for me at home in Marbella. Let's just drop it and forget I said anything, I won't see him again after tonight anyway."

Diane ran upstairs to her room and set about finding something to wear. She had butterflies in her stomach and she couldn't deny that something strange was going on. It couldn't be love, could it? She was convinced that she was immune to that particular emotion.

She firmly believed that love was a concept made up by studio executives in Hollywood just so they could make movies about it. On the other hand she was familiar with what lust was and she was definitely lusting after Oliver. After last night's dancing-in-the-pub shenanigans, she wanted to redeem herself and look as sexy as she could. She picked jeans and a black silk top. It was a barely-there top which she had put in her luggage, not thinking it would actually get an outing. She used her GHD to create waves in her silky blonde hair. She was happy with her reflection in the mirror before she left her room.

She arrived downstairs to wolf whistles from Laurie.

"What? I'm only wearing jeans," said Diane defensively.

"You're only nearly wearing that top too. I can see your boobs if you turn sideways!" Laurie could see Diane was blatantly in flirt mode. She knew she was right not to crash their private party.

"Seriously, Laurie, we call this 'fashion' over here in

Europe," said Diane, making inverted comma signs with her fingers.

"And we call it what it is in California. A Shag-Me Top. Anyway, you look fantastic no matter what it's called. I can't see him being able to concentrate on any fabric other than whatever that top is made of."

The doorbell rang. Diane hurried out and swung open the front door. Oliver stood there, a broad smile across his handsome face. She had to order herself to stop grinning from ear to ear.

Luckily Laurie interrupted the awkward "will we kiss or shake hands" moment.

"Hello again, Oliver."

"Hi, Laurie."

"Diane, I forgot to tell you," said Laurie anxiously. "We're meeting with that person I wanted to see tomorrow morning at eleven."

Diane frowned. "Sorry, you've lost me. We're meeting who tomorrow at eleven?"

"You know. Seamus." Laurie made eyes at Diane, wanting to be discreet. "Mrs. Murphy managed to get an appointment."

Diane would kill that bloody woman. "Oh, right. Eh, OK. That's, *em,* great."

"I know. Mrs. Murphy said I'm lucky to be seen so quickly, so I don't want to miss the appointment."

She sounded as if she was talking about an actual consultant not a feckin' backwater quack doctor, thought Diane.

"Seamus Sullivan?" said Oliver. "He's a legend in these parts. I remember when we were kids, he cured everyone of everything going. The doctor's waiting room in the village used to be empty while there was a queue a mile long outside Seamus's door."

Oh for the love of God, thought Diane. He believed the hocus-pocus too. What was wrong with everyone?

"You see, Diane? He must have a gift," said Laurie.

Diane didn't know what to say. She didn't want to dash Laurie's hopes but there was no way that she could let her kid herself into believing that Seamus whatshisname could help her actually have a child when some of the best medical brains in the world couldn't help.

"He cured my father of a bad case of shingles once," Oliver went on. "The spots were about to meet around his middle and he stopped them in their tracks. It involved a bit of blood though."

"OK. OK. Sorry to interrupt this fascinating chat but we've got to go," said Diane, grabbing Oliver by the arm and leaving Laurie to an exciting night of Scrabble with Jesus.

They walked to his car.

"You don't really believe in that stuff, do you?" Diane asked.

"What? Seamus? Of course I do. You should have seen my father's middle – there were loads of them and they were –"

"Alright. You can spare me the details," said Diane, definitely not caring to think about Oliver's father's midsection. "You have to admit it's all a bit far-fetched. I'm

126

worried. I don't want Laurie to end up worse off than she is now."

"Laurie seems to be open to it so she'll probably get some good out of it. It's the people who don't believe in anything who end up with nothing. I don't want to pry, but I hope she's not ill. She seems like a lovely person."

"She's not. Please don't repeat this to anyone, but she's desperate for a baby. She's got it into her head that she's infertile."

"Well, she's going to see the right man to fix that."

"Ah, come on! You don't really believe that hocus-pocus?"

"If you grew up in this village, you'd believe it too."

"Eh, I don't think so. I believe in cold hard facts. And evidence."

"Diane, you have to believe in things even if there's no proof or scientific evidence present. We all need a bit of magic in our lives."

Diane was about to launch into an argument against believing anything of the sort when her phone rang. Serge's picture came up on her screen and she stared at it for a second.

"You want to take that?" he asked.

"Nah, it's nobody," she said, ending the call and putting the phone back in her bag.

Diane and Oliver went through every room in Ballygra Castle in their heads and in doodles on the back of the restaurant's cocktail napkins. Diane was surprised that he had such strong ideas about the style he wanted to create. James, her ex-husband, had never got involved in any aspect of the design of their palatial home and had never even expressed an opinion other than "Yeah, that's nice" when asked what he thought about certain rooms.

"So no regrets about giving up the bright lights of London to come back to Ballygra? Don't you think you'll miss the buzz of the big city?" said Diane as the waiter put espressos in front of them.

"The plan is we'll be too busy to even notice."

Oliver was nervous about the move but not because of leaving London and moving to the village in the middle of nowhere where he grew up. It was because they had staked so much on making this project work. There was a lot riding on the hotel's success.

Oliver and Richard had been best friends growing up and couldn't wait to get the hell out of Ballygra and head for the bright lights of anywhere. They didn't care if it was Dublin, London or New York just as long as it wasn't West Cork.

They moved to London and Oliver got a job as a trader for an international bank. Richard trained in the kitchens of the most famous chefs in the city. They both worked crazy hours and were both enormously successful at what they did. One day Richard told Oliver he was going out on his own and was going to open his own restaurant. Oliver heard himself telling Richard that he wanted in. He told his boss he was leaving, cleared out his desk and never looked back.

The two boys from Ballygra were cocky and clever and they made a great team. Oliver looked after the financial side of things and Richard looked after all things culinary. They put every penny of their savings on the line, took out huge loans and opened up a restaurant in the middle of Chelsea. They courted the media and took whatever publicity they could get. Soon the Irish pair of cheeky chappies were the toast of Chelsea.

If Oliver thought he put in long hours on the trading floor, he was in for a shock. The difference was that he loved what he and Richard had created and would have worked every hour out of every day if he had to. They got a Michelin Star within a year and they were off and running.

"A Michelin star! I'm impressed. God, you guys must have been unbearable though," said Diane.

She remembered when James's bank got a European banking award and James was singled out as being the banks MVP. The amount of backslapping and whooping and hollering that went on was embarrassing. For a long time it seemed like James had vacated his body and a massive ego walked around in his stead.

Oliver laughed. "How did you know? We were so bloody full of it, we could hardly stand ourselves, never mind each other after a while. If I met me then, I'd think I was a complete asshole."

"And you've changed?" she asked with an arched eyebrow.

"Hey, hey. Yes, I've changed. Don't you agree that I'm disarmingly charming right now?" he said with mock seriousness.

"Oh, totally. I couldn't imagine you ever being an asshole," said Diane, laughing. He was unbelievably handsome, charming, funny, self-effacing. She liked him a lot.

"Seriously, I was. Ask Jenny, Or her father for that matter."

"Jenny? Is she your girlfriend? I didn't know. Not that I should have known, of course ... I mean ... I just didn't ..." Diane was acting like an idiot. She hoped that he hadn't noticed.

"My wife. Jenny was, well, she is a beautiful young woman." *His wife. His bloody wife?*

"You're married?" Diane said. She knew it all along. Guys like Oliver didn't roam free around the countryside.

"I was. Jenny's my ex. She's her daddy's little princess. And her pop happens to be the East End's answer to Tony Soprano. I didn't know this when I asked her to marry me but I found out about him pretty quickly after we got engaged."

Diane couldn't get over how relieved she was to hear that Jenny was his ex.

"How did you meet her?"

"She was waiting tables at the restaurant in Chelsea. Not that she needed the money. It was her father's idea to teach her about real life. He wanted her to realise that money didn't grow on trees. Anyway, I stupidly started something with her. She was beautiful, sweet and she adored me. I was lonely. I spent so much time at work that I never met anyone who didn't work for us or who wasn't a customer. It started out as a bit of fun but next thing I know I'm asking her to marry me. Looking back, I think I lost my mind a bit. I was living on adrenalin, drinking too much. Barely getting any sleep. Sorry, this is probably very boring for you. We can change the subject."

"No, please. I want to hear about it."

"OK, so she agreed to marry me and next thing we're going to meet her dad. I thought that he'd be some middle-aged guy who worked in insurance or something. When I saw him, my gut told me to run away. I should have trusted my instincts. He is the most savage human being I have ever met. He has scars all over his face where he was knifed by some rival crime lord about twenty years ago. The first thing he told me was that he wasn't happy. You might not think it, but lowlife scumbag thugs can also be very traditional. He reckoned that I should have asked his permission before I asked his Jennifer to marry me. I swear to God, I was never so scared in my life. Then he sort of softened and said that he would love me because Jenny loved me. He said we'd all live happily ever after. It didn't sound like a blessing. More like a threat really." Oliver stopped to take a drink of water from his glass. "When it all started to go wrong between us, I knew I was in trouble. He had pretty much ordered me to make his little princess happy. I tried to make it work but we were completely unsuited to each other. We made each other miserable. She ran back to daddy and told him we were getting a divorce."

Diane couldn't imagine how Jenny let someone like Oliver go. Nor could she imagine Oliver making any woman miserable.

"So what happened then? Did Tony Soprano try to kill you?" she asked jokingly.

"Worse. He cornered me one night when I left the restaurant. It was like something out of a movie. He got his heavies to bundle me into his car which had blackout windows. He then threatened to cut off my balls with a rusty blade."

Oliver was still wincing at the thought of it. Beads of sweat started to appear on his forehead.

"Are you alright?" Diane asked, alarmed.

"I'm OK, thanks. I'm sorry but it still brings me out in a cold sweat."

"I can imagine. I've worked with a few of his type."

"Oh right. I never thought about thugs needing decorating advice."

"I'm a barrister by profession. I took a bit of a sabbatical recently."

"Beauty and brains. You're almost too good to be true."

Diane couldn't help but feel thrilled by his words. What the hell was happening to her? She needed to get back on an even keel. She changed the subject back to him.

"Was he serious? The dad. He wasn't really going to do it, was he?" She was shocked that something like that could actually happen and grateful that his bits and pieces were still intact.

"He sounded pretty damn serious at the time. Only for Jenny showing up I might be minus a few of my parts right now. She knew he had come to see me and she followed him to the restaurant. She banged on the window and begged him not to hurt me. It wasn't my proudest moment, watching my twenty-three-year-old wife beg her father not to cut my nuts off."

"Twenty-three? *Wow!* That's pretty young," said Diane. It's a wonder Jenny's father didn't kill him just for cradle-snatching, she thought.

"Anyhow, that's in the past. I've still got all my equipment and it's in perfect working order. And I dearly hope that I'll never see my ex-father-in-law again. All's well that ends well. Do you fancy a drink somewhere?"

Diane could have listened to him all night but she had to think of Laurie at home playing Scrabble.

"I can't. It's not fair to Laurie. We're meant to be on holiday together and I feel bad for leaving her home alone."

Back at the O'Neill house, Oliver put his hand on hers when she started to get out of the car. "Thanks for all your ideas tonight. I'll be using a lot of them. Especially the grand piano."

She looked at him and his face was inches from hers. She

could feel his breath and smell the faint whiff of the whiskey he had after dinner. In the dim light of the car she could still see the outline of his handsome face. His lips looked like she could sink into them like feather pillows.

"I was thinking," he said, "that I ..."

"No. Don't say anything. I feel that way too, but we're never going to see each other again and we should leave it at the *what if* stage," she said breathlessly, still wanting nothing more than to feel his soft touch.

"Oh. I was just going to say that I'll drive you and Laurie to Seamus's place tomorrow. You'll never find it on your own."

Balls. Mortification. Why didn't she keep her big mouth shut?

"But I'll bear in mind what you said," he said, grinning.

Chapter 21

The taxi dropped Sarah and Suze at the hospital and Sarah burst through the doors. Whatever restraint she had managed to show on the journey had completely evaporated when she saw the sign for the hospital.

Joe and Paolo were still in the waiting room, looking drawn and worried.

"Where is she?" she cried.

"Come on, I'll get the nurse to take you to her," said Joe, taking her hand and leading her to the nurse's station.

Paolo was left sitting there like a spare wheel and Suze's heart went out to him

"Tough day?" she asked kindly, sitting down beside him.

"Very. She is so very small and she has so much pain. It is hard to see," said Paolo sadly in his wonky English.

"It's terrible but she's in the right place and you guys got her here quickly. Let's just hope and pray that it's not meningitis."

"How was your trip?" asked Paolo, trying to distract from the gloomy situation.

"Short," said Suze and smiled at him. "We managed to have some fun though. It was nice to be together again, even if it was only a couple of nights."

They sat there and the conversation was stilted due to Paolo's imperfect English and the fact that Suze couldn't concentrate on very much, thanks to her time with Jesus. She was glad to see Joe come back to the waiting room.

"Any news?" Paolo asked.

"No, not yet."

"How can they still have no news? It's been hours for God's sake!" said Suze, utterly frustrated on all of their behalf.

Joe resumed his seat beside Paolo.

"They're treating her with antibiotics. Her temperature is dangerously high and they can't seem to get it under control. Whatever they're using for the temperature is stopping the antibiotics having the effect they hoped."

"Jesus Christ, they're bloody doctors! You'd think they'd have overcome this problem before. Poor Sarah. And Tom. How is he? Is he working on her?"

"No, he can't. He's as helpless as the rest of us. In fact, I think it may be worse for him because he's probably seen all this before and he can't do a damn thing."

Joe had seen Tom in Rosa's room and he was indeed worrying just like any father. Joe was ashamed of himself for thinking otherwise.

They sat there for what seemed like an eternity with still no update from anybody. Every time a person in scrubs appeared the three of them sat up with a mixture of excitement and dread.

Suze couldn't bear it anymore. She had done this to her own family. She had made Peter, Paul and Emma be the people waiting to hear from the doctors whether their loved one was alive or dead. She had tried to end her own life. She still found it hard to dwell on. It seemed like a lifetime ago. Her family had to sit in a room just like this one for days on end, waiting. She couldn't believe she had done it to them and wanted to burst out of there and tell them she was sorry.

"I'm sorry, I have to go. Tell Sarah I'll come back tomorrow. And call me if there's any news. You have my number, Joe?"

Once she was satisfied that Joe did indeed have her number, she left the hospital to get a taxi to her old house.

Suze paid the driver and got out at the house where her old life used to happen. It was only when the taxi had driven off that she noticed there were two cars in the driveway. Peter's work van was there along with a swanky new black Audi. Suze didn't know any of Peter's friends who drove an Audi, especially a sporty model like this one.

Something made her not use her key to let herself in and not ring the doorbell. She really wanted to see him, to talk to him, but what if he was busy and didn't want to see her?

She couldn't see any sign of life at the front of the house so she went around to the side. They had never used the bolt on the side gate and Peter was still in the bad habit of leaving it unlocked, thankfully. She looked in the utility-room window and saw through to the kitchen where Peter was standing. He had his back to her. He looked like he was chopping something. Vegetables?

She could see the stove and it looked like there were two pots simmering on the gas. Peter turned the knobs a few times to get the gas regulation he wanted. He must be making dinner for himself and whichever pal he had over. It was strange to see him being so domesticated. He never cooked when they were together. Suze used to do it all. It wasn't that he refused to do it or didn't want to, it was just the way it was with them. She was like an employee who didn't take holidays in case their boss realised that they weren't needed in the first place. Suze reckoned if she did everything, she couldn't be fired from her life. Look where that sort of thinking got her. She had tried to fire herself from the life she had in spectacular fashion.

It was good that Peter was doing things for himself. Suze went through his pals one by one, wondering which one he was cooking for. They were all lads' lads and having one of their mates cook dinner for them wouldn't be their thing at all. Then a penny dropped and she thought about the dating website. Was it one of them? The car looked like a man's car but of course it could belong to a woman.

Peter looked pretty good, she thought. He had on jeans and a shirt that she hadn't seen before. It was fitted and she noticed that he no longer had the love handles hanging over his jeans. When had that happened? Suddenly Peter turned around and Suze ducked out of sight.

She didn't consider what she was doing was spying on him, but she didn't know what else it could be called. And she didn't want to be caught. She went to leave but decided to have one last sneaky peek. She was sorry she did. She looked. Ducked. Looked again.

A woman was handing Peter a glass of wine which she had obviously been pouring while Suze was wondering which of the guys he was entertaining. So it was one of his online dates. She was lovely. Gorgeous even. Then Suze noticed the soft light in the kitchen area. The table was set with linen that Suze didn't know they had and candles were lit between the two settings.

Never in his life had Peter set a table like that for Suze. On her birthday or their anniversaries, when the kids had reminded him of the date, he had put a paper napkin on a tray and brought her tea and toast in bed. She felt gutted.

She told herself to leave, that what was happening in the house where her old life had happened was no longer any of her business. But she couldn't go. She wanted to look again. He was grinning at the woman. Whoever she was, she had obviously said something funny. He had a lovely smile. He looked like the old Peter, the one she hadn't seen for years and years.

Suze barely looked at the woman. She was totally drawn to Peter. All she could see was the guy who had practically begged her to marry her, he had loved her so much. She was barely out of school at the time. But now obviously wasn't the time to say she was sorry for what she had put him through. It was time for her to go.

She flagged down another taxi and headed back to Howth.

───

Suze let herself into her little cottage and picked up the post. There was a handwritten envelope. She recognised Seán's writing.

Dear Suze,

I wanted to let you know that I've gone away. I feel a change of scenery will do me good. You know how I feel about you. I wish things were different but I hope you understand that I can't stay knowing you are so near but so very far from me.

Your "friend",
Seán

Suze's heart sank. She wasn't sure she was ready for him to be gone. Why was her life full of complications all of a sudden? When she left for her break away, things were chugging along just fine. In the space of a few days, she had sex for the first time in years, fancied her ex-husband again and scared Seán off to some far-flung location.

It sounded like it was a page from someone else's life, not a chapter in boring old Suze Jackson's book. She was exhausted and decided on an early night. She called Sarah to find that there was no change. She would keep her phone by her bed in case of any update during the night.

She called Laurie. She hadn't replied to the texts from Laurie and Diane earlier, and she knew they would both be worried. Unfortunately she had no good news to relay. She told Laurie again that being in Dublin would be no use to Sarah and that the two should stay where they were. She asked about Diane and Laurie told Suze that she was out to dinner with the guy who came to breakfast.

"Oh, he was nice, wasn't he?" Suze had only vague recollections of Oliver as her mind had been full of Jesus Martinez over breakfast.

"He's very good looking. Of course Diane won't admit it, but it's obvious she really likes him. She went out dressed to kill."

Suze then wondered if staying in West Cork was a good idea after all when Laurie told her that she was going to a quack doctor in the hopes that he'd help her conceive.

"You're not seriously thinking that some barmy old guy is going to wave some magic wand and, hey presto, you're with child, are you? I'm sure the countryside is littered with lunatics like that. Old guys who spend far more time swigging poitín than is good for them!"

"Why can't you guys just be supportive? You know, it would be nice if you didn't treat me like some kind of halfwit!"

"You're far from being a halfwit, Laurie. You've been a great friend to me and I want to be there for you too. It's just that I care about you. We all do. Nobody wants to see you get your hopes up only for them to be dashed. Just be careful, that's all."

"I know. I'm sorry. Wanting this baby is almost all I can think about. I'd do anything to conceive at this stage. Well, almost anything. Don't worry, I won't be having sex with strangers or anything weird like that!"

"Oh, glad to hear it. That would be weird, wouldn't it? How's Jesus by the way?" The stranger she had sex with that very morning.

"He's been holed up upstairs ever since you guys left. He took your room by the way. Your claim to fame can be that you and Jesus Martinez slept in the same bed!" said Laurie, laughing.

If only she knew, thought Suze. It seemed like a dream to her now. A fabulous sexy dream, but a dream nonetheless.

"I know he's Kevin's friend but I just don't get what Kevin sees in him. Maybe if I played Xbox, I might feel differently," continued Laurie.

"Oh. Has he said anything about *em* ..."

"About what?"

"Oh, I was just wondering if he had ..."

"What?"

"I was just wondering if he'd said anything ... about me."

"*Eh*, no. I don't think so. I mean, he's been sulking around the place and looking pretty miserable ever since you guys left this morning. But I think that's just his personality. He's pretty immature."

"Oh."

"Suze, what is it? Did he do something to upset you?"

"No. He didn't upset me at all. We had sex actually." Suze had to say it out loud. She had to say it to check if it was real. And it was.

"You're joking?"

"No. Jesus and I had sex. He heard me get up for some painkillers and I don't know how it happened really, but he ended up in my bed. And then we, you know, we did it."

"Are you kidding me? You and Jesus? Oh my God, Suze! You're a bloody dark horse!"

"Is he really miserable?" said Suze. She hoped he was. She wanted to be the woman who made a Hollywood heartthrob sad.

"He is. He refused to have dinner tonight. Even when Maria finished with him, he still ate. But never mind that, tell me all about it."

"I don't know what to say other than it was amazing." She meant it. It was like nothing she had experienced before and sadly she realised that it was probably something she would never get the chance to do again. With Jesus anyway. "We know he has a thing for ugly women."

"What are you talking about?"

143

"The girlfriend. The East German shot-putter with the moustache."

"Suze! Don't say that. You're not ugly. Not even close. You're gorgeous and I'm sure you're a lot more interesting than most women he's slept with."

"I don't know about that. We didn't do very much talking."

"Bloody hell."

"I saw Peter tonight," said Suze. "I went to our house. I mean his house. He was making dinner. He had a woman with him."

"Oh? I get the impression that you're not over the moon about it?"

"I wanted to see him. I was in the hospital and it really hit home what I put him and the kids through. I wanted to see him and to tell him how sorry I am. I just assumed he would be home alone. The last thing I expected was for him to have female company."

"So what was she like? Did you meet her?"

"I didn't go in. I looked in through the window. I don't know why I'm upset about it, but I am. I feel like going back over there and asking him what the hell he is doing bringing another woman into my home. But it's not my home anymore. I just feel sad that it's all over. Really over."

Laurie was having none of it.

"Suze, you can't have double standards. You just told me you had sex with Jesus Martinez. I think that trumps Peter having a gal pal over, don't you?"

"It's not about trumping anybody. I thought I didn't have any feelings for Peter anymore and what I felt tonight took me by surprise, that's all."

"What did you feel? What do you think is happening?" asked Laurie. "I mean, Peter is Paul and Emma's father and he will always be a huge part of your life. But as far as both of you moving on, that's what I thought you wanted?"

"I don't know exactly. When I was sitting in the hospital, waiting for news about Rosa, I put myself in Peter's shoes and I felt so bad for putting him through all that. He sat there day in, day out, hoping and praying that I'd get better – and what did I do in return? I went to Diane's house. I picked my friend over my husband. I needed to tell him I was sorry. Not just words sorry. I wanted to tell him that I felt what it was like. That I knew what I'd done was almost unforgivable. Then when I saw him being Mr. Domesticated with that woman who, by the way, is at least ten years younger than him, I don't know … I think I'm jealous."

"I think it's a case of you don't want him but you don't want anybody else to have him either. I'm sorry but I don't see any other way to explain it." Laurie was exasperated.

"I know, you're probably right. I don't want him. Why would I want him now when I thought he was the root of all my problems for all those years? Just forget I said anything. It just feels like everything is all over the place. Seán is gone. He left a note to say he couldn't be around me right now. I think I need to crawl under a rock and stay there until everything blows over."

Chapter 22

Peter and Natasha had been seeing each other frequently. They had been to movies, the pub, out for dinner and even spent a Sunday hiking in the Wicklow mountains. Peter had eventually surprised himself by asking her to come over to his house. He said he'd cook dinner. He surprised himself because he had never felt that it was his house to ask somebody over to. He always felt it belonged to the family unit and wasn't to be used for his entertainment alone. But he was being stupid. Of course the house was his. If the others didn't like it, then they'd have to lump it and get used to it.

He also surprised himself because he couldn't cook anything that would impress anybody over ten years of age. He didn't think spaghetti bolognese would cut it with Natasha. He wanted to make something special for her. He needed to impress. She drove a brand-new Audi and her clothes looked like they cost a fortune. Peter was no expert on fashion or fabrics but hers felt expensive. Not that he had been feeling her clothes but when he took her arm or took her coat, the materials seemed luxurious somehow.

He didn't ever remember Suze's clothes feeling like that and he imagined that Natasha didn't shop anywhere on the high street. That's not to say that she was flash. She wasn't. She didn't wear lots of jewellery or anything. Peter was glad of that. He wasn't a fan of the bling.

Natasha only wore diamond studs in her ears and a diamond drop on a necklace. And a watch. A nice clunky one. Peter would have bet the diamonds were the real deal. Natasha herself was the real deal. Being with her made him think that anything was possible.

She told him about a tender at her work. They were looking for quotes for construction of a new office block near the docks.

"Ah sure, they wouldn't be looking for fellas like me. It's the bigger firms that do that sort of stuff," he said.

"But you're a contractor. You could do it just as easily as the bigger firms, as you call them, can," she argued.

"Ah, I don't know. I don't think it's my sort of thing."

"Peter. You're a building contractor. The tender is for a building, so it is your sort of thing. I think you should at least put in a tender for it. Who knows? You might just get it."

"I wouldn't even know where to start. But maybe I'll have a look at it," he said, wanting to please her. Wanting to impress her really. He honestly had no ambition to be a big-time builder. He was happy with his life as it was. But Natasha was making him feel like he was wasting opportunities, going with the flow instead of trying to make something of himself.

"You don't need to hire anybody yourself. You just need to know how to coordinate the whole build. I'll help you, if you like."

He was a bit disconcerted at the thought of Natasha giving him a hand with something he had been doing for almost all of his adult life. But Natasha had sown a seed in his mind: he could do more than he was doing now.

Now, Natasha with her fancy car and her expensive clothes, her perfectly coiffed hair, perfect make-up and great body was in his kitchen pouring him a glass of wine. And he was cooking dinner for them. If somebody had told him a year ago that this actual scenario would be a reality, he would've told them to get a grip. Told them that they were dreaming.

After he invited Natasha round for dinner, he had to scramble to find something to cook. He took a day off work and surfed through the TV channels until he saw a food programme. There were heaps of channels dedicated to just cooking. He couldn't believe it. Cooking was almost as popular as sport was. He watched carefully and took notes.

After about five hours, he was almost cross-eyed from watching the box and he was starving as well. But he was still no wiser about what to cook. He decided while watching all that TV that he liked Jamie Oliver and the way he cooked.

He went to the shopping centre and bought every one of Jamie's cookbooks and brought them home.

Five hours watching telly was followed by five more hours poring over the books, until he found a recipe he was happy with.

It was butterflied leg of lamb with rosemary and garlic. Jamie, of course, had a big feckin' brick oven out his back garden while Peter had to make do with the double oven fitted into his kitchen. The book said that his butcher would butterfly the lamb and this was one of the main reasons he picked it. Initially he had no idea what butterflying meat meant. He would have thought it meant stuffing red admirals somewhere into the lamb's insides.

The butcher in Malahide did indeed butterfly the meat for him and gave him a few hints as to how to make a great gravy with the juices. He liked this cooking lark – everyone he met in the butcher's and the grocers seemed very willing to help him make the meal a success. The dinner was a little bit *meat and two veg* but he didn't trust himself with anything finicky for a first time.

Natasha seemed to like the aromas coming from the kitchen. She was definitely impressed by the sauce he had made and was making all sorts of approving noises.

"*Mmmm*. You made that yourself? It's not out of a packet? It's really good."

"Out of a packet? Please! No packets were harmed in the makin' of this dinner," he said, clinking glasses with her.

It felt so good to be having a conversation with an actual

grown-up in his house. Emma reverted to child mode when she came home. She would tell him about some kids in college who he had no clue about. She spoke about them as if he should know who they were by now. Suze probably would have known or else she knew how to play the game better than he did.

"You're putting me to shame. It's the opposite in my kitchen – nothing fresh is ever harmed by me. I have to admit, I'm not very domesticated. I hope that doesn't put you off me," Natasha said, lifting the lids and looking into the other pots.

Was she off her meds? Put him off? Nothing could put him off her. Except if she took out her teeth or something or unscrewed her wooden leg. He looked at her and she smiled. She had a beautiful smile and the teeth looked like they were all her own.

"Sit down, it's nearly ready," he said, lighting the candles on the dining table.

Natasha sat down and Peter spread her napkin out on her knees. He was nervous now. He wanted everything to be perfect. The smell of garlic was pretty strong. The recipe had said to use six cloves but he only used three.

He carved the meat, put some on their plates and placed the remainder on a platter between them. His garlic-and-rosemary roasted potatoes were a golden crisp colour and he was really pleased with himself.

He down opposite her. He poured them some more wine and told her to tuck in. She delicately cut the meat and ate small bites. He ate too, but not so delicately. It was good, if he said so himself.

He looked over at her and she wasn't gagging, thankfully. She was making yummy noises and soon their plates were wiped clean. Peter wanted to jump up and down with delight. Inside he was. He was sure Jamie would be proud of him.

"That was really delicious, Peter. I didn't realise you're such a good cook."

Peter couldn't hide his delight. He felt like the king of the castle and wanted to ask her to feed him some grapes.

"But you're very fond of garlic," she added.

He had hoped she hadn't noticed it. It was actually burning his throat.

"I only used three cloves and the recipe said six. Just as well I didn't go for it," he said proudly.

"But there are four still on my plate – I didn't eat them all – and three on yours," she said, indicating his plate.

"Oh, I mean I used three whole cloves – you know, when they're all stuck together."

"That's a head of garlic, Peter. Those small bits are the cloves. You used three whole heads? We'll be reeking for a week."

Thankfully, she was laughing. "I was thinking there was something funny going on," he said. "I'm sorry, Natasha. Maybe if you eat mints nobody will get the whiff off you. You won't be kissin' anyone tonight, wha'?".

Peter wanted to kick himself. He wanted more than anything to kiss her.

"I suppose not," she said.

Did she sound disappointed? Peter thought she did. He looked over at her in the candlelight and he decided that he would be kissing her, bad breath or not.

"Dessert?" he asked as he cleared the main-course plates.

"Sure. If you promise there's no garlic in it!"

"Yeah, it said to crush up a clove into the whipped cream but I left it out," he said with a laugh.

"Putting your own stamp on recipes now? You're quite the expert!"

The dessert was meringue with lots of fresh cream and berries. He had sprinkled icing sugar on top to finish it off.

Natasha sat back, agog at the gorgeous-looking dessert.

"This looks amazing. Peter, I've got to tell you, you're becoming more attractive to me with each course."

"Are you sure it's not the wine that's doing it?"

"Hey, you're always playing yourself down. No, it's definitely the food."

She unsettled him a bit. She was a woman who didn't play games. She went after what she wanted and she seemed to want him. He wasn't sure why. He knew she had gone through a few disastrous dates and he knew she liked him, but why exactly? He was a mid-forties, almost-divorced builder. Hardly a catch. Frankly, he thought she could do much better for herself.

"I have a confession to make," he said suddenly.

Natasha stopped mid-spoonful. She looked apprehensive. She stared at him and waited for him to speak.

"I didn't make the meringues. I bought them in the supermarket. Pre-made. I tried to make ones during the week but I kept burning the shite out of them, had the oven too high I must've."

"I don't think I can stay here after hearing that," she said.

"I know. I'm deeply ashamed."

"If you promise it'll never happen again, I'd be willing to give you another chance," she said, trying to hold in the laughter.

"You're a very understanding woman."

She was gas. The night was going better than he thought. Apart from the excessive use of garlic, the dinner was a resounding success.

"Coffee?" he asked as he cleared more dishes.

She stood up and started to help him load things into the dishwasher.

"No, thanks."

"Leave those. I'll do them later," he said.

"Won't you be busy later?" she asked teasingly.

"Will I?"

"Yes. Very," she said as she started towards the stairs.

Suze tossed and turned for hours. Her mother used to tell her to count sheep when she couldn't sleep as a child. She now knew that it was just one of those ridiculous things you said to a child to try to soothe them. It hadn't helped her then and it wasn't helping now.

Lately, when she couldn't sleep, she'd walk up the garden path to Seán's. He hardly slept either. They used to be like a pair of insomniacs sitting in his kitchen sipping hot milk in mostly companionable silence. On the occasions where either of them wanted to talk, they were both good listeners.

What he was going to do with the rest of his life was mostly what kept Seán awake nights. He had sold one company and was stuck. He needed to come up with another killer idea just to prove to himself that he wasn't just some flash in the pan who happened to get lucky. Suze tried to explain to him that most men would love to have his problems. Millions in the bank and houses scattered around the place. Lately he had even seen the funny side of his "problem".

Suze worried mostly about screwing her children up. Having a mother who tried to top herself was a big burden for any kid to bear. Suze and Seán were somehow always able to sort each other's lives out and make everything alright even if it was only a temporary fix. She would miss their midnight talks.

Tonight, Suze was consumed by the image of a handsome Peter chillaxing in their old kitchen. Peter stirring a pot and holding out a spoon for that woman to taste whatever it was he was cooking. He had never ever cooked a meal for her. You couldn't count the birthday tea and toast. She thought of the card from him for her birthday to the cottage this year. It was a funny one, something about women and shopping. He had signed it: *Best wishes, Peter*. She noted the absence of "*love*". She didn't mind at the time. "Love" wasn't really appropriate after all that happened. But it bothered her now. Just because she didn't love him, did that mean that he automatically didn't love her? She didn't think so. She got up out of bed and got into the car. She needed to know if that woman had stayed over. She reasoned that she wouldn't have. Surely to God they weren't going to just hop into bed with each other after knowing each other for five minutes.

And the woman. Suze hadn't studied her but there was something utterly familiar about her. As if she was well known. But what would Peter be doing with anybody famous? She went through lists of women in her head. Women in the tennis club. Women who worked in any of the shops she frequented. Parents of friends of Paul and Emma, though she looked a bit young for that. Nothing sprang to mind and yet Suze was convinced she knew her from somewhere.

She turned onto the motorway and drove until she reached the turn-off into the estate where their old house was. Her car was still there. At four o'clock in the morning. Suze needed to warn Peter that women like that existed. He had lived a sheltered life and Suze worried for him. It was all her fault of course. She never let him do anything for himself. She never even allowed him to iron his own shirts.

He'd think he'd never manage on his own and fall for the first woman who showed a bit of interest in him. With all

155

these thoughts running through her head, Suze realised she was still sitting outside her old house with the engine running. It was full-on stalkerish behaviour. She didn't want Peter to discover her, or get herself arrested, so she drove off back in the direction of the motorway and Howth.

Chapter 23

Rosa's temperature had risen to a dangerously high level. The doctors were frustrated and had no idea what to do next. The antibiotics they were drip-feeding her were the strongest they had and when Sarah asked what would happen if they didn't work, the doctors could only say that they "weren't there yet".

Sarah and Tom stayed in the room with Rosa, watching monitors and suffering as only parents of a sick child can. Nurses and doctors scuttled in and out of the room at regular intervals and not for one minute were they not scared for their daughter's life.

"Why did this happen to us, Tom?" Sarah asked when they were alone.

"I don't know, Sarah. It's just one of those things. Why not us? The doctors don't think it's meningitis but it's some type of virus. They're liaising with other hospitals to see if they've come across it. It's not anything that anybody has done. It's just one of those things that babies can pick up."

"Do you think that it's because we didn't want her? Do you think we're being punished?"

"Sarah. I'm dealing with medicine and facts here. I refuse to think about things that we have no control over. But if you're asking me if some vengeful god is getting back at us through Rosa, then no, I don't. I was the one who suggested getting rid of her. If a vengeful god was going to go after anybody, then it's me. You're both off the hook."

It was exactly what Sarah wanted him to admit.

"Yes, it should be you. You're the one who should be lying there with drips coming out of every limb. You're the one who should be suffering, not Rosa!"

Tom looked at her, aghast. He didn't actually believe they were being punished in the first place, but Sarah sure did. She hadn't forgiven him for his stupidity when she told him she was pregnant. He had tried and tried to make it up to her. He had tried to get her to let him be a part of their lives. He had said he was sorry a thousand times but she was never going to forgive him.

"You know what, Sarah, you just go right ahead thinking that I am the Devil Incarnate. You go ahead and exclude me and blame me for every bad thing that ever happens to you and Rosa. I have tried my hardest to show you that I'm sorry for what I said back then. And I am. Hand on heart, I was the stupidest bastard on the planet. But people make mistakes. We're all allowed to make them. We're also entitled to be forgiven if we try to atone for our mistakes. The most annoying thing about it is that you're so intent on making me suffer that it's impacting on your own life."

"I'll have you know that my life is hunky-dory, thank you very much."

"Oh boy, have I got news for you, Sarah! You're making a complete mess of everything. May is trying her best to rescue The Bakery but you're not helping her. She's asking you to make decisions and you're fobbing her off, telling her you're too busy to do this and that. You do know that The Bean Machine are about to put you out of business? You do realise that May wants to take over The Bakery once she has her degree? You do also realise that you don't let her look after Rosa even though she's her baby sister? She wants to help you. She wants you to let her into your world. You two used to be so close and she's afraid she's lost you. She thinks you don't trust her and her confidence is rock bottom. So that's two things in your life that are most definitely not hunky-dory. Do you want me to continue?"

Tom wanted to cut his tongue out. He had just blown up whatever chance he might have of ever getting back with Sarah and of them ever being a family. He wanted to take it all back but at the same time somebody had to tell Sarah the truth. Her friends didn't realise how bad things had got. They all had parts of the picture but he could see the whole.

"I'm sorry. I'm out of line. Forget I said any of that."

"It's going to be pretty hard to forget."

She didn't argue with him. She didn't tell him he was

159

wrong or that he had no right to speak to her like that. She didn't say any of it because she had a feeling he might be right. But she couldn't think about the mess she was making of her life right now. Not while Rosa was fighting for her little life.

Another nurse came in and they had to discontinue their little "chat". Sarah was sure that the nurse could feel the tense atmosphere in the confined space of the child's room. Tom had to get up and leave and it was like someone released a valve when he was gone. The air became breathable again.

The nurse hit an alarm that presumably called for the doctor and pressed buttons on the machine beside Rosa's cot bed.

"*What's happening?*" screamed Sarah. She couldn't take it anymore. She was living on her nerves and each one of them was shot to bits.

"Her temperature is coming down. I think the antibiotics are working."

Sarah couldn't believe the words coming out of the nurse's mouth. She watched as more doctors and nurses came in and out of the room and eventually declared the temperature to be broken.

Tom had reappeared and he was shaking hands with his colleagues and thanking them for the care they had given to his little girl.

"We'll keep her under observation for another twenty-four hours. She's not out of danger yet but her temperature

160

coming down is good news," one of the doctors said to Tom and Sarah.

Sarah buried her head into Tom's chest and he put his arms around her and held her while the tears of relief flooded.

Now that there was a possibility that Rosa would recover, Sarah felt all of her anger leave her body and hope take its place.

Chapter 24

Peter woke up and stretched himself out on the bed. When he touched off a leg that wasn't his, it took him an instant to remember that Natasha was still there. He turned around and looked at her sleeping face. He nearly had to pinch himself to see if it was all real. He had made love to a beautiful woman when he had thought that he'd never have sex again after Suze left him.

He felt like jumping out of bed and doing a dance that involved a lot of bumping and grinding. *We're still in business, bud,* he said silently to his willy. He didn't want to think about how he got so lucky meeting Natasha because he reckoned that over-analysing his situation might suddenly make her disappear.

They had left a trail of their clothes from the kitchen to the bedroom. By the time they got to the top of the stairs he was wearing only his boxers and Natasha was down to some very sexy lacy bits of silky black material that somehow passed for underwear. Everything was gone by the time they both crawled onto his bed.

He thought she was gorgeous when they had their first date but the sight of her naked took his breath away. And she was giving it all to him. He had given her a lot in return, he thought happily as he looked at her still sleeping while remembering them going at it for the second time. Twice in one night. Jesus Christ, that hadn't even happened since he and Suze were teenagers.

Natasha wanted to please him and be pleased and she told him what she wanted him to do to her. This was a new departure for Peter who had been completely in the dark before as to what it was that a woman wanted. Natasha seemed to understand that he wasn't a bloody mind-reader and her instructions were clear and precise. And they worked if her moans and groans were anything to go by.

He thought he was past it. He thought he was on the scrapheap but there was life left in the old dog yet. He could still taste the damn garlic and he went into the bathroom to brush his teeth and wash his mouth out. He hoped that Natasha would want to go round three when she woke up.

When he got back to the bedroom she was putting on her underwear. She smiled at him when she saw him.

"How'rya," he said, coming around to her side of the bed and kissing her.

"I have to brush my teeth. The garlic is making a comeback this morning," she said with a laugh.

163

Peter didn't know what to do. Should he get back into bed? Should he be waiting for her when she re-emerged from the bathroom, looking all seductive like? He tried a few positions, lying down, leaning on one elbow and then full frontal no bed covers but decided that he looked like a total knob.

He'd be better off out of the bed altogether. He got up again. He was worried that she had come to her senses overnight and realised that she could do way better than him. Maybe she'd tell him that she had made a big mistake and thanks for dinner and the ride but she'd be seeing him. *Fuck*.

She came back into the bedroom and started to get back into bed.

"What? You don't want to join me?" she asked in a sexy voice.

"What do you think?" he said as his desire for her was obvious.

After more lovemaking, Peter and Natasha made their way downstairs where Peter made her some breakfast. It was like a dream and Peter was happier than he remembered being in a long, long time.

Eventually Natasha announced that she had to go home. He didn't want to let her go. He'd had such a great night and it wasn't just the sex. She was great. She was open and fun and no subject was off limits. He didn't know what was next for them. They had done all the dates and they had now done the sex. Was that the zenith? Was their match now considered a success and over because of it? Would she even want to see him again?

"I've got a meeting to go to for the next few days. I'll call you when I'm done," she said as she got up to leave.

"You don't have to make up stuff. You can just say you don't want to see me again if that's what you want. I'm a big boy, I can handle rejection," he said, not meaning it at all. The last thing he wanted was her to reject him.

"I really do have a meeting. The firm are doing a big recruitment drive so I'm going to be up to my eyes in work. Really. Of course I want to see you again. I had a lovely time last night. Didn't you?"

"Yeah. I did. I had a brilliant time. I'll probably have to lie down for a week to get over it, but I had a great time. I was just trying to give you an out if you wanted one."

"Well, I don't want an out. I'll see you in a few days."

And she was gone. He missed her already. The smell of her perfume hung in the air for a while and he breathed it deep into his nostrils. He looked around the kitchen and the pots and pans from last night were still waiting for someone to wash them. He put everything big and small into the dishwasher and started to tidy the kitchen.

He was singing to himself as he wiped and sprayed the surfaces. He heard a car in the driveway and hoped she'd come back. What had she forgotten?

He opened the front door with a huge smile but was greeted not by Natasha, but by Suze.

"Suze, hiya. What are you doing here?" he said, unable to keep the disappointment out of his voice.

"Were you expecting someone else?" she asked, knowing full well that his squeeze had just left.

Suze had been parked down the road for over an hour. She had been about to give up when she saw the black Audi reverse out of their – his driveway.

"Eh, no. It's just I wasn't expectin' to see you, that's all," he said as he held the front door open for her.

"I'm not interrupting you, I hope," she said.

"No, I'm just tidyin' up. Do ya want a cuppa?"

"Sure, yes, thanks," she said as she looked around the kitchen.

Jesus, the smell of garlic would knock a horse, she thought as she watched him ease his way around the kitchen like he had never done before. He had moved a few things and he took out mugs that they didn't own when she lived here.

"So, how are you?" he said as he handed her a mug of tea.

"I'm fine. Good really. I wanted to see you because I have something I want to say to you," she said seriously.

Peter knew this day was coming. They had been apart for over a year now and it was only right that they should make it official. A divorce would give them official permission to get on with their lives.

But Suze started telling him about Sarah's little girl and the possible meningitis diagnosis.

"I was sitting in the hospital waiting room waiting to hear if Rosa was going to live or die and all of a sudden I knew I'd put you through hell and I wanted to tell you that I'm sorry. Truly sorry. I sat there and I felt the tension of the nurses and doctors scurrying around and I felt as helpless as you must have felt."

Peter was sorry for little Rosa but he had no idea why she was bringing up this stuff. All that was in the past. Yes, it had been bad, but it was over now. Why was she raking over this old ground?

"I think we may have made a mistake. Well, I made a mistake. I want us to get back together, Peter."

He could only stare at her. Where was this coming from? He thought that Suze and Seán were an item way over in Howth. Seán was mad about Suze and she was living a few hundred yards from his doorstep. Every time the kids went over, Seán was there. They told him. It didn't bother him now. OK, it did at first. After all, he was after handing his wife to Seán on a silver platter. After Suze's suicide attempt, she couldn't go home to him. He was determined to do something good for her. They discovered the rundown cottage when he was doing up Seán's gaff in Howth. He had done up the cottage for her – he just didn't realise that Seán would be part of his gift to her as well. He had never asked her out straight but it was obvious Seán was crazy about her. It didn't take a genius to figure it out.

"But what about Seán? I thought you two had a thing goin' on," said Peter.

"Nothing ever happened with Seán. Something nearly happened once. In Venice. But it didn't. I thought I wasn't able to have, you know, a relationship with a man after the, well, after I tried to kill myself. Then recently I found out that I can."

"How?"

"How what?"

"How did you find out that you can?"

"It's not important but, believe me, I've got no problems in that department," she said, her voice dropping into a quasi-sexy tone that he had never heard from Suze's mouth before and which he was pretty sure didn't suit her.

Suze had obviously been through a terrible time and Peter didn't want to do anything that would push her over the edge again. Why the hell couldn't she pick Seán? Why him? Why, when he had just had the night of his life, was his ex-wife asking him to get back together with her?

He didn't know what to think about it. Suze was not an unattractive woman. In fact, she looked better now than she had during most of their marriage. She was happy in her work and she loved her new house and her newfound freedom, and it reflected in her appearance.

This new Suze was a virtual stranger to him now so why was she of the opinion that they had made a mistake by breaking up? One thing for sure was that no matter what delusions were implanted in her brain he was not what she was looking for.

He was about to say as much to her when she stood up

and let her coat fall to the ground. She had nothing on underneath except for a black lacy corset thingy. Jesus wept. Hadn't he seen enough black lace for one twenty-four hour period, he thought as the sweat started to bead on his forehead. In fairness to her, she looked bloody great but there was no way he was going there.

"Do you want to see a bit more?" she said, loosening some strings on the corset. He was about to shout no when he heard a key turn in the door.

"Aw, Jaysus, Suze. Put your coat back on!"

"*Hey, Dad!*" Emma called from the hallway.

Peter bolted from the kitchen to the hall to give Suze a few precious extra seconds to gather herself together. This was turning into the craziest day he had ever experienced, and he could badly do with a pint.

"Hiya, love," he said, giving his daughter a long hug.

"What's Mam's car doing here?" she asked, strolling into the kitchen where Suze was sipping her tea with her coat buttoned up again.

"Emma, this is nice. I called round to say hi to Dad. I've been neglecting him lately."

"Not at all, I'm well able to look after meself," said Peter. He didn't want to give Suze any reason to think he felt neglected by her at all. Or give her any encouragement whatsoever.

Chapter 25

Diane and Laurie had received a call from Sarah telling them that Rosa was out of danger and was responding well to the antibiotics she was on. The relief almost made Diane soften her stance on the trip to Seamus, the seventh son of a seventh son.

"I'm nervous. I don't think I'll be able to keep any food down," Laurie said over breakfast.

"I want it on the record that I think you're mad," said Diane.

"Always the lawyer. Look, I know this is a long shot but I bet if there was something that you wanted as badly as I want a baby, we'd be partaking in some fairly dubious stuff too."

"I don't think we would," said Diane.

There was nothing for it now but to go and see the guy. They would let him do his hocus-pocus stuff and Laurie would fly back to LA, to her actual doctors. And hopefully she would get pregnant the traditional way.

"So how was dinner with the handsome Oliver?" asked Laurie.

"Fine."

"Fine? Is that it?"

"Yeah. It was fine. We had dinner. We discussed the style they're going for. It was fine."

Laurie knew the overuse of "fine" meant that things weren't "fine" at all. Diane was suddenly in a bad mood, Sarah's good news forgotten.

"Do you want to talk about it?"

"There's nothing to talk about. He's calling here to take us to the quack's place. He said we'd never find it on our own."

"That's very kind of him."

Diane didn't say a word. Laurie decided she wasn't going to get anything out of her so she dropped it.

"Suze and Jesus slept together," she whispered.

"What?" said Diane, shaking her head vigorously. "God, for a minute there I thought you said Suze and Jesus slept together?"

"I did. They did. Keep your voice down. He's probably moping somewhere around the place and I don't want Mrs. Murphy to hear either."

"Hold on a second. You mean our Suze? And Jesus? *Jesus* Christ Almighty?" said Diane. "I'm sorry, but you'll have to give me some context. Not that Suze's not a good-looking woman but he's so *em* ..."

"Gorgeous?" asked Laurie.

"No. So fucking annoying," said Diane. "When did it happen? How?"

"The night she twisted her ankle, seemingly. He came to her aid. And a bit more besides. And that's not all. She thinks she has unfinished business with Peter. Her emotions are all over the place, Di. I'm worried about her. She went to Peter's and he had some woman over for dinner. She now thinks she may have made a mistake by leaving him and thinks she might still love him. It seems to me like she could be heading for a bit of a crisis. You know what I mean."

Diane knew exactly what Laurie meant and she was worried too. A lot had happened in Suze's life and she had worked hard to resolve all the issues. Diane hoped that it wasn't all about to unravel. Suze had always led the less glamorous life of all four of them. She had been the typical suburban housewife while the others seemed to be living the life she craved.

It was strange but, since the suicide attempt, she seemed to be living the life she wanted to live all along. She was barely recognisable from the empty shell of a person she had been. She even looked different. Better. So why was she looking back now? Peter was her past. She was going to risk her whole recovery by going back there. They would need to intervene to stop her doing something stupid.

Just then they heard tyres on the gravel driveway.

"He's here. You're taking this with a large pinch of salt, yeah?" Diane asked Laurie.

"Yes. Don't worry about me, I haven't gone gaga. Let's just see what happens."

"Morning, ladies!" Oliver said cheerily as they walked outside.

He kissed Laurie on both cheeks and opened the back door of the car for her. He was a real charmer, thought Diane. It was her turn and he was about to kiss her. She was sure he was aiming for her lips – his were hovering dangerously close to hers – but, at the very last second, he kissed her on the cheek. He was teasing her and she wanted to slap him.

"No tractor today?" said Diane sarcastically.

"No, it'd never take the three of us," he replied, enjoying playing with her.

Diane hated this scenario. She was never the one doing the chasing. She made up her mind that she would have him begging her to kiss him. She didn't know how she'd do it but she would.

There was plenty of chitchat going on between Laurie and Oliver on the way to Seamus's place. Diane didn't trust herself to talk so she listened to their chatter and fantasised about being naked with Oliver. It was no harm to fantasise. It didn't mean that she wasn't happy with Serge, did it?

The morning was bright and fresh and the view of the town and the sea below from the top of the mountain they were on was breath-taking.

"I can see why you chose Ballygra for your hotel," said Laurie, taking it all in. "Kevin and I will definitely be guests when it's finished."

"It would be our great pleasure to have you both," was all he said.

Diane knew he had to be dancing a jig inside, but on the surface he remained professional and unruffled. He was such a cool customer. An endorsement by one of Hollywood's leading couples would be worth the world to him and Richard.

"Thanks for taking us. You're right, we'd never have found it," said Laurie as he pulled up outside a rundown stone cottage.

They got out of the car.

There was a half door which was opened at the top. Diane's scrunched her nose at the smell of something wafting out through it.

"He's always brewing up some potion or other," Oliver explained.

Diane shuddered.

"You have to go in by yourself," Oliver said to Laurie. "You'll find him in the room off the kitchen."

Laurie began to look like she had just made a huge mistake by coming.

"Go on, you'll be fine," said Oliver.

They watched her open the half-door and go inside.

"I hope she'll be OK in there with him," said Diane. "He's not dangerous or anything, is he?"

"It depends on your definition of dangerous!" Oliver laughed. "No. He's not going to do her any harm if that's what you're afraid of. He might ask her to drink some of that nasty brew he has boiling on the stove, but that's about as bad as it'll get."

Diane was somehow not reassured by the fact her friend might only have to drink some poisonous liquid. They really shouldn't have come.

"Don't look so worried. She's only a few feet away from us. Nothing bad is going to happen."

Diane hoped he was right. She sat down on a stone seat which happened to overlook the sea below.

"It's beautiful here. Spain is wonderful, but there's something so rugged about this place," she said wistfully.

"And do you like rugged?" said Oliver cheekily.

"I'm purely talking about the landscape," said Diane.

"Me too. What did you think I was talking about?"

Diane looked at him. That face, those lips. He made her skin tingle and he was leaning in to her now. He had his arm behind her back on the seat.

"See down there, between the cluster of trees, that's Ballygra," he said, leaning in closer than was absolutely necessary.

"Oh yes," she said, feeling his breath on the side of her face.

She turned to say something to him but he was right there. Right up in her face. Then his lips were on hers. They were soft like she knew they would be. His arm was now pulling her close to him and his other hand was inside her jacket, around her waist. She put her arms around him and then they were really kissing. There might be magic happening inside the cottage but what was happening outside on the stone seat was magic too.

Diane could feel the hot sun on her face and didn't know if it was the sun or his kisses which were making her feverish. He put his hand under her light sweater and touched her skin. It was like he was shooting electrical currents through her body and Diane wished they were somewhere private. And comfortable too would be good. She touched his skin too and knew she had the same effect on him. There were no thoughts of Serge. There was only Oliver.

"This is going to lead to me having to take all your clothes off right here if we don't stop," said Oliver breathlessly as he reluctantly stopped kissing her.

"You started it," said Diane, disappointed that it had to end.

"I know I did, but I can't finish it. Not here."

He said it so adamantly and held her so possessively that she almost melted into him.

They sat on the stone seat and took in the amazing view of the wild Atlantic below them. They were so lost in their own thoughts and fantasies that they forgot all about Laurie.

When the cottage door opened and they heard her come out, they sat away from each other and hopped up to ask how she got on.

Diane thought she looked funny and luckily Oliver saw it too. He caught her before she hit the ground as she keeled over.

"What the hell has he done to her?" shouted Diane.

Laurie had fainted. There were no marks on her, or signs of any distress but she was out for the count.

"This is normal. A lot of people say that they get a weakness afterwards," said Oliver calmly. "Let's get her into the car."

"A weakness? She's unconscious! Don't you think we should go inside and find out what that madman has done to her first?"

"Trust me. She'll be fine. It's a good sign, believe it or not. Now open the door and I'll lie her down on the back seat."

Diane did as she was told, despite her own reservations. She really wanted to confront Seamus and ask him what he had done to her friend. She sat into the back of the car and took Laurie's head on her lap.

Oliver got it and drove off.

Diane stole glances at him in the mirror. His furrowed brow was reflected back at her as well as his beautiful brown eyes.

The journey along the bumpy roads felt like forever to Diane. When they got back to the O'Neill house, Laurie was still out cold. Like Oliver, Mrs. Murphy wasn't surprised either. She plumped up the cushions on the couch in the good room as she called it, and Oliver laid Laurie down.

The three of them stood over her, not sure what to do.

"Hey, what's up?" asked Jesus, coming into the room.

They had forgotten about Jesus. Diane tried to steer him out of the room before he saw Laurie, but it was too late.

"What's the matter with Laurie?" he asked hysterically. "Is she dead?"

Diane cursed herself for not getting to him on time. Jesus was like a child and they tried to explain that she had a little fainting spell. Mrs. Murphy had to take over and take him into the kitchen where she fed him some of her home-made scones spread with home-made blackberry jam. That seemed to quieten him down for now.

Diane and Oliver sat in the good room, waiting.

"How long?" asked Diane.

"Dunno," he said.

"She will wake up?"

"Of course she will."

Diane bloody well hoped so. She could imagine trying to explain this to Kevin. It might go something like *"Well, Kevin, we let your beautiful wife who you love so much go into a rundown cottage with a complete lunatic stranger who thought he had magical powers and who gave her some noxious poison to drink. We thought she was only going to rub his relic but he went for the poison option in the end."* Yes, he'd definitely understand. Who wouldn't?

"It's very common for people to faint after seeing Seamus. Don't worry, she'll come around any time now."

Diane should have made her see sense. She should never have agreed to have anything to do with her seeing that witch doctor. She even thought about getting the police involved. If he was peddling poison, then he needed to be stopped. She should have persuaded Laurie to go and adopt a child in Africa or somewhere instead.

When she heard *rub* and *relic* in the same sentence she should have known better.

Mrs. Murphy came in with a pot of tea for them. Her answer to everything seemed to be a cup of tea. Oliver cheerily talked about this and that to Mrs. Murphy as if there wasn't a woman lying unconscious on the couch.

Diane was just about to scream when Laurie flicked her eyes open. She looked around as if she had no idea where she was. And she hadn't at first.

"You see. It's the smell of the tea that got her to open her eyes," announced Mrs. Murphy.

Diane's eyes couldn't roll far enough back in her head but she was so grateful that Laurie was back that she ignored the old woman.

"What happened?" asked Laurie after a few seconds.

"You tell us. You fainted outside Seamus's cottage. You've been out of it for about an hour. Are you OK?"

"*Em*, yeah. Yes, I'm fine," said Laurie, sitting up and putting her feet on the ground. "I don't remember fainting. The last thing I remember was drinking this stuff that Seamus gave me. He said it would help with my fertility. It smelt like boiled wellies, but you know how desperate I am. I drank it. It didn't taste too bad, considering."

"I thought he had poisoned you. I didn't know what I was going to say to Kevin. I don't think the truth would have cut it. You know, Laurie, maybe you need to forget all about this nonsense and adopt a baby from somewhere. Brad and Angelina have done it. They might even give you one of theirs."

"I won't need to. Seamus told me I'm going to have a baby. He said that I'm not going to just have one baby either. I'm going to have lots. I'm so happy, Diane. I'm going to have children!"

That fucking rotten lying bastard, thought Diane. She would go back up there and give him a piece of her mind. He was probably off his head on homebrew but it was unforgivable of him to give Laurie hope when most of the medical world sided with her doctors in LA who held out no hope at all.

"Don't look like that," said Laurie. "I know you think I'm crazy but I know it's going to happen."

"It's not that I think you're crazy. But that Seamus guy – how can we believe what he's saying? I think if he lived in civilisation, he might be considered to have mental-health issues. Think about what you just said. Don't you think it's all just a bit too far-fetched?"

Diane gave Mrs. Murphy a filthy look. It was all her fault. She had suggested going to Seamus Sullivan in the first place. And Oliver – he was as bad. He kissed like a god but that was totally beside the point right now. What mattered was the mess that was left behind. How would Laurie cope when the anticipated and heralded baby didn't arrive? Who was going to pick up the pieces then?

180

"How are you feeling now?" asked Diane as she lay down beside Laurie on her bed.

"I'm fine. Sorry you were scared. I don't know what happened."

"That old fucker nearly poisoned you, that's what happened. You know I'd never have forgiven myself if anything happened to you. And what would Kevin have said? I should never have gone along with it in the first place."

"I'm not a child, Di. I would have gone there with or without you. I know you don't believe in any of that stuff but, wait and see, I'll have a baby soon," Laurie said with certainty.

"How can you possibly believe that? You've been around a block or two. You're a smart girl who knows what's what. It's ludicrous!" Diane threw her hands up in the air. Laurie had worked for a national newspaper reporting on all things political and financial and how she had managed to switch off her common sense, she would never understand.

"I felt him," said Laurie.

"Felt who? *Seamus?*" asked Diane.

"The baby. My baby. I felt him move inside me. He fluttered like a little butterfly. I could feel him in there. It was beautiful." Laurie looked at Diane with watering eyes.

"But Laurie, how could you? Listen to yourself. This is madness. You need to sleep off whatever drug that fecker has given you."

"I know you think I'm off my rocker. I know you think it's nonsense but I felt my baby inside me."

181

"Do you really think that's possible, Laurie?" begged Diane. "Really? Think about what you just said and tell me that you don't believe it."

"But I do believe it. You never wanted children, so you don't know what the longing is like. I'm not being mean about it but you've no idea what it's like to feel your baby move inside you. I'm sorry but you couldn't possibly understand."

"Nor do you know what it feels like because you don't have a baby moving inside you. For fuck's sake, Laurie, where is your head at?"

"Diane, unless you want us to fall out, I think we need to change the subject. Let's agree to disagree, shall we?"

Diane grudgingly agreed to do just that. She and Laurie were all that was left of their big vacation and Laurie had travelled a long way to be here. It was the least she could do not to fight her on this. She was alive. She was fine. Diane was grateful for that at least. She left Laurie to rest and went downstairs.

Mrs. Murphy was in the kitchen standing at the stove boiling the kettle. As usual.

"If that Oliver Butler fella comes around here again, I'm going to put the run on him," said Mrs. Murphy out of the blue.

"Why? What did he do?" asked Diane. She had hardly found out about the kiss earlier.

"It's all over the village that he's coming in and out of this house just so he can persuade that lovely girl and her husband to come and stay in his castle."

"What lovely girl are you on about now?" Diane asked impatiently.

"That lovely girl upstairs. Mrs. Flynn. That Oliver Butler was always a little feckin' pup. I gave him more than one red ear in my time and, I don't mind telling you, I'll give him another flake if I see him around here again."

"You don't know that for sure, Mrs. Murphy. Maybe you're being a bit hard on him?"

But Mrs. Murphy was in full rant mode.

"I do know it for certain. Sure he was in the pub the night you were all in high spirits. He was asking around that night about where you were all staying. He recognised Mrs. Flynn straight away. He's no ordinary eejit, that fella."

So he did know who Laurie was and all that feigned disinterest was faked. Diane was gutted but she consoled herself with the fact that they had done nothing more than kiss and that all she had given him was the benefit of her interior-design expertise. So why was her disappointment telling her that she had given him more than that?

Laurie thought back to what had happened earlier that day. Seamus was a kind-faced old man and Laurie wasn't afraid of him at all. The house was old and bare, but it wasn't dirty. There looked like there was no technology of any sort in the house, not even a television. The only link to the outside world seemed to be an old wireless on a shelf. Seamus certainly lived the simple life. He sat her down and took her hand in his. He looked deep into her eyes, into her soul, she felt, and he asked her why she was there.

"I want a baby," she said simply.

He kept looking at her, into her, and Laurie didn't feel uncomfortable as you would if a complete stranger was staring at you.

"Close your eyes."

Laurie did what she was told.

"Picture yourself and your babby. Look at his face and know him. You're his mother."

He still held onto her hands as images of motherhood flickered on and off in Laurie's mind.

"Feel the weight of him. Feel what it's like to carry him. Feel what it's like to hold him in your arms. Smell him and fill yourself with the scent."

Laurie felt her face soften. She felt the stress leave her brows as the joy of motherhood overtook her.

He held her hands for a long time. Laurie wasn't in a hurry to leave the movie that was playing on the screen of her mind. It was the happiest movie she had ever watched, and she would happily have stayed in Seamus's bare, white room forever.

He eventually brought her back to reality.

"Are you alright, girleen?" he asked.

She was anguished to be back in the real world without her baby who she had been smelling and holding and feeding for the past while.

"Don't worry, *a ghrá*. You've seen him in your mind so you'll be holding him before long."

"Yes." But Laurie was inconsolable. Sobs wracked her body and she doubled over in the chair to try to manage the spasms.

Laurie couldn't make any sense of what was happening. She was so happy she thought she would burst but the emotion was too much to bear. The sobs eventually became less violent and that's when Seamus went to get a glass of the concoction that was boiling on the stove for her. If Seamus had asked her to walk on broken glass, she would have done it. He was a miracle worker and he had given her the one thing in life that she wanted more than anything. She drank and thanked him from the bottom of her heart.

Chapter 26

"I'm a total screw-up," cried Suze down the phone to Diane.

"I don't think you're alone there," replied Diane.

"I went to Peter's to try to seduce him. I only had underwear under my coat. I dropped my coat and stood there almost in the nip in my old kitchen. I told him I wanted him back."

"OK, you win – you're a total screw-up," said Diane as she tried to get her head around the scene in Suze's old house. "What did he do?"

"He told me to put my coat back on," said Suze, bursting into tears.

"*Ouch!*" And it was still hurting if Suze's cries at the far end of the phone were anything to go by. "You have to consider that it must have been a bit of a shock for him to see you like that. I'm sure it caught him by surprise."

"*Then Emma came in!*" wailed Suze.

This was getting worse even though Diane had thought that wasn't possible.

"Christ. Poor Emma. She must have run out of the house screaming!"

"No, I had my coat back on by then."

"Thank God for that." This was totally out of character for Suze. She was normally so reserved and uninterested in sex as far as Diane could tell. "Do you mind me asking if you're still taking your medication?"

"I stopped taking it before the holiday. I thought we'd be having such a relaxing time that I wouldn't need it. I don't want to get too dependent on the pills, Di. I don't want to be on them for the rest of my life. Do you think that what I did has anything to do with not taking them?"

"I think it's demonstrating that a side effect of not taking them is acute nymphomania," said Diane.

"So Laurie told you about Jesus?" said Suze.

"She did. I was just getting my head around that and now you drop this bombshell. Suze, I think you need to go back to your doctor and get her to write you another prescription. I don't think you're going to be taking the medication forever but you're not ready to go cold turkey yet."

"Mrs. Murphy told me the reason why Seamus has the gift," said Laurie when Diane walked into the kitchen.

The teapot was out again and the kettle was whistling

away softly on the stove. Diane wondered where it all went wrong. She had envisioned a week sipping cocktails on a beach, not drinking enough tea to sink a battleship. Nevertheless she accepted when Mrs. Murphy offered to pour her a cup.

"You know how I feel about all this, Laurie. I thought we had agreed to disagree."

"He had a baby. It's buried underneath the stone seat outside the cottage," said Laurie, undeterred.

"Well, he's a bloody miracle man if he had a baby. Is this documented in some medical journal somewhere? Or in the local library at least?" said Diane harshly.

"Of course he didn't *have* the baby. But guess who did?" asked Laurie, completely enthralled in the telling of the story.

"And how would I possibly know that?" Diane wanted to forget that Seamus Sullivan even existed.

"Joe's mother. According to Mrs. Murphy, that is."

Mrs. Murphy shuffled uneasily as Laurie said her name. She had obviously been telling tales out of school. But this was juicy and Diane was interested all of a sudden and wanted to hear more.

"Sheila O'Neill, as she was then, and Seamus were sweethearts. Lovers. Sheila got 'in trouble' as Mrs. Murphy puts it but they didn't tell anybody. They were trying to hide it for as long as they could. You know what it was like in those days – she'd almost have been burned at the stake for having sex outside marriage. She asked Seamus to run away with her, but he couldn't go. He had the gift and he had to stay here and cure the locals of their various ills. He loved Sheila but he couldn't run away with her. The poor things didn't know what to do. One day when they were together, Sheila went into labour but the baby was stillborn. They buried the baby's remains in the garden of Seamus's cottage. Later on, he built a stone bench over where the baby was buried. It's so sad, isn't it?"

"It's completely messed up, that's what it is. This country has a shameful past. You know I'm not Granny O'Hara's biggest fan, but there's no way a woman or a girl for that matter should ever be ashamed of herself for having sex, doing the most natural thing in the world."

Diane heard Mrs. Murphy give a little snort. Mrs. Murphy who lusted after Eddie O'Neill for her whole life without ever getting a rub of his relic.

"Do you think Joe knows?" Diane asked Mrs. Murphy.

"There's nobody knows, only a handful," she replied. "I only know because Eddie used to rant and rave after he had a few drinks. He left her with no choice but to go after their parents passed away. He had seen her swollen belly. He was no fool. He also noticed that it had disappeared. He confronted her about it one night soon after her parents died. He pretended to be all concerned. The poor girl told him. She should have kept her mouth shut, so she should. He was very violent that night. He hit her and he could've killed her if she didn't make a run for it. You see, it was a sin. We were told from the pulpit every Sunday that it was a sin to have lustful thoughts and especially to act on them.

I'm ashamed to say I didn't know any better. I thought he was right doing what he did. Not hurting her, don't get me wrong. But I thought he was right to bawl her out. May God forgive me."

"He sounds like a really great guy. I can see why you devoted your life to him," said Diane sarcastically. She wanted to say more but she could see that Mrs. Murphy was already ashamed enough of herself for what happened all those years ago.

"*Ara*, he didn't know any better. None of us did. If I ever saw Sheila again, I'd ask her forgiveness and that's for sure."

Diane believed her. These people had lived in a time where the Church ruled with an iron fist. It would take a brave person to stand up to an association like the Catholic Church and poor Sheila couldn't have taken them on without coming off a very poor second.

"Why didn't Sheila run to Seamus?" asked Laurie. "They must have been in love if they risked having sex in those days. Why didn't Seamus man up and do the right thing?"

"Sure Seamus was a gentle soul, the gentlest you'd ever meet. Sheila wouldn't tell Eddie who the father was. She was afraid he'd kill him. And he would have. Seamus would have been no match for Eddie. Seamus wouldn't lift a finger against another human being and Sheila knew that full well. If she ran to Seamus, Eddie would've found out. She left on her own to protect the man she loved."

Laurie had tears running down her cheeks as Mrs.

Murphy portrayed the story of the young lovers and their dead baby. Even hard-hearted Diane felt a stirring of pity for Granny O'Hara, the poor old dear.

"So? Do you want to do something for our last night in the sticks?" Laurie asked Diane.

The week in the country wasn't nearly as uneventful as Diane had feared it would be. She had to admit that being kissed by Oliver was the highlight.

"I dunno. Do you?"

"I suppose we could go to the pub again. If they let us in, that is."

"Sure, why not. It's not like there's many other options. Any other option really."

Laurie went upstairs while Diane made a phone call to Serge.

She had a few missed calls and she felt bad for not picking up. This time it was Serge's turn not to take her call. Diane was relieved that he didn't answer. What would she say? Would he sense that things had shifted? That her feelings for him had changed?

She put her phone back in her pocket and went to make her way upstairs.

"The poor crater. She's probably tired what with the babby and all," butted in Mrs. Murphy as Diane started to climb the stairs.

"What bloody babby, I mean baby? She's not pregnant. Seamus Sullivan is a quack and most probably a crack addict or something. So don't start with any of that bollo— nonsense."

The tirade had little or no effect on Mrs. Murphy.

"Will I go with ye?" she said.

"Go where?" asked Diane, wondering what she was on about.

"For a drink. I like a glass of sherry on the odd occasion. I'll get my coat."

"Oh for f… Yeah. Sure. Whatever."

Laurie came downstairs.

"Mrs. Murphy is coming with us." Diane pulled a face. "So what about Jesus? Will he be OK here on his own?"

"He doesn't want to come. He says he wants to get an early night. He has his phone and he has WIFI. He'll be grand."

———

The pub was busier than it had been when they were there less than a week before. Like on the previous occasion, every single head turned to look at them when the door opened. The bartender gave her a funny look but Diane acted like nothing had happened. She ordered a glass of wine and a sherry for Mrs. Murphy. Laurie was having a sparkling water because of the non-existent baby she was all of a sudden carrying.

Diane and Laurie sipped their drinks. Mrs. Murphy downed her sherry like it was a shot of tequila. Diane went to the bar and got her another. Every eye in the place was on Laurie. Diane could see people stealthily taking photographs with their mobile phones. Some people were less discreet and came right up to Laurie and attempted to take selfies.

"We would have been better off staying at home," Diane said to Laurie when she returned to the table.

"It's fine. I'm on such a high right now that nothing can bother me."

Mrs. Murphy was sitting between Diane and Laurie with her coat buttoned up and her handbag held tightly on her knees as if someone would run off with it. She seemed completely oblivious to the photo-taking that was going on.

Laurie noticed that her glass was empty again and went to the bar. She was half tempted to buy the bottle at the rate Mrs. Murphy was knocking them back.

"For fuck's sake," Diane said as the old woman floored the drink Laurie had just bought. "You'd want to slow down there."

"Ah sure, I'll have another one if you insist."

Diane went to bar again. The pub was now full. The young bartender attended to her immediately.

"Another sherry, please," said Diane, indicating the old woman at their table.

"Sherry? I would have taken you for more of a champagne kind of girl," said the familiar velvet voice.

"It's not for me. It's for the party animal over there. She's knocking them back like there's no tomorrow."

Diane felt like she had suddenly come alive. The old pub no longer seemed like the rundown shebeen it was. It was disco lights and glitter balls just because he was in it.

"I know," said Oliver. "She'll just keep sinking them. Then she'll fall down. She has form."

Diane was about to pay the bartender.

"No. Let me. Can I get you something? And Laurie?"

He waved in the direction of the two ladies at the table. Laurie smiled broadly at him.

"No, we're grand, thanks. I've still got a drink and Laurie's on the water because she thinks she's pregnant."

"She could very well be."

"Oh, please. Don't."

"So you didn't feel anything magical happen in Dooneybeg?"

Diane couldn't look at him. She felt magic of some sort but it was nothing to do with Laurie and her phantom pregnancy.

"I don't believe in magic," she said flatly. "I'll better take this over to Mrs. M."

Diane put the sherry in front of Mrs. Murphy and turned to Laurie.

"Oliver said she'll drink until she falls down."

"Shit. I'd better take her home," said Laurie.

"I'll go too," said Diane.

"No, you stay," said Laurie, making eyes in Oliver's direction. He was still standing at the bar.

"I don't have anything I want to say to that man."

"He likes you, Diane. Something's going to happen between you two."

"Don't be ridiculous –" Diane didn't get a chance to finish her sentence as Oliver arrived over to their table.

Mrs. Murphy picked up her glass and drained it in seconds.

"Eh, I think it's time we got going," said Laurie.

"Sure we're having a lovely time here."

"We'll end up carrying you home, Mrs. Murphy. We don't want you getting plastered," said Diane.

Oliver spoke directly to Diane. "Don't go."

"Yeah, stay, Diane. I can manage on my own."

"It's not fair. It's our last night."

"Diane, stay, I'll be fine." Laurie was not taking no for an answer.

Diane let her coat fall back onto the seat.

Laurie said goodnight and Mrs. Murphy slurred something at her that she didn't understand as they left.

"What? You don't want to run out after Laurie?" Diane said. "I know that you've only been hanging around hoping to get a celebrity endorsement for your hotel."

She was glad he had the decency to look embarrassed.

"OK, OK. When I saw Laurie here in the pub the other night, I had to pinch myself. This isn't exactly the French Riviera, you know. We don't get A-listers around these parts. And a celebrity endorsement is just what Richard and I need. But when I met you, I forgot all about that. Don't get me wrong, I would be delirious if Kevin and Laurie Flynn stayed and tweeted about it. But you have to believe me when I say that my only reason for calling to the house that morning was to see you."

Diane felt herself going to jelly inside. He softened all her hard edges and made her feel fluffy and frilly. She hated it.

As she sat there beside Oliver, she couldn't stop thinking about the kiss that day outside Seamus's house. The kiss that turned her back into the girl she was before she became hard and cynical and immune to love. She wanted to grab him by the lapels of his jacket and kiss him hard on the mouth.

"Did you hear me?" he said.

"Eh, sorry, I was miles away. What did you say?" If only he knew where she had been in her imagination.

"I was asking if you thought that, along with the grand piano in the foyer, there should be one in the drawing room as well. Or is that too much?"

Bloody hell, didn't he want to talk about anything else?

"I think maybe a baby grand in the window of the drawing room. It's more for relaxing so it would be out of the way of the sofas and armchairs."

"You're right. Good idea. There was something else I wanted to ask you. Would it be OK if I call you sometime?"

"You mean to ask for more of my interior-design advice? I'll have to start charging you."

"No. Not about interior design. Diane, I feel something for you. I felt it the night we were dancing over there," he said, pointing to the juke box in the corner. "I think you know what I'm talking about. When we kissed outside Seamus's, I didn't want it to stop. I've thought about nothing else but finishing what we started and kissing every square inch of your naked body."

He was looking at her intensely with those chocolate pools he had for eyes, and she did know what he meant. She felt it too.

"I have a boyfriend, you know that. It's not a good idea."

She hated saying it to him. She wanted him on a very basic level. Her body was crying out for his. She wanted to feel the weight of him on top of her. She wanted to feel his mouth on her skin. Her heart was telling her to say yes but her head was telling her to stay a million miles away from the possibility of falling in love with him.

"I hope you don't live to regret your decision," he said.

"I'm regretting it already."

He took her hand in his and they sat there in the middle of the noisy pub and let themselves feel the thrill of touching each other's skin. He started to rub his thumb along hers and she felt stirrings in the pit of her stomach. She needed to get out of the pub and run after Laurie and Mrs. Murphy. She shouldn't still be anywhere within the vicinity of the outrageously sexy man who was beside her caressing her hand with his. She tried her hardest not to look at him but when she did he mouthed two words to her.

"My place?"

She got up and followed him out of the door without hesitation. People shouted goodnight to them but she didn't hear a thing outside her own heart beating out of her chest with the anticipation of what was to come.

He stopped at a house close by that he and Richard were renting temporarily. He put his key in the door and pulled her inside. He took her in his arms and kicked the door closed behind them.

"Is there anybody else here?" she asked.

"Richard is in London. We've got the place to ourselves. But I have to warn you, the walls are thin so when you scream the neighbours might hear you," he said breathlessly into her ear.

"When I scream? You're very sure of yourself," she said, taking off his jacket, then his shirt as he helped her out of her own clothes.

"Don't say I didn't warn you."

———

Diane did scream. Several times. She didn't give any thought to the neighbours. She'd never see them again, after all. She didn't give any thought to anything or anyone outside the four walls of Oliver's bedroom.

The next morning she extricated herself from his embrace without waking him. She hated the thought of leaving him, but she couldn't stay. The car was booked for eleven. It was already eight-thirty and she hadn't even packed. Her head was a complete mess. She was going back to Spain. To Serge. To her shop. Yet all she wanted to do was stay in bed with Oliver and never leave his side again. She quietly got dressed and opened the door.

"What are you doing?"

Suddenly he was by her side, catching her by the arm and trying to drag her back to him.

"I have to go. The car's coming at eleven. I need to …"

"Come back to bed."

He wouldn't let go of her hand.

"Oliver! I can't. My life is in Spain. I have to go."

She looked into his sleepy brown eyes and kissed him goodbye. She didn't say a thing. She didn't trust her own voice.

Chapter 27

Diane walked back up to the O'Neill house where the car was waiting to take them home. To take her away from Oliver.

Diane walked into the house. Mrs. Murphy was at her usual spot by the stove with the kettle on the boil.

"Everything alright, Mrs. Murphy?" asked Diane.

"Sure everything's fine and dandy. I'm amazed at the hours you young ones keep these days. In my day, you came home at a decent hour and slept in your own bed."

Diane was about to give the nosey old cow a piece of her mind but Laurie arrived into the kitchen.

"Forget it," she mouthed to Diane, leading her out of earshot of Mrs. Murphy.

"How is she not in a coma today?" Diane asked Laurie.

"I'd say she has the constitution of a horse, that one. But never mind her, what about you? Tell me everything."

"We talked in the pub. We agreed that nothing was going to happen between us because of, well, Serge, among other things."

"Oh. So what were you doing all night?" said Laurie.

"I said that we agreed that nothing was going to happen. Then we went back to his and shagged each other's brains out."

Laurie clapped her hands together. "Well? What was it like?" She liked Oliver. Apart from his good looks, he had been very kind to her after her visit to Seamus.

"It, the sex, was amazing. I mean, he's gorgeous, he's sexy and he knows his way around a woman's body. But it's more than that. I left him a few minutes ago and I feel like I've left a part of me behind."

Diane was embarrassed. She didn't normally talk like this. She didn't normally feel like this either. The men in her life before Oliver performed different roles. They were father figures. Oliver was her equal and the dynamic scared her.

"Sorry. I sound like a sap. You know I don't believe in all that bullshit. I'm just tired. I'm sure a nap in the car on the way back will sort me out."

"It sounds to me like you're in love. It does exist, you know," said Laurie.

"No offence, but I don't really buy that."

"Well, offence taken. That nonsense, as you call it, is the very basis of my life. At least I'm open to beautiful things happening to me and open to all of life's possibilities. You're so closed off to things because you think you're so bloody cool. But you're not cool, you're emotionally stunted."

Laurie stopped. She wanted to run a mile from what she just said to Diane. She stood there waiting for the tirade of abuse that she deserved to get, but it didn't come.

Diane got up and went upstairs without a word. It would be a very long car ride back to Dublin.

———

"I'm not going with you," Diane announced to Laurie.

"*Aw*, come on, Diane. I'm sorry. I shouldn't have called you emotionally retarded. I just –"

"Emotionally retarded? Earlier I was emotionally stunted. Make your mind up for fuck's sake."

"What you do is your own business, Di. I promise I won't say another word about you and Oliver."

"It's not the reason I'm not going. I've got a lot of things to think about before I go back to Spain. I need to take time out." Diane couldn't face Serge right now. She needed to be clear about how she felt about Oliver first.

"I am really sorry. I didn't mean to hurt your feelings. I said those things because I care about you."

"I know. Now go. Go before you miss your flight. And call me when you get back to LA."

They hugged goodbye.

Jesus looked chirpier than he had when they arrived first. He was having a moment with Mrs. Murphy before he got into the taxi. She gave him some freshly baked scones in case he got hungry on the drive.

"I'm sorry the week didn't turn out like you planned," said Laurie.

"Things seldom do," said Diane, closing the car door and going back into the house.

Mrs. Murphy and Diane stood at the front steps and waved Laurie and Jesus off.

"I suppose I'll have to be staying around for you."

"You don't have to. I'm a big girl, I can take care of myself." But Diane knew that nothing made Mrs. Murphy happier than fussing over people in the house where she had worked for over fifty years. "Stay if you want to. I don't mind one way or the other."

"I will so, I will. I think it'd be for the best. Sure how are you going to manage the stove? You'd hardly be able to boil the kettle." Mrs. Murphy tut-tutted her way into the kitchen.

Diane went to her room and started to unpack the things she had spent the last while packing. What the hell was she doing? She and Serge were on easy street. They had an immense fondness for one another and they were great together. They gave each other their freedom. Diane thought it was what she wanted. She had bragged to her friends that they had the perfect relationship, great companionship and great sex.

But she had to face it. All the sex she had with Serge didn't come close to the meeting of bodies that happened with Oliver. It was ridiculous but it felt like their souls connected somehow. He had wormed his way under her skin and she felt as if his skin was hers and hers his. The fireworks of last night were still ricocheting through her body and she had to lie down on her bed.

Oliver hadn't asked anything of her, she knew that. She knew they probably didn't stand a chance. But one thing she did know was that she wanted more for herself than what she was settling for with Serge.

She wanted to be loved and missed when she wasn't there. She knew now she wanted the whole package that came with falling in love. She wanted the fireworks. Laurie would laugh at her right now, she thought. Laurie who always told her that love was the only thing that mattered. Diane argued for her own choices. Until now. So this is what Laurie and Kevin have, she thought. The lucky bastards.

Her thoughts were interrupted by the sounds of Mrs. Murphy charging around changing bedclothes as if there were more guests waiting to be accommodated.

She went outside. "Can I help you with that?" she asked.

"Not at all, girleen. I'll be done in a jiffy. I've been changing beds in this house for over fifty years. But I think that this will be my last time. There'll be new people come into the house and they won't need the likes of me at all."

Diane almost felt sorry for the poor thing with her sad face.

"Would you listen to me gassin' away and not a child in the house washed! I better get on with things. I'll be going to the village later to get something for the dinner. Let me know if there's anything you want." She bustled out, cheered up by having somebody to fuss over for another day.

Diane was having an afternoon coffee in the kitchen when Mrs. Murphy arrived back.

"That Oliver fella is up to his old tricks," she announced.

"Oh yeah?" said Diane. Her stomach churned and she had a feeling she didn't want to know anything about his old tricks.

"I was in the butcher's getting a bit of meat for the dinner," said Mrs. Murphy, busily emptying various shopping bags. "I got some lamb chops, I hope you like lamb. Some people can't take to the taste of it at all, at all. One meat tastes just like another from the supermarket but when you get a good butcher the taste can be too strong for them."

"Mrs. Murphy! What about Oliver?"

"Oh, that fella. Yes. Well, it seems like he's got himself a woman. From London, of course. He went to the airport earlier and brought her back here. He's a divil alright, that one." She paused and looked pointedly at Diane. "He seems to prefer them young."

Just when Diane thought that maybe they'd be able to get along, Mrs. Murphy brought her devastating news and insulted her all in the one sentence.

"Well, it's his business what he does, I'm sure. He's a free agent," said Diane with mock cheeriness.

Diane told Mrs. Murphy she was going for a walk and

grabbed her jacket off the coat-stand. Was Oliver that much of a Casanova? Had he moved on to his next conquest already? Something told her that Mrs. Murphy got her wires crossed but she had to see for herself. The castle wasn't far from the house so she started to walk along the narrow windy roads.

She relived the night before in her mind. She thought about his mouth and his hands and what he did to her. The more she thought about it, the more convinced she was that Mrs. Murphy was mistaken. She could see the turn for the hotel ahead. She walked up the tree-lined avenue and stopped dead in her tracks. Oliver was walking ahead towards the hotel. He had his arm around a woman with long red hair. She was looking up into his face and laughing.

Diane's stomach turned to jelly and she thought she might be sick. She turned and ran back in the direction she came from.

"Look, I'm sorry about the lamb chops and everything but I'm not going to be able to stay for dinner after all. Something's come up back home that I have to deal with. Thanks for everything," said Diane to Mrs. Murphy when the taxi pulled up to take her back to Dublin.

"Sure it's been a right pleasure getting to know you lovely girls. I hope you come to visit again sometime," said Mrs. Murphy, firmly shaking Diane's hand and placing her other hand over it too. "You know, if you stopped acting so high and mighty and smiled a little bit more, you might get on better with people."

"*Eh*, thanks. I'll bear that in mind," said Diane, heading for the door.

Chapter 28

"Hello! Anyone home?" Peter called from the doorway of the tiny cottage.

Suze was sitting at the kitchen table working on her column. She had received a letter from a woman who was getting urges to call on her ex-husband even though they had been separated for months. Suze had told her to stay strong and not to give into these urges as they were not a true reflection of her actual feelings. The urges were just a manifestation of her own loneliness. Well, that was what Suze had reckoned it was all about in her own case.

When she saw Peter standing in her doorway she wanted to run away. But the tiny cottage didn't afford her any hiding space. She had to face the music.

"Peter. I, *eh*, I, *em* ..." What could she say? *I'm sorry for turning up at your place and acting like a cheap whore. Please rest assured that it will never happen again. Thanks for calling. Goodbye.*

"I didn't know whether I should come over or not but I didn't want to leave things the way we left them the other day. I was freaked out, you know. I wasn't expectin' you to, well, I wasn't expectin' … you know."

"You mean you weren't expecting your emotionally unstable ex-wife to turn up at your house wearing only tacky underwear under her coat?" offered Suze.

"Ah, it wasn't that bad – the underwear didn't look that tacky," he said, laughing.

Good old Peter, always good at breaking the ice. Suze felt herself smile too. God, it was so embarrassing to have done what she did. At least Peter didn't argue with the fact that she had been emotionally unstable. She still had a long way to go before she could call herself sane. If indeed that day ever came. She had taken Diane's advice and was back on her regular medication.

"I don't know what came over me. I stopped taking my meds and I think that had something to do with my behaviour, although I do take full responsibility for what I did."

"You're making it sound like you tried to knife me or somethin'. I've seen you without your clothes on before, remember?"

Suze felt herself going red again. Of course they had seen each other naked. They knew every square inch of each other's bodies even though there was considerably less of both bodies present now.

"That was different. We were married then. I had no

right to barge in on top of you and do that. Just so you know, I'm sorry and I'm very embarrassed."

"Just so *you* know, I'm not complainin'. You look good. For a woman in her forties." He laughed again.

She wanted to hug him. For being sweet Pete. For being the person who was always there to catch her when she fell.

"You're not bad yourself. When I saw you in the kitchen the other night cooking for that woman you had over ..."
Shit.

"What night? What are you talkin' about?" asked Peter.

"The night after the hospital with Sarah and Rosa. I got this thing into my head that I had to tell you how sorry I was. It was like the most compelling thing I ever had to do. I drove over to the house and saw a car outside. I looked in the window and I saw the two of you. I'm sorry, Peter, I didn't mean to spy on you or anything. It's just that, oh, I don't know. I needed to see you. I can't explain what came over me."

Peter was quiet. She wanted him to say something. Anything. She sounded like a stalker. Maybe she really was a bona fide crazy person.

"So let me get this right. You came to my house. You spied on me through the window. You saw me and Natasha. And you came back the following day with hardly a stitch on. What am I meant to make of all that?"

She could see that he was genuinely trying to work out in his head what the hell was going on.

"Look, I wasn't myself. I thought I'd made a big mistake by leaving you. I thought I wanted you back and, worse, I thought you might even want me too. When I saw you with that woman, I was jealous. It's irrational, I know."

"Suze. You tried to kill yourself just to get away from me. Why would you think that you wanted me back?" said Peter, utterly bewildered.

"I don't know, Peter. All I do know is that I'm sorry. I'm sorry for what I put you through and I'm sorry for calling over to your house. Both times." She was utterly ashamed of herself and she expected Peter to walk out and never want to see her again.

"If you'd come back to me anytime in the last year I would've been thrilled. It's all I wanted back then. To have you home with me. But we've both changed now, there's no going back. I don't want to go back." He didn't say the words to hurt her. He needed her to know that he had moved on.

"I know. Honestly, I know that deep down. Peter, I'm so sorry."

"It's alright. We both have a lot to be sorry for. But it's in the past. Time to move on with our lives, yeah?"

"Yes, yes, it is. How is Natasha? Is it serious with you two?" asked Suze, grateful that Peter was being so understanding.

"Well, it's early days. I can't talk for Natasha but I'm keen alright. She's great. She's away a lot with work but we spend whatever free time she has together. She works in IT. There's probably a fancy name for it, wha'? A software engineer or somethin'."

"She's not a software engineer," said Suze.

"She is. She works for that iBuy crowd down the docklands. I should know. I'm the one goin' out with her."

"She works for iBuy alright. She's the Vice President of European and Middle East Operations. She's not a software engineer."

"Nah, she can't be. What would a vice president of anythin' be doin' with the likes of me? You've got it wrong. What makes you think that?"

"I thought I recognised her when I saw her in the kitchen with you."

"The night you were spyin' on me?"

Suze was ashamed all over again.

"Yes. I thought that we knew her from somewhere. Like she was someone well known or something. But then it clicked with me. I'd seen her in the papers. The *Indo* magazine did a spread on her a while ago."

"*Jaysus.*"

"I googled her. There're loads of pictures of her online. It's definitely her, Peter. She's a really big deal."

Chapter 29

"May, will you take care of Rosa for a few hours?" asked Sarah.

"Sure. Where are you going?" May was unused to her mum asking her for any help whatsoever.

"I'm going to get my hair and nails done and then I'm going out to meet Suze for lunch." Sarah couldn't believe she was saying those beautiful words. *Lunch, hair, nails, done.*

May couldn't believe that her mum was going out and going to leave Rosa behind in her care.

"*Eh.* OK. Great. Rosa and I are going to have lots of fun, aren't we?" she said, tickling her little sister's tummy and making her laugh.

The sight of her two beautiful girls almost made tears come but Sarah beat them back. There had been enough tears and heartache in the days gone by. It was about time to leave all that behind.

"May, I'm sorry I've been such a pain lately. Actually, I know I've been a pain since Rosa was born. I don't know how to explain it exactly but I thought that Rosa was my problem and that I had to deal with her. It took thinking that I was going to lose her for me to realise she's not a problem but a beautiful blessing."

"It's OK," said May, hugging her. Her mum was there all the time but she wasn't the same mum as she was before Joe left and before she had Rosa. She was a duller version of the colourful woman she once was. But May would settle for any version of Sarah, she loved her so much. "You're still the best mum in the world in my eyes."

"Thanks, love. I mean it. I'll make it all up to you somehow. And we'll kick The Bean Machine's ass!" Sarah hugged her back, even though she had no idea how they were going to pull that one off.

"Well, go on. Go have fun with the Ladies Who Lunch," said May, ushering her mum into the hall and out the front door. She didn't want her to start crying or to change her mind about going. This was progress and she didn't want anything to stop it.

Sarah pulled up outside the restaurant. It was a beautiful autumn day and she felt like she had been reborn. Nothing had changed but everything had changed at the same time. She had adjusted her thinking. That was all it took.

Tom had been harsh with her but every word he said was true. She had shut everyone out. She didn't want their pity even though pity wasn't even on their minds. She felt like every single person she met thought she was pathetic for getting pregnant in the first place. But everybody had their own stuff going on and she eventually realised that the only thing that mattered was what she felt.

She felt truly blessed and happy for the first time since that night with Tom. The night she realised that she was capable of turning a man on. She realised that Joe wasn't gay to hurt her and cause her pain. He was gay because, well, because he was. Sarah had somehow blamed herself for that too. She thought if she was more attractive and more of a woman she could have prevented it from happening. It took a long time for her to come to terms with it and to accept that the years they had together were not wasted but just different chapters in the book of her life.

"*Whoa!* You look flipping amazing, Mrs. O'Hara." Suze had almost given up on ever seeing the glam side of her friend again.

"It's amazing what not having baby vomit on your clothes can do for your appearance," said Sarah, hugging Suze.

"No, really. It's good to see the old Sarah back. How is Rosa?"

"She's perfect. She's gorgeous and pink and smiling and almost walking." Sarah took out her phone to show Suze the latest pictures she had taken.

"That whole hospital thing was scary. How did you cope? I nearly had a nervous breakdown and I'm not even family," said Suze, remembering the horror of the waiting room.

"It was hell. A hell I hope to never go through again. Really, all I want is for my kids to be healthy. After that, anything is a bonus. One thing it did do, though, was that it helped me see straight. I was a mess. I'm sure you could all see it but I just couldn't see it myself."

Suze looked at Sarah and nodded. They were old friends. Sarah didn't need to explain herself to Suze.

"And Tom?" asked Suze.

"He comes around pretty regularly. I told him he's welcome anytime. I don't want to get into all the legal stuff about access and shared custody. He seems to be happy the way things are."

"But what about you and Tom?"

"There is no me and Tom. I don't think he's interested in me like that anymore. He seems quite content to call and see Rosa. Of course the fact that he's not begging to see me anymore makes me want him!"

"Of course he wants you. He's crazy about you. Work on him. Make it so that he can't ignore you."

Sarah was tired of thinking about how to get Tom to fancy her again. She thought that maybe childbirth made women less attractive to men and she worried that he saw her only as a mom now and not a desirable woman.

"You know that The Bean Machine are planning on opening a shop beside The Bakery? I'm going to be screwed if it goes ahead. I'm way behind where I should be on that front. May has her knickers totally in a twist about it for the last while but I've been so busy shutting everybody out that I was living in blissful ignorance about the whole thing."

Sarah had seen the planning application and it looked like The Bean Machine had complied with the conditions laid down, and their grand opening was now only a formality. All of Sarah's hard work would mostly go up in smoke if they opened. The Bean Machine's history in other towns had shown that. Her online store would probably be the only part of her business to survive. She wanted the whole of her business to survive because May wanted to be a big part of its future. She had to make it happen for her.

"I've heard about it. Don't worry. Things will work out in the end. And if they don't, then it's not yet the end," said Suze. "I'm in therapy again. I'm working on my positivity."

Suze told Sarah about Peter and the stalking incident. She also told her about the coat and what was underneath. Sarah laughed until she thought she'd be asked to leave the restaurant.

"It's not funny, Sarah. It was the most embarrassing thing that ever happened to me."

"I'm just thinking about Peter's face. It must have been priceless."

"Laugh all you want. Jesus didn't laugh when he saw the goods," Suze said, taking a forkful of lettuce leaves.

"Jesus saw the goods? You mean he actually caught you naked? Did he walk in on you?" Sarah was laughing again –

she thought she might never stop laughing now.

"No, he didn't walk in on me. He took off my underwear. He saw the goods if you know what I mean. He saw and he tested. And he liked."

"*What?*" Sarah almost screamed, causing the other diners to stare. "Holy shit, Suze! You and Jesus Martinez?" She had lowered her voice on the last two words.

She wasn't laughing now. She was seriously impressed by Suze's revelation. He was a bit of a baby and very annoying but there was no denying he was a thing of utter beauty.

"So what's the story? Are you going to see him again?" she asked eagerly.

"That's the strange thing. I'm not longing to see him. I feel like he did me a massive favour though."

"What do you mean?"

"I orgasmed. I honestly thought I'd never have one again. I know you guys are always telling me that I'm great and this and that. But deep down I didn't feel like I was desirable. Jesus convinced me otherwise."

"Actions speak louder than words, I suppose. So do you think you're ready to start something with Seán? He's been waiting patiently."

"Seán's gone," said Suze sadly. "He said he can't be around me. I don't blame him. I've rejected him so many times. I've been rejecting him since we were kids really."

"You know, life was so much easier when we were married. This single life stuff is very complicated."

Chapter 30

"I don't know how to say this, Joe," said Sarah, holding his hands across the table.

"You're not dying, are you?" he asked.

"Me? No. Why are you being so dramatic?"

"You summoned me back from Rome. You asked me to lunch, told me you had something to tell me and now you're holding my hands across the table. What the hell am I supposed to think?"

"It's your mum," said Sarah.

"My mum is dying?" said Joe, shocked.

"Nobody is dying, Joe."

"Then what's going on?"

"Laurie was told something about Ballygra. She called me, she wanted me to tell you."

"So tell me. Please, I'm freaking out right now." He was slightly mollified that nobody was dying but he knew it must be serious nonetheless.

"Your mother had a baby," said Sarah.

"Make some sense, please, Sarah."

"A long time ago."

"Yes. And he's sitting opposite you right now. *Helloooo!*"

"She had a baby before you were born. It was a baby boy. He was stillborn."

Sarah let the words sink in.

Joe couldn't fathom any of it.

Sarah poured him a glass of water from the carafe on the table.

He took a gulp. "She didn't meet my father 'til she came to Dublin," he said then. "So I take it that he wasn't the father."

"No. She was in love with a local boy in Ballygra. Seamus Sullivan is his name. He's still alive. He's a faith healer, a seventh son of a seventh son."

Joe had never heard of him and had no idea what his lineage meant. His mother rarely spoke about her life before she moved to Dublin. She used to say that she had no good memories of her time in the country so Joe stopped asking her about her young life. He assumed it was because of the hard times that she lived in and because of the fact that her parents had died.

He always thought it was odd that she never wanted to visit her brother who lived in her home place but she left him in no doubt that it wasn't something that was on her list of things she wanted to do. When she got the news that

Eddie had died, Joe had offered to come back from Italy and take her to the funeral. She told him she'd say her own prayers for her brother, that she didn't want to make the trip.

Joe put it down to her advancing years and the several hours it would take to drive there. She had called him again recently to say that Eddie had left the house to her. She made it very clear that she didn't want it. She wanted Joe to get rid of it.

"What did this guy Seamus Sullivan do? Did he take responsibility for getting my mother pregnant?" asked Joe.

"He did – but they were both terrified. You know what it was like in those days. They were very young – your mother was only seventeen – and they were scared witless of what their families would say if they found out. It seems that your mother went into labour when she was with Seamus. The baby was already dead when she delivered him. They buried the baby in a grave they made themselves." Sarah decided that now wouldn't be the time to tell him about Seamus's gift for healing infertility.

"My poor mother. How did she keep this to herself for all these years? How can someone hide something so monumental and pretend it never happened. I have to talk to her about it, Sarah. I have a right to know about my brother."

"There's more, Joe. There's more and it's worse."

Joe motioned for the waiter to come over. He ordered a shot of whiskey for himself. Sarah passed but she couldn't blame Joe for needing a drink to fortify himself.

"Tell me," said Joe when he had taken a gulp from his glass.

"It seems that Eddie had noticed that your mother had put on a bit of weight. He wasn't an idiot. When your grandparents died, Eddie got the house and he seemed to have turned into a bit of a tyrant. Your mum had been close to him growing up but even so she couldn't tell him she was pregnant. Once he noticed the bump was gone, he asked her about it. She was vulnerable and emotionally very fragile so she told him everything. Everything except who the father was. He beat her, Joe. Badly by all accounts. But she never told him who the father was. She managed to grab a few things and she left the house. She left Ballygra in the middle of the night, black and blue, and walked as far as the nearest town and got a bus to Cork and then on to Dublin. That's why she couldn't bear to go back there. I can't say I blame her."

Joe was distraught. Sarah had known he would take it badly. Sarah had cried when Laurie told her. The gentle woman hey called Granny O'Hara didn't deserve what had happened to her.

"That fucking bastard! If he was alive right now I'd kill him myself," said Joe.

"You'd have to get in line. He was a nasty piece of work, but he's gone now. What's important is that your mum is alive and so is Seamus. I wonder if she would like to see him again. Do you think she would want to talk about it after all this time?"

"I don't know. Will you come with me to talk to her?" pleaded Joe.

"Of course I will."

———

Joe let himself in with his key. His mother had the television at full volume and she didn't hear them come in. She was watching a quiz show and had a pencil and paper in her lap, playing along.

"*Mum*," said Joe loudly over the sound of the TV.

"*Jesus, Mary and Joseph!*" said Granny O'Hara, almost jumping out of her skin. "Are you trying to give me a heart attack?"

"You can hear that television in my apartment in Rome. You need to get a hearing-aid, Mother," said Joe.

"I told you I don't need a hearing-aid – they're for old people."

Sarah smiled at her absolute denial that she was in fact an old person herself.

Granny looked at Joe and Sarah suspiciously. It had been a long time since they had called to see her together. She liked Paolo but it seemed she always hoped that it was just a fad. Sarah knew she loved her like a daughter and would love to see Joe and her back together again.

"It's lovely to see the two of you," she said.

They sat down.

"Mum, we have to talk to you," said Joe. "About Ballygra."

"I told you to get rid of it. I don't want to set foot in that place again and I know that you'll never go there either. Just get it ready for sale and do what you like with the money. I don't want any part of it."

Sarah hadn't heard Granny be so dogmatic about anything for years. As she got older, she got vague but there was no mistaking her strong feelings about the house in Ballygra.

"It's a lovely house," said Sarah. "May might like to visit it someday. Maybe you'd like to take her there."

"I don't want my grandchild anywhere near that place. Sell it, Joe. That's all about it."

"Mum, I don't know how to say this but Mrs. Murphy, Eddie's housekeeper, told the girls something."

Granny shifted in her seat as if she sensed something unpleasant was coming.

Sarah wished they could spare her any more pain. She tugged at Joe's sleeve and looked at him. "Maybe we should let Granny get back to the TV, Joe."

"No. Mum, I need to ask you something." Joe wanted to spare his mother too but this was too major to brush under the carpet any longer.

Granny sat straighter up in her armchair.

"Well, go on," she said.

"Mrs. Murphy said that you had a baby. Before me."

He hated himself for asking her. He could see by her expression that she was still holding on to the shame.

"So you're listening to idle gossip now? Is that it? Some

busybody like Celia Murphy is telling tales and you're all ready to believe a wan like her. Well, my God, it's no wonder I got out of there when I did!"

She was angry and Joe let her rant. She had every right to rant and rage all she wanted. Joe pulled his chair closer to his mother's. He sat close to her and held her hand. She couldn't look at him. She looked out the window and anywhere else except into his eyes.

"You don't have to talk about it if you don't want to," he said gently.

It seemed like she didn't.

Sarah left the room and it was just the two of them in the silence.

Joe sat and continued to hold her hand. He could see her eyes water in her side profile. He was sorry he'd brought it up. Maybe there was no truth in it after all. What did some old woman like Mrs. Murphy know about something that happened all those years ago anyhow? Maybe she was mistaken. Confused. Maybe she had mixed his mother up with some other poor girl.

"He was beautiful," she said simply.

Joe had never seen his mother this sad before. She was always upbeat, making light of everything and generally being annoyingly happy-clappy. He wondered now if it was just a cover-up for how she was really feeling inside. She had buried a child who she had hardly been able to acknowledge in the first place. Life was a bitch sometimes.

"He was perfect. He had a little button nose. I'll never

forget it. We didn't know what to do. I remember the water. I didn't know what it was, but I ran over to Seamus's because I knew it was something to do with the baby. It felt different. There was a lot of pressure and I was afraid that the baby was coming and I didn't know what to do."

His mother bit her lip and Joe could feel her fear. She was only seventeen, the same age as May. At least if it happened to May, she would have the support of Sarah and him. His mother was alone in the world apart from Seamus.

She was quiet again but Joe didn't hurry her. He sat and allowed her to tell her story in her own good time.

"Seamus had a bit of knowledge of medicine and things. He was told he had a special gift and he had healed people. He was calm. We went to one of the unused sheds away from the house. He got clean blankets and he made sure I was comfortable. The pain was shocking and I was terrified. His father was around the place for a while. He was tending to the cattle, I remember, and his mother was gone to visit some sick relative. We could hear all the comings and goings. Seamus was keeping an eye on the door. He was trying to soothe me. I almost passed out from the pain."

The tears were falling down her face now. Joe held her hand still. Cows in the fields were better tended than his poor mother, he thought angrily.

"I was tired. I thought I was going to die. I think Seamus thought I was going to die too. He was scared. He didn't know what to do but he stayed with me. I begged him not to go anywhere. He wanted to get a doctor. I wouldn't let him go. I begged him to stay with me."

Joe never felt sadness like it in his life. His kind mother who loved him unconditionally. When he told her he was gay, she took it in her stride and welcomed Paolo into the family with open arms. She had such capacity for love despite what she had been through that he could only admire her and love her all the more for it.

"Then he came out. He was only a scrap of a thing but he was perfect. He probably died in my womb a bit before he was born. I think that now. He was like a doll. Every time I see one of those dolls, you know the ones that look like a new-born baby, I think about him. I pray for him every day, you know. I pray for God's forgiveness every day too."

This made Joe mad. He knew it wasn't the time for Church-bashing but he couldn't help himself. His mother was a product of her time but he was also a product of his.

"You did nothing to need forgiveness for, Mum. What you did is not a sin. You loved Seamus and you had a baby. Just because some middle-aged men who have never been in love tell you that it's a sin to have sex outside of marriage, that doesn't make them right. You did nothing wrong."

Joe knew that his words were falling on deaf ears. Religion was far too ingrained in his mother not to have left its indelible mark on her soul.

"What did you do with him then?" he prompted.

"It took us a while to realise he wasn't breathing. We thought we did it. We thought it was our fault. We wrapped him up in a blanket. I cleaned myself up and we went over to the house. There's a bit that overlooks the sea and it's a beautiful place. His father was gone by now too. He had been calling for Seamus to go to town with him but he couldn't find him, so he went on his own. It was a godsend. We were able to bury our baby together. Seamus dug a hole. It was deep. I wanted him to hurry up in case anyone came back. We would be killed if they caught us. We could have been arrested. Seamus asked me what we would call him. I said Michael. After my father. We kissed him and we covered his face with the blanket and put him in the ground."

Her shoulders were shaking uncontrollably as she recounted burying her baby. Joe felt the tears welling in his own eyes. Now that he had a name, Joe felt that he could picture the little fella who looked like a doll. The perfect little boy with the button nose.

"What about Seamus? Why didn't he help you after that?" asked Joe.

"I suppose Celia Murphy told all about the run-in I had with Eddie. He beat me up and down the house but I wouldn't tell him who the father was. He would have killed Seamus. There's not a doubt in the world about that. I knew from that day on that I could never ever see Seamus again so I packed what I could and I left that godforsaken house. I swore I would never go back there again."

Chapter 31

Peter was livid with Suze for sticking her nose in where it wasn't wanted. And he was equally mad with Natasha for lying to him. He had checked online and there she was. Vice President. Why did she do it? Was she making a complete fool of him? He had been stupid enough to think that they could have a future together.

They didn't have to get married or anything, though maybe one day, who knew? He had thought about them going on holidays together. He looked up places on the internet where they could go. Just the two of them. He was going to surprise her with a week away somewhere nice. Greece maybe. But Natasha could go anywhere in the world she wanted to go. If she really was the Vice President of iBuy, she probably owned a Greek island, for fuck's sake.

He needed to calm himself down. He didn't want to go into her workplace with all guns blazing and get kicked out by security. He'd only prove to her that he wasn't worth telling the truth to.

He paced up and down outside the offices where all Ireland's bright young things were going in and out with woolly hats and plugs in their ears. He eventually went inside. The lobby was all cool marble and funky artwork on the walls. He went up to a desk which was slap-bang in the middle of the floor.

"How'r'ya. I'm here to see Natasha Redmond," he said to the young man behind the desk. He looked like Paul. He had the same lazy way about him and Peter was half-expecting to be addressed as "dude".

"Do you have an appointment with her?" the young man asked, busily checking a computer screen.

"Eh, no. No, I don't. But you can tell her it's Peter. Peter Jackson."

Peter put his hands in his pockets and waited while the young fella rang her office. She was probably somewhere up on the top floor in her floor-to-ceiling glass office. The young fella had turned his back to Peter while he spoke into the headset. She was probably telling him that she was too busy.

"She will be right out. Actually, there she is." The young fella motioned behind Peter.

He turned around and she was walking towards him, every inch the VP. She was wearing a black pencil skirt with a black silk blouse and high heels. How the hell did she manage to look so sexy at work too? It only convinced Peter all the more that he was just a plaything to her.

"Peter! What are you doing here? What a lovely surprise. C'mon, my office is over here," she said.

She led him into a nearby office. Peter closed the door behind them. The office was enormous, with a big, shiny, mahogany desk its centrepiece. There were clocks on the wall, showing the times in Dublin, Dubai, New York, Hong Kong, Beijing and Sydney. There were devices of all sorts on her desk, smart phones, tablets, PCs and Macs. Peter had only recently been introduced to the digital age.

She put her arms around his middle and stood on her tippy toes and kissed him. He didn't want any of that carry-on. He stood firm and didn't embrace her or try to kiss her back.

"Nice office," he said.

"Yeah, it's grand," she said, looking around. "It belongs to my boss. I can work anywhere once I have access to the internet. Sometimes, I sit in the open-plan office."

"Oh, do ya? Yeah, I'm sure ya do," he said, getting angrier the more she lied.

"Peter, what's wrong? Did something happen? Are you alright?"

"Why did ya lie to me? This is your office. I know you're the Vice President of Europe and Asia or somethin'. I know because my ex-wife googled you and she told me all about you."

Natasha stood opposite him with her arms folded over her beautiful breasts, looking remarkably calm for someone who had just been found out in a lie.

"So? What do you want me to say? Do you want me to apologise for – for this?" she said, indicating her office.

"No, I bloody don't but I do want to know why you lied to me about it. Why didn't you tell me you practically run the company? I just don't understand why you'd lie about that." Now he sounded more hurt than angry.

"I … I don't have an answer, Peter," she said quietly.

"You'll have to do better than that," he said. He stood while she constructed her story.

"Peter, first of all I didn't mean to lie to you. I mean, I really like you. That's the most important thing."

"I'd say trust and being honest is fairly important too, wha'?"

"You're right. Of course you are. I wanted to tell you but it just didn't seem like the right time. I didn't say anything because in the past, well, some men, I'm not saying you would be like them, but some men were intimidated by me – well, my job title."

"So you thought I'd be intimidated because you're so successful and I'm just an ordinary joe, is that it? You thought that poor thick Peter would think he wasn't good enough for ya. Jaysus, no wonder you were tryin' to talk me into takin' on those big contracts. You were tryin' to make me into some bigshot like yourself. There's no way a bloke who's just an ordinary builder would be good enough for you."

"That's not it at all, Peter. I told you about those jobs because you could easily do them. I told you for you, not for me. Most people don't realise their potential, I was just trying to make you see yours, that's all. I was going to tell you about my job. I was. It's not a big deal. It's only a damn job."

But it was a big deal to Peter. The past year had been a roller-coaster ride and he was dizzy from all of it. He could hardly think straight and hadn't slept since Suze had told him who Natasha really was.

"Natasha, I can't do this. I'm sorry. You should've been straight up. I wouldn't care if you mopped floors for a livin' or ran this company. It's you I was interested in, not what you do. I woulda been proud, ya know. I woulda bragged about ya to me mates. You shoulda told me."

"Peter. Please. Try to understand what I … try …"

But there was no talking to him.

He left her office and walked outside into the Dublin sunshine. As he walked along the river he had to stop himself turning around and running back to her. When Suze left him, she left him devastated. She took his identity away too. He wasn't a husband anymore and he didn't know how to be anything else.

It took a lot of courage for him to put himself out there again, to date online. He had dared to dream that Natasha was his second chance for happiness. He dared to dream that they had a great future together. But he couldn't take lies. Suze had lied all those years and said she was fine but she was far from it. She tried to kill herself, for fuck's sake. No, there was no place for lies in his life.

Natasha banged her fists off her desk. She was furious with herself. With Peter. *Damn this job*, she thought. Damn Peter for not accepting her for who she was. She couldn't figure out who she was angrier with, herself or Peter. It wasn't like he found out she was a stripper or a lap dancer. She was a Vice President of a hugely successful company.

She had started out on her career with the same qualifications as hundreds, no, thousands of others. Natasha knew that she had to set herself apart to stand out from the crowd. No matter what company she was working for, she gave one hundred per cent of herself and then she gave a little bit more. She watched the women she worked with as they climbed up the various corporate ladders only to lose their footing and fall back down to the bottom of the heap where they would have to start again.

She was fed up looking up the ladder at the arses of the men who were higher up than she was. It seemed that no matter how hard she worked, or how smart she was, it still wasn't enough to get to the top. It was about this time that Natasha made the decision not to have a life outside her career.

While her male colleagues were being feted as "Jack the lads" for increasing business she was being called a "tough bitch" for doing exactly the same thing. It pissed her off no end but she wasn't going to let it beat her. When iBuy announced it was opening its European headquarters in

Dublin, Natasha found out everything there was to know about the company.

They had as many women as men in key positions and Natasha set about getting a job there. She was proud of her accomplishments and she felt she fully deserved her place at the table. She wasn't going to apologise to anyone for being successful, not even Peter. But she knew it wasn't the job that Peter had a problem with. It was the fact that she didn't tell him. How could she explain it to him if she could hardly explain it to herself?

She had been on many dates with *beginagain.com*. Each one more painful than the last. On the first one, when she told her date about the true nature of her employment, something changed between them. She couldn't explain it but no invitation on a second date was forthcoming. She didn't put two and two together straight away. Maybe he just didn't like the look of her. But she knew it wasn't that. She knew it because so many other women disliked her and shielded their husbands from her at parties in case she'd try to make a grab for them. They needn't have worried. Natasha knew what she wanted and those women's husbands weren't on her wish list.

The second date, she didn't fare much better. When she told him what she did, he told her she must be a tough bitch. The very same crap as she had to put up for years working for different companies. Well, she didn't have to put up with it in her social life. This time she made her excuses and left. After a few more dates ended in much the same way, Natasha decided to dumb herself down. She regretted it now.

Chapter 32

Sarah couldn't stop thinking about what Suze had done to try to get Peter back. She was in awe of Suze's boldness even though Suze admittedly wasn't thinking straight. Sarah really needed Tom to see her as a woman again, the woman whom he swore he was in love with before Rosa was born.

When he went on that rant in the hospital, Sarah thought she would never speak to him again. She hated hearing him say those things to her. But when the anger started to abate, mortification started to kick in. There was no denying that he was right.

Tom had made her see sense before she completely messed up her relationship with May. She owed him a huge debt of gratitude. She had blown the chance of her and Tom, May and Rosa becoming a family. He had made mistakes. He had said he was sorry. What more could the poor guy do? Now it was up to her.

So how was she going to put herself back on his radar? She wondered if she should take a leaf out of a self-confessed crazy-woman's book. Desperate times called for desperate measures. She went upstairs.

She looked at herself in her mirror and decided she needed the help of a little bit of fake tan. Laurie had given her a bottle of some non-stinky stuff she got in LA. It was organic and cost an absolute fortune. It must be good because Laurie always looked amazing and never sat out in the sun.

Sarah showered, defuzzed and applied the tan. She waited until the fake tan dried in and then put on her sexiest underwear. She looked good. And not just good for someone who had a baby, but good-good. As she stood there she thought about Tom running his hands over her body, touching her breasts, touching her between her legs. It had been way too long since she'd had sex and she wondered again why she had been such a stubborn fool.

She regretted all the times they didn't have together but she hoped that she could put it right tonight.

She phoned Tom and told him she wanted to call to see him. She didn't want any interruptions so May was going to baby-sit Rosa. Sarah told May she was going to dinner with Suze and that she might stay the night with her just in case they drank too much wine at dinner.

She examined herself in the mirror again. Her hair was in loose curls around her shoulders so she tied it up into a grip. She put on a pair of high sandals and then put on her coat. She looked like any woman on a night out with her gal pal.

"Good night, my darling girls," she said downstairs, kissing both of her daughters.

"Tell Tom I said hi," said May who was playing peekaboo with Rosa.

"What? I'm going out with Suze!"

"Yeah, right. You're getting ready for two hours to go out with Suze. Whatever! Enjoy," said May, smiling.

"OK, OK. I am going to see Tom. I'm going to see if we can, you know …"

May had her hands over her ears, making a humming sound. She didn't want to know.

Of course she didn't want to know, what was Sarah thinking?

Sarah drove the few miles to Tom's house. Her nerves were shot and she almost turned the car around and drove back home. She cursed herself for not wearing anything substantial under her coat. This was a crazy stunt to pull. The thought had dawned on her that if things didn't go well, she'd end up sitting in a buttoned-up coat for the whole night. How weird would that be? By the time she got to Tom's house her mind was racing so much she couldn't get out of the car.

If he had dinner ready for them, she would have to refuse to take off her coat. She could say she had a cold maybe. God, what was she doing? She argued back and forth in her head as to whether she should in fact go back home and put some bloody clothes on. She was about to put the car in reverse when he tapped on her window. *Fuck.*

She pressed the button and the window went down.

"Hi. Are you coming in or are you going to sit out here all night?" he said.

"*Em. Em.* I'm looking for my earring. I think I dropped it."

"You're wearing two earrings. How many ears do you have?"

Shoot! Of course, her hair was all drawn back and he could plainly see.

"Oh. Yes. Not these earrings. It's a pair I was wearing the other day. Not to worry, I can look some other time. Like when it's bright, that'd be better."

She got out of the car and followed him to the front door.

She went in and the first thing she noticed was how hot it was. He must have the heating on full belt, she thought. She began to panic just a little. She could feel herself beginning to sweat. This was a very bad idea. It was a bad idea when Suze did it so she should have bloody well known better.

"Here, let me take your coat," he said with his hand out to her.

"Eh, no, it's OK. I'll keep it on for a while if you don't mind," she said.

"Sure. I've the heating at its highest setting so it will soon warm up. And I've lit the fire in the sitting room. Come on through."

Excellent! The house was like the Bahamas and now there was a huge log fire roaring in the grate to boot.

Sarah sat down on the couch. She could feel the sweat start to trickle down her back. She knew it wasn't just because of the coat, the fire and the heating. She was also sweating in sheer panic and embarrassment. If she was going to seduce Tom, she'd better do it quickly before she turned into one big puddle of water.

"Wine?" he offered.

"Yes, please. White. Cold – very cold," she said a little too quickly. "And ice. Please. Lots of ice."

She took the wine from his hand when he came back and downed half the glass in one gulp. Tom gave her a strange look but she didn't care. She felt like she was in a turkey bag. Her face was burning from the fire and wine and she knew her hair would be taking on a life of its own in the heat.

"What's wrong, Sarah? You look really uncomfortable. I'll take your coat. It's really hot now."

She gulped down the rest of the wine. "Can I have a glass of water, please?" she said. "With lots of ice."

Tom looked at her quizzically and went back to the kitchen.

Sarah jumped to her feet, quickly opened her coat and flapped it around her, trying to cool herself down. She buttoned it up again hastily and sat back down just as Tom came back into the room.

He handed her the glass of iced water and she drank it down.

"What's wrong, Sarah? I'm worried about you. You're not ill, are you?"

Sarah could see that his worry was real. His wife had died and she saw in his eyes how scared he was now.

"No, I'm not ill. I think I may be sick in the head but otherwise I'm fine. I've done something very stupid though."

"Whatever it is you can tell me." He sat beside her and took her hand.

"I came here to seduce you," she said simply.

The words were beautiful music to his ears. He could see that she was embarrassed and way out of her comfort zone and he felt a surge of love for her.

"I've got nothing on under my coat except my undies," she said.

Poor Sarah, no wonder she couldn't take her coat off, he thought. This gorgeous woman, the woman he loved so much, who he thought no longer loved him, was sitting there telling him that she was wearing nothing but underwear underneath her coat. How many guys got that lucky, he thought? He moved towards her and put his hand on the unevenly tied buttons. He opened them slowly, one by one until the coat fell open around her. He took her face in his hands and kissed her glossy lips.

He missed those lips every day. He stood, took her hand and pulled her up from the couch. The coat fell to the ground and he admired her. She was a little softer than before she had Rosa but she was still as beautiful. And she knew it too. What woman would do this if they didn't know how good they looked?

"Thank God," she muttered into his mouth between kisses.

"Yes, thank God you're here," he said.

"No. I meant thank God I could take that bloody coat off," she said, kissing him passionately.

"You're probably too hot in that too," he said, opening her bra and letting it drop to the floor. "And those," he said, slipping her panties down her legs. "Better?"

"Much," she answered, tugging at his clothes and taking off his shirt, jeans and underwear. She had forgotten how gorgeous he was. How was that possible?

"So – you wanted to seduce me," he said. "Go ahead."

She was still wearing her killer heels, aptly named because they were bloody well killing her right now, but she was at his full height. She pulled him towards her and his need for her was the only thing between them.

The next morning, Tom brought her coffee in bed. He was still naked and she hoped he was planning to stay that way. She kissed him and slipped out of bed to use the adjoining bathroom.

Tom lay back and anticipated making love to her again. Suddenly he heard screams coming from the other side of the bathroom door. His heart almost stopped. He hadn't been able to shake the sight of her sweating and looking ill the night before. There was something she wasn't telling him after all.

He rushed to the bathroom and flung open the door. She was standing there, not covered in blood or looking harmed in any way.

"*What is it?*" he cried.

"*Why didn't you tell me?*" she shrieked. "*I'm feckin' orange. I thought the fake tan came up straight away. I didn't realise it developed overnight. I look like Donald Trump!*"

"To be honest, I thought it was the look you were going for," he said, laughing.

"*Get out, get out!*" she shouted, turning on the shower. She was beyond embarrassed. Firstly she showed up at his house sweating like a woman going through the menopause and now she looked like she belonged in a circus.

At least he was laughing and not running a mile in the opposite direction.

Chapter 33

"What's going on with the shop next door?" asked Diane.

"You must be the only person in Ireland who doesn't know. The Bean Machine are opening next month. My days here are numbered," said Sarah sadly.

"But I expressed an interest in that shop ages ago. The agent told me he'd let me know if anybody else was interested," fumed Diane.

She had known the estate agent since her lawyer days and they had brokered a few good deals together over the years. "That sneaky little fucker! I'm going to have to have a word in his ear. What do The Bean Machine want opening right beside an existing coffee shop? Sounds like bad business to me."

"That's the point. Most places don't remain open for long once The Bean Machine move in. They annihilate the competition therefore making no existing business, therefore no actual competition," said Sarah. "Anyhow, why did you talk to the agent about it?"

"To open La Choise Part Deux, of course," said Diane. Now that she was no longer under threat of being arrested or her assets seized, she was thrilled with the idea of bringing her concept store to her hometown. She missed being in Ireland when she was in Spain and she missed being in Spain when she was in Ireland, so having a foothold in both countries made perfect sense to her.

"Really? That's wonderful, Di. Malahide would be the perfect place for La Choise. Don't worry about next door, I'm sure there'll be other locations. In fact, The Bakery could be up for sale before too long." She sighed.

"Don't say that. Don't even think it. And anyway, it wouldn't be right to buy The Bakery. It's been part of Malahide for so long now, I don't think the locals would take kindly to anybody moving in or capitalising on your misery."

Sarah knew it was true that The Bakery was part and parcel of village life years ago and as the village grew into a town, The Bakery grew with it. Sarah had seen her customers turn from children into adults with their own children and from glamorous women to stylish old ladies. It was as much a part of Malahide as the Grand Hotel. But that didn't stand for anything in the face of the multinational express train that was coming her way at high speed.

"It's so frustrating. It's like I'm fighting with my hands tied behind my back. I went to the bank to see if they'd back my plans to expand but when they heard the words 'The

Bean Machine', they started to get all fidgety and nervous. Next day I got a letter to say they wouldn't be offering me any facilities. Even my bank knows I'm screwed!" Sarah threw up her hands.

"It's not over 'til it's over. It may look like nothing will stop it now but you just never know what's around the corner," said Diane cryptically.

"Like what?"

"Oh, I don't know. Tell me all about Dr. Tom," said Diane, changing the subject. She didn't want to get Sarah's hopes up but she had a piece of information in the back of her mind that she thought might work in Sarah's favour.

Sarah started to tell Diane all about the great seduction she had planned and how it all went so badly wrong but incredibly right at the same time.

"When did you and Suze start going to Slut School?" asked Diane. "I don't know about you two. Remind me not to ask you for any sex tips, won't you?"

"As if you would. We all know you don't need any help in that department. You get whoever you want. You don't know what it's like for us ugly girls!"

And Diane did always get whoever she wanted. Up until now.

"If only you knew," sighed Diane.

"What?"

"I didn't get the boy this time. The boy's not interested in 'this'," said Diane, pointing at herself. "I know! It's hard to believe."

"What are you talking about? Serge is crazy about you."

"Who said anything about Serge? I'm talking about Oliver."

"Who the hell is Oliver?" asked Sarah, completely at sea.

"The guy who came for breakfast in Ballygra. The morning after you took on the Beyoncé challenge and failed miserably."

Sarah felt herself going red again. She really was a terrible singer and why she had the urge to sing the most unsingable songs in the world when she was drunk was a huge mystery to her.

"Oh, him. He was very nice about it. Hey, he was really cute too. *Wow, Dianawana has a crushie poo!*" said Sarah as if she was talking to Rosa.

"I don't have a bloody *crushie poo* and please don't ever talk like that around me. It's not even that cute when you're talking to a baby."

"But you do have a crush on him?" asked Sarah, dying to hear more and stunned by this turn of events.

"I have something. I'm not quite sure what it is exactly but I think about him all the time. My heart speeds up and I think I'm going to faint. This is all in the full knowledge of the fact that he is shagging a young one."

"Hold on, am I missing some important piece of the puzzle? I thought he just called for breakfast."

"We fucked. Not at breakfast. A few days later. He was amazing, by the way. We said goodbye and he moved on to a young tart. The end."

"Don't say 'fucked', Di. It sounds so crass. Say you made love, it's much more romantic."

"And what's romantic about him picking up his next victim from the airport the day after we did it? I think *'fucked'* is utterly appropriate."

"Who is she?"

"I don't know. She is much younger than I am and obviously important to him if he flew her over from London."

Diane twisted her hands in her lap. Screw him. She hated feeling like this. She had seen lots of women turn to quivering messes when they talked about how their boyfriends broke up with them and how they were broken-hearted and couldn't live without them, *blah blah blah*. Diane thought they were pathetic. They only had themselves to blame for leaving themselves open to getting hurt in the first place.

"How do you know all this?" asked Sarah.

"Mrs. Murphy heard it in the butcher's," said Diane.

Sarah thought she heard a slight sniffle. She thought she had to be mistaken but for the first time she could remember, Diane looked vulnerable.

"This is very serious, Diane. I hate to tell you this, but I think you're in love."

"I know," said Diane as she started to cry.

Sarah didn't know what to do. This never happened before. She sat beside Diane and held her hand. Diane didn't try to pull her hand back but let Sarah hold it for a while. Then she dried her eyes and wiped her nose with a tissue.

Chapter 34

Suze had looked forward to this day since Paul was born. And considering how long she had thought about it, she really shouldn't still be debating over what to wear. It was a big day and it was tricky to pick an outfit that was appropriate for an important daytime event.

Paul's graduation. She had seen the photographs in her head thousands of times. Her and Peter, the proud parents, with Paul standing between them in his cap and gown. If only she had taken notice of what she was wearing in the photographs in her mind, she thought ruefully. She tried on dress after dress and almost the entire contents of her wardrobe were on her bed.

It was November but the day was bright and fresh and not at all cold. She eventually picked a red wrap-over that skimmed her hips and had a slight gathering around the middle where she needed some forgiveness shown. She put on her black heels and was satisfied that she looked her best before she left the house. Peter had said he'd pick her up and they'd go together.

He had stopped being mad at her, thankfully. She had apologised so much that he eventually told her he'd never speak to her again if she said she was sorry one more time

Emma told her that there were no signs around the house that he was dating anybody. Certainly Natasha was nowhere to be seen. Suze wished it had worked out for them. Even though Natasha made her feel like a frump, she wanted Peter to be happy even if it was with a younger, more successful, better-looking woman than her. No, really she did.

She heard a car horn beep from outside. He was early, feck it. He'd be giving out yards that she was always late for everything and that no matter how much time she was given, she was never ready on time.

She had a last look at herself in the mirror and was mildly satisfied. She grabbed her coat and keys and went out to join Peter.

"You look lovely," said Peter as she got into the car.

"So do you," said Suze, looking admiringly at her ex.

"Divorce suits us," he said, laughing.

"It does," agreed Suze. They had started the process of making their separation official.

"I know you've been looking forward to this day for, well, forever," said Peter, putting his hand on Suze's.

Today wouldn't make sense without Peter, she thought.

He was as important to her as the kids themselves were. They were completely intertwined and no divorce court could undo the ties that bound them together.

"I'm so proud of him. I know I'm going to cry when he goes up to get his parchment," said Suze, checking in her bag to make sure she had lots of tissues.

"Me too. Not the cryin' bit but I am really proud of him. We might have done a lot wrong but we did most things right with the kids. They've turned out to be great human beings."

Suze thought she heard his voice break a little bit.

She hoped not. She needed Peter to be strong today or they'd both be basket cases and make a total show of poor Paul.

"By the way, Emma said she'd meet us in the hall. She has lectures this morning and she'll come right over."

"She better make an effort to dress up," said Suze. She didn't want Emma turning up looking like a hippie when she and Peter had made such an effort. Paul would be in a suit too and Emma would completely ruin the family photographs. Family? Well, they still were a family. Of sorts.

"I told her to make sure she wore somethin' decent. I told her not to be annoyin' you," said Peter, turning into the university campus.

"You did? Thanks, Peter." What people wore was never normally on his radar. What he wore was never normally on his radar. But Suze had to admit that he looked great lately. He was dressing in clothes that were flattering and suited his new slimmer body.

251

"Any more online dating?" she asked as they got out of the car .

"Nah. I'm steerin' clear of all that. I'm tellin' ya, there's mad women out there. Natasha was the only one I met who wasn't a bleedin' nutter. And she turned out to be a liar. I'm thinkin' about becomin' a priest if ya must know." He pressed the zapper, locking his car.

"Father Peter. It has a nice ring to it," said Suze as they walked inside to see their son being conferred.

They sat in their designated seating and Suze was delighted that Emma was already seated, looking glammed-up and fabulous. Suze thought she would burst with happiness. She wondered momentarily what the root of that happiness was. She thought of what Peter had said. They had done a lot wrong but they got the children right.

She looked across at Peter. He and Emma were sharing a joke of some kind. They were always close, that pair, thought Suze. It used to annoy her no end that she was never 'in' on their jokes, but she was no longer threatened by their closeness.

People were shuffling around in their seats and chattering noisily when someone did a quick '*one two, one two*' on the microphone that got everyone's attention.

A minute later a speaker approached the microphone. He welcomed everyone to the conferring ceremony and informed the gathered students and their families that they would first hear a few inspiring words from a guest speaker.

Suze looked over the heads in the hall and tried to pick

out Paul from the others. It was hard as they were all dressed in black gowns. She reckoned he was sitting in the second row about five from the end. She was about to ask Peter if he thought it was in fact Paul when she heard the name "Natasha Redmond".

She saw Peter's face drop. Sure enough, Natasha was making her way up to the podium.

Peter looked as if he either wanted to throw up or get up and run out of the place. But he couldn't go anywhere as there were far too many people on either side of them. Poor Peter, thought Suze.

Suze wasn't listening to the content of Natasha's speech as she was too busy looking at her. She was a beautiful woman. She looked like she was airbrushed somehow. There wasn't a hair out of place and her dark hair was wavy but not flyaway, a look that Suze knew was almost impossible to achieve from way back when her hair was longer.

She wore a simple black dress, making Suze feel like her red wrap-over was vulgar and showy. And, for the love of God, she was giving the class of 2019 their last inspirational talk before they set out to conquer the world. Suze looked around and Emma was in raptures. She saw her mouthing "*She's amazing*" at Peter when Natasha finished her speech.

Peter just nodded and tried to pull himself together. The ceremony proper got under way. Natasha was handing them their scrolls and Peter's misery continued unabated. It took another forty-five minutes for his personal hell and the ceremony to come to an end.

They left the hall and went out to the gardens where photographers were milling around the place. Here comes the moment I imagined in my mind for so long, thought Suze as the photographer asked them all to smile for the camera. Paul looked happy and understandably proud of himself. He was chilled as was his normal persona but he also had an edge today. Suze watched as Peter embraced Paul and the two men clapped each other on the back.

As soon as the photographs were over, Paul wanted to head for the restaurant. Typical, thought Suze, always thinking of his stomach first. Suze had booked lunch for them close by in the Merrion Hotel. She had wanted to book somewhere special and had in fact picked the Merrion out as the place they'd go to celebrate the momentous occasion years before.

"I think you should stay and say hello to her," Suze said, taking Peter aside.

"Nah. She's probably gone anyway."

Suze rubbed his arm, trying somehow to soothe him. She might not still be in love with him but she wanted to spare him any pain, even though he looked like nothing could ease the turmoil he was going through.

Then she saw Natasha. "Oh my God. Don't look now but I think she's coming over," she said through gritted teeth.

Of course Peter looked.

Natasha was trying to tread carefully over the grass in her Jimmy Choos and Suze felt her pain. Her own heels had dug into the grass and were as mucky as a farmer's wellies.

"I'll go on with the kids. See you there when you're ready," said Suze. She made a little wave gesture at the approaching Natasha and took each child by the arm and led them away.

"What's Dad doing?" said Emma, looking back and trying to free herself from her mam's grip.

"He met someone he knows. He'll follow us over," said Suze, intent on dragging Paul and Emma out of the campus.

They walked the short distance to the hotel where they sat in the beautiful Georgian dining room and admired the opulent surroundings.

Paul and Emma were chatting about the ceremony and the conversation got around to Natasha Redmond's speech.

"She's incredible," said Emma. "I love that she's totally comfortable with who she is. She doesn't make any apologies for being a woman and being at the top. I want to be like her someday."

Suze listened as Emma recounted what she knew about the newly appointed president of iBuy.

"She makes millions of dollars a year according to the papers. That includes her stock options, of course."

Of course, thought Suze. Millions of dollars. Jesus Christ, no wonder men found her intimidating. One thing for sure was that money didn't impress Peter. He had no great need for the things that money can buy. He wasn't fond of travelling and never wore jewellery. He dressed casually and didn't care for designer labels. Whatever about

Natasha herself, Natasha's money would do nothing to impress him.

"Where is Dad?" said Emma for the third time. "We never spend time together as a family. You'd think he'd make an effort!"

Suze reassured her that he'd be there soon.

"Paul, will you choose the wine, please? It's your big day after all," she said, trying to change the subject.

Paul picked up the wine list and ordered a bottle of French white and Spanish red. Suze wondered what she'd do for her next trick to keep their minds off the absent Peter.

"There he is. Dad, Dad!" said Emma, standing and waving at him. "Who's with him?"

Suze turned around to see Peter and Natasha coming towards their table. The restaurant manager would have a heart attack. They had insisted that she confirm numbers two weeks in advance and she was sure he wouldn't be impressed with an extra guest. But maybe she didn't intend to stay?

"Oh my God, it's Natasha Redmond!" said Emma incredulously.

Suze could see her brain working, trying to figure out why her good old dad was steering Natasha Redmond, one of the most influential businesswomen in Ireland or indeed the world, towards their table.

"Room for one more?" asked Peter as he introduced Natasha to his family.

Natasha had known he was there. She heard Paul Jackson's name being called and a young man who was the image of Peter stood in front of her. She felt like she had just been kicked in the gut. It had been almost two months since she'd seen Peter but she wasn't over him.

She busied herself with her work which gave her little opportunity to wallow in her misery. Whatever little time she had to herself was spent thinking about him. She had driven to his house but didn't have the nerve to get out of the car. She could broker deals with governments to save millions of tax dollars for iBuy yet she couldn't walk up to Peter and tell him she wanted to be with him.

The fear of rejection was too crippling and she reckoned that if she didn't give him the opportunity to reject her then there was still a flicker of hope for them. She had spoken to the students about what lay beyond the fear and she needed to go to that place herself.

She saw him pose for photographs with Suze and the kids, and she stood by until they finished. When it looked like they were ready to leave, she knew she had to make her move or leave him alone forever.

When he turned and came towards her, she could feel her heart beating out of her chest.

"Natasha. How'r'ya," he said.

"Hi, Peter. Congratulations on Paul's graduation. It's a special day for you."

"Yeah, it is. Great speech by the way," he said, even though he hadn't heard a word she said.

"Oh, thanks. Yes, I think it's important to keep telling young people that anything is possible. Especially at this time in their lives."

"And do you believe it?" asked Peter.

"Of course. Look at me. I'm just an ordinary girl from Dublin and look where I am now." She didn't mean to go there but it was like the big elephant in the room. "Look, Peter, I'm not going to apologise for what I've achieved. It's pretty bloody good."

"I'd never ask you to apologise for who you are. I think you're amazin'. I know that you must've worked like crazy to get where you are and I admire you for that. I'd never expect you to play that down. Look, I should have understood when you told me why you lied. I shoulda listened to you."

"I shouldn't have lied to you. I should have known you weren't like those other creeps I met. Peter, do you think there's any way that we could start over again? You know? Maybe go out on a first date, pretend the last few months never happened?"

"Are you kiddin' me?"

"OK. Sorry. I should have left it alone. Forget it. I lied and you can't forgive me, I get it." She was ready to turn on her heels and run for the nearest whiskey bottle.

"Wha'? I mean, are ya kiddin' asking if I want to give it another chance. Of course I want to try again. I can't believe it. I thought I'd messed up for good."

He took her in his arms and she melted into him,

breathing in his familiar smell of soap and Hugo Boss.

"This is terrible, but I have to go. Suze has lunch booked for ages and she'll be goin' ballistic." But he didn't want to go. He didn't want to let her out of his sight for another minute. "Will you come with me? I want you to meet the kids. Please?"

Of course she'd go. If he asked her to go to the moon and back, she would.

Chapter 35

"Dean Burke, please," Diane said to the receptionist.

"Do you have an appointment?" asked the girl, scrolling through her boss's appointments for the day.

"Tell him Diane Foster is here. He'll see me."

Diane sat down to wait. She wasn't waiting for long. Dean came out of his office at the back and greeted her with a friendly hug. He had sold Diane and James their mansion in Malahide back in the day. James had also recommended him to some friends and Dean made a killing. He was only a whippersnapper then but he was able to start up his own Estate Agency as a result of those first few commissions and had a soft spot for Diane since.

"Diane, how are you? You look fantastic by the way," he said warmly.

"I'm pissed off, Dean, that's how I am."

"Come into the office and tell me all about it," said Dean,

steering her in the direction of his office. He had no idea what Diane being pissed off had to do with him but he was sure he was about to find out.

As usual Diane went straight to the point.

"I see there's a Lease Agreed sign on the old Cummings building," she said.

"Yes, indeed there is. Sweet deal. The Bean Machine are moving in. Tied them in for twenty years with terms and rent reviews every five. That's good business even in this climate." Dean sounded very pleased with himself.

"I'm sure it is a sweet deal. But didn't you tell me that you'd alert me to any suitable properties that came up in Malahide. The Cummings building would be perfect for La Choise. *Absolutely one hundred per cent perfect.*"

Dean was blushing and Diane enjoyed his discomfort.

"I thought you were looking for something nearer the Marina," he said, trying to squirm out of it.

"That's bullshit, Dean, and you know it. I never even mentioned the Marina when I asked you to keep a look-out for me."

Diane knew he wanted the ground to open up and swallow him. Serves the little prick right, she thought.

"I'm sorry, Diane, but the Cummings premises is more suited to The Bean Machine than to a clothes shop."

The bull in Diane had just seen the red rag. La Choise wasn't just a clothes shop. It was an experience. And it was going to be a very bad experience for Dean. If he thought his day couldn't go down the toilet, then he was in for a rude awakening.

"And this Bean Machine, they're a big multinational, aren't they?" she said.

"They're one of the biggest on the planet. They've got over three thousand stores in Europe alone. Worldwide, it's at about twenty thousand or so. We should be delighted they picked Malahide to open another store."

"Yes, I suppose we should. We should all come out and wave our flags when they open their doors. Another faceless generic coffee chain in our midst," said Diane dryly.

"You can't stop progress, Diane," he sighed, as if he himself had singlehandedly tried and failed.

"You know, I had a friend of mine, a lawyer, look over old Mr. Cumming's lease conditions. Anyone can have a look-see, you know. Seeing as how his portfolio of properties is now run by a fund manager."

"Right," said Dean, sitting back and waiting for the bang. He picked up a pencil and started chewing on it, a nervous habit of his.

Diane hadn't come here just to haul him over the hot coals for selling out the lease from under her nose. She had bigger fish to fry and he could feel himself starting to tense up.

"Did you know that Mr. Cummings expressly forbid his properties being leased to multinationals? He didn't want any big grocery chains or fast food outlets moving in and ruining village life. He expressly ruled those companies out."

Diane let this sink in. She could see Dean was about to bite off the top of the pencil he had been chewing.

"Don't you think that The Bean Machine would be considered the type of company that he had in mind?" she said.

"The Bean Machine is not fast food. It's a coffee house and serves only the finest quality pastries to accompany its main product which is in fact the coffee. Where did you get this nonsense, did you say?"

"Karen Kelly of Kelly, Clarke and Son." Diane had just made that up. Her friend Karen practised alone. She had to big her up to scare Dean.

"Excuse me a moment," he said, dropping the mutilated pencil and picking up his phone. He stood and left the office.

He was obviously worried. Diane was grateful for her legal background. Karen emailed her the lease and she went through it with a fine-tooth comb.

The condition in the lease had obviously been ignored by legal parties on both sides to suit their needs. The fund wanted a tenant and the tenant wanted a particular location. Who cared what some old guy who actually owned the property wanted? Especially a dead old guy Well, Diane did for one.

Dean came back into the office, looking a bit less strung out, which worried Diane.

"Yes, I checked out that clause. You're correct, there is a condition in the contract but as Mr. Cummings who wrote the original lease is now deceased, it is no longer applicable. It seems his wishes died when he did."

"I think you'll see in Clause Six, condition five, third paragraph that any living relative can reinstate Mr. Cummings' original contract at any time. He was obviously a wise old man who knew that times would change. He was savvy enough to leave it to his descendants to do the right thing." Diane was scrolling through her emails on her phone.

"But there are no descendants that we know of so that's a moot point, surely," said Dean, sensing another blow was coming.

"Actually, do you know what? I've got Mr. Cumming's nephew in the car. He's quite elderly now so I didn't bring him in. We're on our way to my solicitor to put in an objection to the lease but I wanted to give you the heads-up first. After all, you've been so good to me," said Diane sarcastically.

Take that, you little fucker, she thought and left the office where Dean saw his considerable commission disappearing in a puff of smoke.

Diane wished that everything was as easy as that to fix. She wished that her last meeting with Serge had been as quick and painless.

"What has happened, *mi amor*? You are different," Serge said when he met her at the airport.

"Nothing. I'm fine. I'm just tired. We had a lot of late nights," she said, touching him on the hand. She had tried to stop him coming to pick her up but he insisted.

She sat and silently looked out the window.

Back at the apartment, Serge didn't let it go.

"Do you miss your friends, is that it?" he asked.

"Yes, I do miss them. They've been part of my life for so long and I find it so lonely here without them."

"You have me," he said, pulling her into his arms.

Diane didn't embrace him. She held her arms upright between his chest and hers. She knew she couldn't hold him or make love to him again. She started to cry.

"Did that make you cry, my sweet?" he asked, holding her at arm's length.

"No, no. I know it's corny but it's not you, Serge. It's me. I can't ... I'm sorry, I can't do this anymore," she said, pulling away from him. She wished he'd intuitively know. Just so she wouldn't have to say it.

But he wasn't letting her off the hook that easily.

"Has something happened?" he asked.

"Yes." Would he make her say it?

He stood there looking at her, waiting for her to finish.

"I met somebody else. There's no future for us but he made me realise that I can't be with you. I'm sorry, Serge. I think I love him."

The words hung in the air between them. Serge went to her bedroom. Diane stood rooted to the spot in the living room where they had been having their conversation. He emerged a few minutes later with his things in a bag. She presumed he had removed his clothes from her closet, his toiletries from her bathroom. And was about to remove himself from her life.

He swept past her and stood at the front door.

"You will have to leave my family's shop. She will not have you there after this," he said.

What? Surely he wasn't that petty? Surely the arrangement with his mother wasn't dependent on whether she was sleeping with her son or not?

As it turned out, the lease *was* dependent on her sleeping with Serge and Diane received her marching orders from Señora Messine the following day. She didn't even try to argue the legalities with the family. She wanted to go home. She was tired of missing her friends and she feared she might drink herself to death if she stayed here alone.

Chapter 36

"Go down there again? No bloody way," said Diane firmly.

"But Laurie's coming. And Kevin. And Jesus. It's the least we can do," argued Sarah.

"I'm snowed under trying to get orders for the new shop. It's the worst possible time for me."

Diane had unsurprisingly secured the lease on the shop next door to The Bakery. Sarah was thrilled by the totally unexpected turn of events. And she loved having Diane so nearby. It was like the old days.

"Look. There's no way around it. Laurie wants us all to spend Christmas together in Ballygra Castle. You're going to have to make the time and that's that."

"Oh, for fuck's sake. But I'm not staying long. One night and that's it."

At least Sarah had the good sense not to mention Oliver.

Diane's nerves were bad enough as it was with the grand

opening of her own store which was planned for the beginning of December that she couldn't risk thinking about Oliver and the way he made her feel.

She had no intention of pining over him for long more. There was a brand new year just around the corner and her resolution was to forget him and his sexy, crooked-toothed smile. But, until then, there was lots to be done.

She had sourced a whole new winter range from all of her suppliers and La Choise 2 was almost ready to open. She looked around her new shop and she had to admit it was stunning even if she did say so herself. Everybody else said it too, mind. She had women banging her door down trying to buy things from her even before she opened. They had seen her website and wanted first dibs on the fabulous clothes. She was glad of the distraction of the shop. Otherwise she would go crazy.

"Is there any teeny-weenie chance you'd let me try on some of the ball gowns? I really want to look amazing for Tom. I want something that'll make his eyes pop out on sticks," said Sarah.

There was a Christmas Ball planned for Christmas Eve in Ballygra Castle. There would be magazines and newspapers there taking photographs of the grand opening and of all the glitterati who were invited. Kevin Flynn was the big name but all of Ireland's beautiful people were invited to attend, ensuring it would be the most talked-about event of the year.

"I thought you already wore the eyes-out-on-sticks outfit.

You know the one you had on under your coat," laughed Diane.

"Ha ha. I'd like something with a little bit more substance this time," said Sarah as she started to flick through the dresses hanging on the rails.

"Hold on, Sarah. Those dresses cost a fortune. I'm sorry but I don't want greasy paws all over them," said Diane, running over to rescue her garments.

"I don't have greasy paws. We all can't go to work dressed like we're straight off a catwalk," said Sarah, wiping the front of her apron. She had just popped in when The Bakery's lunch rush had died down.

"Sorry. That was mean of me. OK, let's see. What colour are you thinking?" said Diane, trying to make it up to her.

"Black. Definitely black. I want it to scream 'sexy'," said Sarah, getting excited about finding the perfect dress.

"OK, wait there. I have one in the back. I wasn't sure about it because it's taffeta and there's not much call for it. But if it's screaming sexy you're after, this is it."

Diane disappeared into the storeroom while Sarah ran into the dressing room and started to take off her apron and jeans. Diane came in with swathes of black material and started to remove its plastic protection. Sarah saw the watermark pattern and loved it straight away.

"Take off your bra, you're not going to need it," said Diane, trying to find where the zipper was amid all the material.

Sarah did as she was told and stepped into the acres of fabric. It looked like a big black mass until Diane started to make sense of what went where.

Diane wouldn't let her look in the mirror until she had kicked off her own heels and given them to her to wear.

"Right. You can turn around now," said Diane.

Sarah screamed. And so she should have. Diane almost screamed too. It was fabulous. It had transformed Sarah from a pot-washer to a goddess in seconds. The transformation was mesmerizing. Diane had long been an advocate of clothes making the woman, but even she was amazed. She could see that there were tears forming in Sarah's eyes.

"No way, Sarah. No crying. This dress does not deserve tears. Maybe from other women who want to rip if off you and have it for themselves, but not yours. Now, step out of the dress and I shall wrap it for madam."

"Do I have to take it off?" cried Sarah. She could look at herself all day in this dress. She had never felt more like a woman before in her life.

"What? Do you want to wear it making cupcakes? Of course you have to take it off. Just think the next time you wear it you'll be wowing the man of your dreams. Tom's a lucky man."

"Yes, he is. And I'm a lucky woman. I'm so glad that we got back together. I can't imagine being without ..." Sarah stopped speaking.

Diane busied herself helping Sarah out of the dress and went to put it in a box for Sarah to take it with her.

"I'm sorry, Diane."

"For what? I'm glad for you and Tom. You belong together. You don't have to apologise for being in love. I don't need a man in my life to be happy. I have all this!" Diane indicated her fabulous shop and it's even more fabulous contents.

"I wish things had worked out for you, Di. You deserve it just as much as any of us. I don't know much about Oliver but he's a total idiot for passing you over for a woman half your age."

"God, thanks, Sarah. That makes me feel much better."

Chapter 37

Suze's first column for *gorge.com* was a roaring success. The first interview was with Natasha Redmond. Suze had seen the effect that Natasha had on Emma and she knew that the readers would admire her too. It was odd at first. Suze asked Peter to ask Natasha if she would agree to the interview.

Suze wouldn't have blamed her if she said no, that it would be too weird, but she needn't have worried. Natasha agreed and Suze went to her home in Sandymount to meet her. It was one of the old period properties, old style elegance on the outside and super-modern on the inside. It was the beginning of December and Suze couldn't help but imagine how amazing the house would look like decorated for the festive season.

Suze was used to her limited living accommodation and Natasha's home seemed to go on forever. It was spread out over three floors and was decorated in neutral tones. There was lots of art on the walls which added just the right amount of colour and texture to the generously proportioned rooms. Suze preferred a cosier look but she had to admit that Natasha's house was stunning.

It was awkward at first when Natasha answered the door to let her and the photographer in. Suze didn't know whether to ask after Peter or if that would be considered too personal a question at this early stage. So Suze just treated Natasha like any other interviewee and set about finding out what made her tick and how she had become so successful.

By the end of the interview Suze admired Natasha about as much as Emma did. Natasha was the youngest of eight children born in the inner-city Dublin. She remembered mostly being left to her own devices to get herself through life. She got herself ready for school from as far back as she could remember. She thought her father might have taken her the very first day, but she couldn't be sure.

Her parents were worn out by their other seven kids long before Natasha came along. She hadn't been treated badly by any means, only indifferently. One thing Natasha never gave in to was self-pity. There was always food on the table even if there was no money for anything else.

She had no real relationship with her mother and that was still a big regret to her. Her father died of a heart attack when he was in his forties so her mother, already overburdened, was left to fend for herself and her eight children. The older kids left school and started working at an early age, forgoing the rest of their education in order to bring some much-needed money into the house.

Natasha remembered her mother struggling and promised herself that she never would. Luckily, being the youngest and left to her own devices mainly, nobody really noticed that she stayed in school right to the end. She did well and her teachers told her she was a clever child. She carried this with her everywhere. She told herself over and over again that she was clever, even when it seemed that she was going to end up working in Frawleys, the local department store, along with an older brother and sister.

Natasha avoided working in Frawleys by packing herself off to London where she got a job as a PA to a high-flying executive in a PR firm. She was smart and knew that she got her job more for how she looked than for how many words she typed in a minute. It annoyed her but it was better than the alternative which was living at home with no future job prospects.

She worked hard and used all of her wits to move up the corporate ladder. It turned out that even though her boss appreciated her good looks, he encouraged her to go for bigger and better positions within the company. Soon Natasha was an account manager looking after a portfolio worth millions of pounds.

She saw early on how women had to give up all they worked for when they decided to have kids and that's when she ruled that out for herself. She wasn't sad at having to make the big decision not to have children. She knew how much love and affection a child needed and she would never be in a position to give all that. Better not to give it at all than to do a half-arsed job. She had learned that from her own childhood. Her mother just didn't have enough of herself to go around and the pain of it still hurt Natasha as a grown woman.

She was candid and brutally honest and Suze knew that her readers were going to love this interview. Natasha's message for the readers was that they couldn't have it all and not to fool themselves into thinking it was possible. Suze had to ask the question towards the end of the interview that she already knew the answer to but knew her readers would want to know.

"So do you have a special someone in your life right now?" she asked, giving Natasha a knowing look.

"Yes. I do."

"And do you want to tell the readers anything about this someone special?" urged Suze, signalling that she could say anything and that she wouldn't find it awkward. And the odd thing was that it wasn't awkward at all.

"Just that he means a lot to me. He makes me laugh and he makes me happy. That's about it," said Natasha, softening for the first time in the interview.

Afterwards the photographer took pictures of Natasha in various poses around the house. Relaxing on the couch, busy at her desk and cooking in her pristine, brand-new, out-of-the-box, shiny kitchen. Suze thought it was safe to say that it was the least-used room in the house.

"Thanks for doing this, Natasha. I think the readers are going to love it. We're told all the time that we should be juggling kids, home, husband and have an amazing job that takes up most of our lives as well. It's refreshing to hear someone who has the amazing job admitting that some things had to give along the way. You're an incredible person."

"Oh, please. I'm no more incredible than women who stay at home and devote their lives to their kids. They could do my job with their eyes closed but they just chose a different path to mine. If they didn't do what they did, I don't know what kind of world we'd have in the future. At least with good people rearing children, we can all be assured of a bright future."

Suze thought that Natasha was somehow telling her that the choice she made all those years ago to take care of Paul and Emma was a good choice too. Suze shouldn't have cared what Natasha thought, but she was touched by her words. She hoped that they could be friends someday.

Interview number one was taken care of and Suze was still left with the very immediate problem of finding the next suitable candidate to interview. Penny had called all the editorial staff to London for a pow-wow and Suze was to reveal who that "person" was going to be.

There were lots of people out there who were dying to be interviewed. They would agree to anything if they could flog something in return. Suze hoped she wouldn't have to settle for some washed-up soap star who had written a book about losing ten stone, quitting drugs and alcohol or finding God.

She was pretty sure the readers had had enough of all that. She wanted people who made a difference. People who beat the odds. Somebody aspirational. She just didn't know where she was going to find one on short notice. She needed a name. She knew Penny wouldn't think twice about firing her if she didn't deliver.

She was in a taxi from the airport to the centre of London when her phone beeped. The office had been texting her all morning, updating all staff on the agenda for the day. Jesus Christ, Penny could run a small country if she applied the same time and effort to it as she did to the minutiae of running the magazine.

What was it now? The lunch menu options? But it was a text from Penny to say that Jinny Jones wouldn't be attending as Jinny and her column had been scrapped. Jesus, Penny was a mini-Hitler. Suze was terrified her column would be heading the same direction as Jinny's if she didn't come up with the goods.

The taxi pulled up outside the office and Suze tried to forget her fears and took the lift to the eighth floor. The rest of the staff were assembled in the boardroom and Suze grabbed a coffee and sat down as Penny was calling the meeting to order.

Suze had taken a sip of her coffee when Penny looked straight at her and asked her who her next interviewee would be.

Suze almost spat the coffee back into the paper cup but instead she swallowed the coffee and heard herself say "*Jesus Martinez*".

Penny's eyes actually lit up and Suze could see she had to restrain herself from getting up and leading a conga line around the boardroom. Suze started to panic inside but hoped it didn't show on the outside. How was she going to deliver? She had his number. She'd had it since Ballygra. She didn't imagine she'd ever call him up. They'd had their fun and their sort of fun wasn't sustainable in the real world.

But if she didn't call him she might as well resign. No, scratch that. Penny would fire her before she could do that. She wouldn't be allowed a dignified exit from *gorge.com* either. Penny would blacken her name and make sure she'd never get a job on another magazine on Planet Earth.

———

Suze dialled the number Laurie had given her for Jesus. She was nervous making the call. Not because of what had happened between them or because she wanted anything further to happen. It was because Jesus was a really big deal. His new movie was breaking all sorts of box-office records and he had millions of followers on social media.

"Hello, Jesus. It's Suze. I don't know if you remember me but I …"

"Suze. Of course I remember. How can I forget? We had a beautiful fuck."

"Eh, yeah. Well … I'm not calling about that."

Suze felt herself blushing. The memory of the beautiful fuck was suddenly the only thing in her mind. She shook her head to get rid of it.

"I want to ask you for a favour."

"What kind of favour?"

"Would you let me interview you? I work for a magazine. It's one of the top ones in Ireland and the UK. We have millions of readers. I know they'd love to find out about you. You know. Your past. How you got into acting. How fame has affected you."

"Of course. I am going back to Ballygra with Kevin and Laurie at Christmas. We can do it then, no?"

"Fantastic. Thank you, Jesus."

Suze hung up the phone and screamed. Not because she was going to see Jesus again but with relief that she wasn't going to get fired. Not this month anyway.

Chapter 38

Sarah was worried about Joe's mother. Joe confronting her about the baby and Seamus didn't have the positive effect they'd hoped for. In fact, it seemed to have stirred up a nest of vipers in her soul. Sarah could see the torment in her eyes. It was as if she felt she was unworthy, having committed such an outrageous sin.

Sarah called Joe and told him he had to do something. And quickly. Joe made a call to the local parish priest. He filled the priest in on what had happened in his mother's past and about the shame she was carrying around with her. The priest agreed to call around and see her.

Father O'Brien rang the doorbell and waited a few minutes for the door to be answered. He knew that old people liked to be sure there were no crooksters on the other side of the door so he waited patiently.

"Father O'Brien! What are you doing here?"

"I wanted to talk to you, Mrs. O'Hara. Is it OK if I come in?"

"Of course. Come on in. And call me Sheila," she said, holding the door open for him.

She opened the door of the "good" room to show him in. When Joe was a child, he wasn't allowed in there. There was nothing good about it, in truth, but at least it was always neat and tidy. There was never an old newspaper lying around or a cushion out of place.

"The kitchen is grand for me, Mrs. O'Hara – Sheila," he said. "I've love a cup of tea."

In the kitchen, Sheila busied herself with putting on the kettle and getting the cups and saucers out of the press.

She cursed May under her breath for eating all the chocolate biscuits. Sarah said she didn't eat a thing at home. Well, she certainly had no bother eating in her granny's house. The priest would have to make do with the plain digestives. Digestives! For a priest!

They made a little bit of small talk while Sheila wondered why he was there in the first place. The parish had only one full-time priest and surely he didn't use his valuable time visiting the elderly?

When they got the niceties out of the way, Father O'Brien put down his cup and said, "Sheila. Your son contacted me."

"Oh," said Sheila. She'd feckin' kill him. She could just

imagine what it was he contacted the priest about too. She didn't need to be a rocket scientist to figure that one out.

"He told me about your first child. About the stillbirth."

She sat motionless.

Father O'Brien imagined that Joe would be getting an earful on the phone later on.

"I wonder if you'd like to pray for him with me," the priest said kindly. Still no response. He got ready to be thrown out on his ear. "Our Lord is compassion and love, Sheila. And forgiveness."

"I would like that," she said eventually.

Father O'Brien started a decade of the rosary and the two sat and prayed for little Michael.

———

When Joe saw the caller ID, he braced himself. His mother never took kindly to anything private being discussed outside the family. But he was ready with his defence and he answered the phone to her.

"Before you start throwing the head, I'm not sorry I did it. You needed to talk to someone and a priest seemed to be the best bet."

"I'm not going to give out to you, son. Father O'Brien and I said the rosary and had a little talk about Michael and, to be honest, I got a lot of comfort."

"Good. I'm glad, Mum. I'm really glad."

"And do you know what, Joe? I'd love to go back to Ballygra after all."

Chapter 39

"Are you nearly ready to leave?" Sarah asked Diane over the phone.

"Look, Sarah, I'm not going to be able to make it after all. It's been crazy here and I've still to organise all the clothes for the post-Christmas sales," said a jaded Diane.

"Oh no, you don't! You're going. You railroaded me into going when I didn't want to. This time you owe me."

"Think about it, Sarah. The place will be nuts. You'll hardly miss me." The last place she wanted to go to was Ballygra Castle. Laurie would have to understand.

"*Hardly miss you?* Of course we'll miss you. I want you there. We all do."

"But you've all got each other. You and Tom. Suze and Jesus. Laurie and Kevin, Joe and Paolo. It's so unfair. I'm never the one who's not having sex. It's a sad reflection on my life when Suze is getting it and I'm not."

"Suze isn't interested in Jesus – you know that," said Sarah. "But if you really feel you can't go, then of course we'll understand. It's a pity that you're going to miss the Christmas Eve Ball and all of the glitz and glamour. Laurie says that even *People Magazine* are sending a photographer. Although you not being there will give some other lucky girl the chance to get 'The Press Dress' award. I might even have a chance in my Screaming Sexy number. I'll be sure to mention where I got it."

Sarah left the words hanging in the air. She knew it would kill Diane not to be front and centre of the biggest event on Ireland's social scene this year.

"*People Magazine?* Fucking hell. Right. I suppose I could go. Just for the Ball. I can leave first thing Christmas morning and me and my misery could be home in time to watch *The Sound of Music.*"

———

Diane looked around her. The preparations for the sale were almost done. She was wrecked. The Christmas rush had been mental. She was sold out of almost everything and was frantically trying to restock before the New Year's Eve onslaught.

She knew on some level that she was trying to distract herself from her life. Once she was busy she didn't have to think about Oliver and his new love. It didn't mean that she didn't berate herself for falling for him, for making that rookie mistake. She had always been in control in her relationships and for very good reason.

Chapter 40

Diane pulled her car up outside the grand entrance to Ballygra Castle. She got out and stared in wonder at the majestic building. It was stunning. The castle walls were up-lit with spotlights and huge trees were adorned by Christmas lights, making it seem truly magical. The only thing that was missing was snow but, knowing Oliver, he probably had taken care of that as well.

She pulled her coat around her and told herself to be strong. She had rehearsed their meeting in her head a hundred times but she was afraid that the reality of him might make her lose all her resolve and turn around and go back to Dublin. Back to some place where there was no chance of seeing him.

Just then the huge wooden door opened. She took a deep breath and felt herself gasp in relief when it wasn't him.

"You must be Diane. You're very welcome to Ballygra Castle," a man said, moving aside to let her step in.

How did he know who she was, thought Diane. Had they so few guests that they knew each reservation by name?

"I'm Richard and it will be my pleasure to have you staying with us."

She recognised him from his television show and his face smiling out of his cookery books. She followed him into the entrance hall where a grand piano was the centrepiece, just as she had suggested, and she could see the baby grand she had also suggested in the huge bay window of the lounge amid more twinkling lights.

"It's beautiful," said Diane.

There was a big log fire burning in the huge hearth which was surrounded by comfortable armchairs and the hall felt warm and cosy despite its huge proportions. A large Christmas tree stood by the piano, glimmering with coloured lights. She almost expected to see Santa and his elves wandering around the place.

"I know we have you to thank. You gave Oliver some really wonderful ideas," said Richard.

"It's better than I ever imagined," said Diane.

"We feel exactly the same. We knew it was special but it's like it came back to life right before our eyes. Oliver told you we fell in love when we saw it," he said, grinning.

So Oliver had talked about her.

"Oh, yes, indeed."

"Are you here alone? We have a double suite booked under your name," said Richard, giving Diane's bags to a porter who took it up the elegant staircase.

"Yes, I'm alone," said Diane. She felt like a total loser when he put it to her like that. She wondered why Laurie, who had taken charge of all the reservations, hadn't booked a single room for her. She felt bad now that she was taking a room that Richard could have sold to another guest.

"I can move to a single room if you prefer," she offered.

"No, no. That's not what I was suggesting. It's just that we were under the impression that you and your partner were coming. Let me just show you to your room."

He led her to the elevator where he pressed the button for the second floor.

Diane wondered if by 'we', Richard had meant him and Oliver. She imagined they were as close as brothers, especially with all their shared experiences in London and turning the castle of their childhood into this wonderful hotel. The odds were that Richard knew that she and Oliver had shagged. He probably pitied her for even thinking she had a chance with cradle-snatching Oliver. But Diane had made sure that anybody's pity for her would be misplaced. She had worn the tightest black jeans she had and a black silk blouse that looked almost indecent as it stretched itself over her breasts and clung to her tiny waist. She had taken off her coat and given that to the porter too. It was working. She had caught Richard steal more than one glance at her on their way up in the lift.

"Will your partner be joining you at any stage?" asked Richard as he showed her to her sumptuous room with its romantic four-poster bed at its centre.

Seriously, she thought, I'll just pay the bloody single supplement.

"Nobody will be joining me," said Diane. "Look, I have no trouble moving to a single room if there has been some mix-up in the reservations."

"No, no. Not at all. This room is allocated to you. Room 630. Mrs. Flynn has made all the reservations. Please enjoy your stay with us." With a smile he left the room.

If there was no problem with her having a double room all to herself, then what was he going on about? Diane was too vexed to think about it so she flopped down on the bed and made snow angels on the sheets.

———————

"It's bloody amazing, isn't it?" said Suze, bursting into Diane's room an hour later.

"Fabulous. I can't believe it's the same place. It's like something out of a fairy tale," said Diane, looking up at the four-poster bed.

"It is. It's like a real castle. They could film a Disney movie in here."

Suze lay down on the bed next to Diane.

"I know you told us not to mention him, but what about Oliver? Have you seen him yet?"

"No."

"What are you going to do when you see him? It's bound to happen, you know."

"Yes, I do know that, Suze, thank you. I do realise that he owns this castle and would most definitely be here for one of the busiest periods of the year for the hotel industry," said Diane brusquely. She didn't mean to pick a fight with Suze but she was a woman on the edge. "I'm sorry, Suze. I'm not sure what I'll do when I see him. Of course I'll try to be all '*I don't give a shit, mate*' but ... I'm not used to being in this, *em*, situation."

"We've all felt like that at some stage or another. You've just been lucky to get away with it for this long. It will be hard, but it won't kill you. And you know that what doesn't kill you makes you stronger."

"I don't want to be stronger, Suze. I want him. I've lain on this bed for the past hour and thought about nothing else but him. Jesus Christ, who have I turned into? This is not me. And I don't like not being me. I need a plan. Can I borrow Jesus?"

"You can do whatever you like with him. He's not mine," said Suze.

"I need to pretend Jesus and I are a couple. If Oliver can have a lover half his age, then so can I."

"I dunno. Being honest is usually the best policy. Why not just be yourself? By yourself?"

"You have a point, Suze. But I need to get out of this situation with as much dignity as I can."

"I suppose."

"OK. I need to get ready. I need to look like a million dollars before I meet Oliver," said Diane, getting up and reaching for her oversized suitcase.

"So much for not staying for long," said Suze when she saw the amount of luggage Diane had brought along.

"I couldn't decide what to choose so I just brought everything. What am I going to wear?"

She started taking out one gown after another.

Suze was amazed by the dresses that were being pulled out. They were all from the shop in Malahide and each one cost an absolute fortune. Suze spotted a silk dress with a chiffon fishtail in the most gorgeous shade of pink she had ever seen. She ordered Diane to try it on.

"Pink? It's not my colour. I don't even know why I put this one in," said Diane, studying the dress at arm's length.

"It's beautiful. And with your blonde hair, it would be stunning."

Diane stripped herself of her all-black outfit and literally transformed herself in front of Suze's eyes.

Suze could barely speak.

"What? It's awful? I knew it. I told you I didn't know why I included it," said Diane in reply to Suze's silence.

"No. Look at yourself," said Suze.

Diane turned around and looked in the full-length mirror. It was, well, it was certainly different and not a colour she had worn before.

"You're a vision."

Diane almost laughed at Suze's description but she took another look at herself and agreed with her friend's assessment. She looked totally different from her normal self. She had worn gowns to more events than she cared to remember but she had never looked like this. The dress hugged every curve and moved with the natural rhythm of her body as if totally in synch with her. Diane had never known such a fabric and checked the label to make a note to herself to order more of the same for the shop.

"I am a bloody vision," Diane said. "Bloody hell. This dress and Jesus Martinez will have Oliver regretting his decision to pick a mere girl over me."

Chapter 41

Joe held his mother's hand as they walked into her childhood home. Sheila O'Hara stopped in the hallway and breathed in the old familiar smell. The staircase was waxed with the same polish her mother used all those years ago.

"We used to nearly kill ourselves on these very same rugs when we were running mad around the place," Sheila said, pointing at the rugs on the freshly waxed floor. "Do you know, I can nearly hear the laughing of us. We were wild. I don't know how my poor mother put up with us at all."

Sheila walked into the kitchen and saw the old Aga stove where her mother stood for most of her married life. Her dear mother who she loved with all her heart and missed to this day. There was the armchair where her father would sit listening to the wireless and reading his paper after a day out working the farm. When little Sheila passed him he would pull her onto his knee and tickle her until she nearly cried.

All the memories came flooding back to her. And not just the bad ones as she had feared.

"I'm going to be alright," she said to Joe and went to put the kettle on the stove.

Joe watched as she reacquainted herself with the house and all of the memories it held. He could see that his mother was happy to be back in her home place. She had every right to be there and should have been able to enjoy it for all the intervening years. He marvelled again at the amazing way she was able to live without bitterness, despite all the people and things that conspired against her in life.

He was glad to be spending Christmas in West Cork. Everyone had been invited to the castle for a Christmas Ball and he and Paolo were at the ready with matching burgundy-velvet tuxedos. Paolo looked fabulous in his but Joe wasn't sure he'd be able to pull off the look, despite Paolo's protestations.

A car pulled up on the gravel driveway and Joe went out to greet Laurie and Kevin. It was amazing to think that they were both Hollywood royalty and were here to visit his mother in her childhood home.

"Hi, Joe! Thanks for letting us come. I had to come and thank your mum for getting me to meet Seamus."

Sarah had told him about Laurie going to visit Seamus and about some magical powers that Seamus was supposed to possess. Joe was sure it was all rubbish but Laurie seemed to be living proof that the opposite was the case. Laurie wore a smock top even though her 'bump' was barely evident.

"So, you haven't just gone on a carb binge, then?" said Joe.

"Nope. Although now that I'm eating for two, I am indulging myself alright," laughed Laurie. "It's because of Seamus. I don't want to cause any grief for your mum but I need to thank her. And Seamus. You've no idea how long we've waited for this and how over the moon we are."

Joe looked at Kevin who shifted uncomfortably on his feet. He guessed that Kevin wasn't convinced that Seamus held the key to Laurie's fertility at all.

"Well, congratulations to both of you. It's the most wonderful news. Come on in. Mum is in the kitchen. Making tea, of course!" Joe said with a laugh.

He led them in to say hello to his mother. Then he and Kevin left the two women and went to wait for them in the sitting room.

"I really don't know what to say, Joe. It's what we wanted most in the world but I can't actually buy into Seamus being the one who made it happen," said Kevin as they sat on the couch where Laurie had lain unconscious a few months before.

"Hey, the end result is the most important thing," said Joe.

He felt sorry for Kevin. It wasn't like Laurie had sex with Seamus or anything like it, but it must seem weird to be crediting an almost eighty-year-old man with the conception of his own child.

"Don't ask me how I know that the visit to Seamus did it, I just do," Laurie was saying to Joe's mother in the warm kitchen. "I never felt like I was going to get pregnant when I spoke to the doctors in LA. I was at the stage where all I felt was despair and hopelessness. When I met Seamus I felt suddenly full of hope and, I don't know, I felt joy. Oh God, I know this must sound like the lift doesn't go all the way to the top, but I don't know a more honest way of putting it."

"I have to say that when I heard that Celia Murphy was blabbing about what happened all those years ago, I was mad," said Sheila. "She was always the same. Sticking her nose in where it wasn't welcome. But she actually did me a favour. At least now I can remember our little boy and not feel the weight of the world of shame about it."

"I'm glad you feel like that now. It was a different world back then. I'm sorry for what you went through. It was barbaric. I couldn't imagine how I could bear it if anything ..."

"*Ara*, girl, nothing bad is going to happen to you. You've waited too long for this baby and you're going to have a fine healthy little child."

Laurie was overcome with emotion again. She felt guilty for feeling such utter joy when the poor woman opposite her had lost her own precious boy.

"It's because of you and Seamus that we've been so fortunate. I, we, want to thank you from the bottom of our hearts."

"Isn't it great that something good came out of all that

sadness and shame? A lot of good has come out of it over the years from what I hear. You know, I haven't seen Seamus in nearly sixty years. I think it's about time I put that right."

———

"Joe, I need you to take us to Seamus. I'll tell you the way."

"What? Mother, are you sure?"

"I've never been surer about anything."

"I don't know, Mam. It could dredge up old memories. Why don't you leave it for another time?"

"Joe, I'm seventy-eight and Seamus is the same. I don't think we have a whole lot of time left."

Joe picked up his car keys. As always, he was ready to do anything his mother asked him to do.

"Right. Come on. Get in the car."

Joe was already an anxious driver. He almost had a nervous breakdown at the thought of meeting another vehicle – the country roads were too narrow to accommodate one car, never mind two. He shuddered at the thought of how much extra the rental car company would charge to his credit card if he did any damage to the car. He cursed himself for not taking the excess policy. And with the state of the roads, he was convinced that the suspension would be knackered by the time he brought it back to the airport as well.

"Are your eyes closed?" his mother asked.

"No. Of course not. I'm concentrating, that's all."

"You're very nervous. There's sweat on your –"

"Alright, Mam! Stop talking now if you want me to get us there in one piece."

"You should let Paolo drive. Nothing would scare him, I'd say."

"I only have a licence for the scooter, Mrs. O'Hara."

"I told you to call me Sheila. Or you can call me 'mamma' if you prefer."

"OK … Sheila."

Joe continued to sweat while his mum and Paolo chatted. He couldn't partake. He was proper scared. He had hired a small car from the categories on offer. He drove the Ford Fiesta at 30 miles per hour, gripping the steering wheel for dear life. Kevin and Laurie were driving behind them. Kevin had opted for the extra-large variety. It was enormous and took up the complete width of the boreen. How he and a tractor driver would manage to negotiate an encounter and both emerge unharmed, Joe shuddered to think.

Eventually they came to an entrance to an old farmyard and his mum ordered him to take a left turn. Joe wished she could have done this on another trip. She hadn't seen Seamus in donkeys' years and the memories of what happened then could have a terrible effect on her and ruin Christmas for them all.

He sighed with relief as he unbuckled his seatbelt and got out of the car. Paolo helped his mother out her door and they both walked her up to the door of the old cottage.

Sheila knocked on the door and called out Seamus's

name. In pure country fashion, she pushed open the door, not waiting to be invited in.

"Hello, Seamie! Are you home?" she called, reverting to her pet name for him all those years ago.

Joe, Paolo, Laurie and Kevin followed her into the stone cottage. It was basic. Not minimalist. Bare as fuck. Joe looked around and wondered how someone could live there. There was a big pot on the Aga giving off a smell that would stop a galloping horse in its tracks. He thought he would be sick and hoped the smell didn't attach to his clothes or skin. His mother didn't seem to notice it at all. She walked into a room off the kitchen.

Joe, Paolo and Kevin looked around the place in a state of disbelief. There was an armchair beside the stove, and a small red Formica table at the window with two chairs pushed in underneath. That was it. That was all the furniture in the room. There was a shelf with an old-fashioned tea caddy and a few willow-pattern cups and saucers which were all chipped as far as Joe could see.

Laurie stood there, seemingly oblivious, focused on the door Sheila had disappeared through.

"Come in now, will ye?" said Sheila, sticking her head into the kitchen.

They went in.

Seamus was sitting in a chair in the room whose only other furniture was a bed with a plain white eiderdown on it.

Laurie rushed forward, beaming. "Seamus! It's so good

to see you again. It worked and I can't ever thank you enough!" She caressed her bump lovingly.

"It's the first of many, girleen," he said in a voice that sounded stronger than he looked.

"This is Kevin. This is my husband," Laurie said.

Kevin shook his hand.

"*Eh*, thank you, sir. Laurie told me about her visit with you." He couldn't in all honesty say more. The jury was definitely still out on whether Seamus had anything to do with Laurie's pregnancy.

"Sure the lassie did it herself. She let herself feel the babby. That's all she ever needed to do. To have the faith, to believe no matter what."

Kevin made some agreeable noise that was between a word and a mutter and moved back and put an arm around Laurie.

"And this is my Joe and his, *em*, friend Paolo," said Sheila.

Joe shook hands with the man who was his mother's lover before he was born and reintroduced Paolo as his husband. Seamus didn't register any surprise at this but perhaps he didn't hear.

Admittedly when Joe saw Seamus at first, sitting in the chair, he couldn't imagine the man being anybody's lover. He looked small and wizened and old beyond his years. When he looked into Seamus's eyes though, he saw a steeliness that made him think of him in a different way. He didn't have the faraway look of the elderly. Despite his aging body, his mind was still all there.

They made a bit of small talk for a few minutes and then they left Sheila and Seamus alone in the room.

"He's wonderful, isn't he?" gushed Laurie.

"*Eh*, yeah. There's definitely something about him. Those eyes," said Kevin.

"He's the reason we're having this baby, hon. The man is a miracle worker. You should be more grateful to him."

"Of course I'm grateful. You know I am. We're having a baby, for god's sake. What do you want me to do? I can leave him a wad of cash but I don't think he'd have any great need for it, do you?" He indicated the place around him.

"He doesn't want our money. I know that but I want to make some kind of gesture to show him how grateful we are. He did what he did out of love for his fellow man. I know you're sceptical about it, but I know that something happened in this place. I felt the magic happening."

"Maybe we should make a movie about it," said Kevin jokingly.

"You know what, Kevin? I think that's exactly what we should do."

Chapter 42

"How do I look?" Tom stood back and waited for Sarah to give him the once-over.

Sarah was still in her underwear, putting on her make-up. She turned to look at him. Tom Harrison was born to wear a tux, she thought. It crossed her mind instantly how lucky she was to have him back in her life.

"You look like the most handsome man in the world. You could be the next James Bond," she said, with tears pricking her eyes.

"No. No. No. No crying. Tonight is a celebration. All your friends are here. We're going to have a great time," he said, taking her in his arms.

"It's just when I think about all the time we wasted and how we might not even be together now, it just kind of scares me. We're so lucky, you know. To have each other and to have May and Rosa." Sarah was in full flood now. She was freaked out that she almost threw all this away. All this happiness and promise. All this possibility and love.

"*Shhhh* ... stop," he said, dabbing her eyes gently with a tissue. "We are lucky. I'm grateful every day to have what we have. So let's be happy about it. No more tears. You'll ruin your make-up and you spent the last half hour putting it on."

"You go on downstairs," she ordered him.

"But I was going to –"

"Just go. Wait for me at the bottom of the staircase. I'll be down in a few minutes. Please," she added when he seemed to hesitate.

When he left the room Sarah ran and locked the door.

Her fantasy of Tom standing at the end of the stairs as she descended in her beautiful gown was now becoming a reality. She unzipped the bag that held the black ball gown. Like Diane, it took her a few minutes to figure out what went where. She wished Diane was with her now. It wasn't an easy task shaping the beautiful fabric around her. She finally pulled up the zipper at the side and she was in.

She stood in front of the mirror and honestly couldn't find fault with what she saw. It was super-dramatic, super-sexy and eye-wateringly expensive.

The tight bodice showed off her boobs to great effect and gave way to a huge skirt which looked romantic and sexy at the same time. She wasn't full of herself by any means but the dress somehow transformed her from Sarah O'Hara into Scarlett O'Hara.

And her Rhett Butler was at the bottom of the stairs

waiting for her. She picked up a feather clutch and left the room. She walked past the lift and down the magnificent stairs. She heard the orchestra playing in the foyer and she thought how perfect it all was. It was the nearest thing to living her dreams that she had ever experienced.

She saw him at the bottom where she told him to wait. He was talking to Joe and Paolo and the three of them looked around at the same time. Tom had to do a double take even though he had only seen her moments earlier. His eyes almost popped out of his head and locked onto hers as she walked down each stair. He had his hand out for hers as she reached the bottom step. She could feel the tears welling up again.

Her love for Tom and for her family was about to engulf her and turn her into a gibbering mess. Then Tom dropped down onto one knee and it took a few seconds for her to figure out what was going on. The orchestra had stopped playing and all eyes were on Tom and Sarah.

"You're beautiful on the inside and the outside. I love you with all my heart. Sarah O'Hara, will you marry me?"

Sarah looked around her. Joe had buried his head in Paolo's shoulder so that she wouldn't see his tears. Paolo made eyes at her and indicated she should give poor Tom an answer before his knee gave out. She looked at Tom with a beaming smile.

"Yes."

This reality had surpassed anything she could have dreamed up. She could hear cheering and clapping and the orchestra had struck up again and was playing "Congratulations" with gusto.

Tom fumbled in his pocket for the little velvet box he had brought to Ballygra.

"But how? Why? How? I mean, when did you know you were going to propose?" asked Sarah between kisses.

"I knew when you drove me back to Rome from Amalfi. When I got on the plane, leaving you felt like losing a limb," he said. "I wanted to ask you in the bedroom upstairs but you threw me out before I got a chance. I was waiting for another opportunity and when I saw you at the top of the stairs I knew it was the right moment."

"I love you, Tom Harrison. I've always wanted to be your wife. Wait until we tell May. She'll be thrilled."

"I already told her. Well, I asked her. As in I asked her for her permission. She was happy by the way. Her approval is not without conditions though. She wants to be your bridesmaid."

———

There was champagne in the drawing room to celebrate the good news. The night couldn't be more perfect, they all agreed. All except Diane. She still hadn't seen Oliver and the dread of seeing him threatened to ruin her night entirely.

They all chatted noisily and planned the upcoming wedding down to the minutest detail. Then the door opened and Laurie came in with Kevin. They had been at a photo shoot for *People Magazine* and it had run late.

Everyone knew that there was something different about Laurie. The change was subtle and it took the women a few moments to cop on to what it was.

"Oh my God, I don't believe it!" said Sarah, hugging Laurie and screaming excitedly.

"It's wonderful!" said Suze, hugging her in turn.

Diane hadn't a clue what was going on.

"Diane! Aren't you going to congratulate Laurie?" asked Sarah.

Diane was confused. She looked at Laurie and then she saw it. She was literally glowing. A tiny swelling was visible but it was definitely there.

"You're ... oh my God. You're pregnant?"

"I wanted you all to be together when I told you. Yes. I am. And I've got scan photographs to prove it. Don't worry, it's not a phantom pregnancy, Di. It's real. We're going to have a baby."

Diane hugged her but not too close in case she creased her perfect dress which Oliver had yet to get a load of.

"I'm happy for you, I really am. No matter how it happened," said Diane sincerely.

She didn't believe any of the nonsense that happened in Ballygra a few months back but that didn't matter now. The important thing was that Laurie was getting exactly what she wanted.

"It's a boy," said Laurie.

"You found out at the scan?"

"No. Seamus told me."

"Well, I suppose he has a fifty-fifty chance of being right."

"So we're still agreeing to disagree?" asked Laurie.

"We are," said Diane. "But I'm genuinely thrilled for you. It couldn't happen to a nicer couple than you and Kevin."

"I'm thinking of calling him Seamus," said Laurie.

"Jesus, could you not call him something a bit more glamorous? Like Summer or River. Seamus? Seamus Flynn? It's just not Hollywood," said a dismayed Diane.

"A bit like Kevin, you mean?"

"Yeah. He'll never make it with a name like that," said Diane, laughing.

The dinner gong sounded and they started to file out of the drawing room in pairs. They were interrupted on their way by a few carefully chosen celebrity photographers who were going to publish their images and that of the castle in some of the most high-profile newspapers and magazines on the planet.

Diane posed with Jesus. Suze had filled him in on why Diane wanted him at her side. He was great. He acted as if he was besotted by her. The photographers asked her to pose on her own and asked what label she was wearing. She was actually in a good mood by the time they were ready to sit for dinner. She got La Choise's name out there and she had a handsome toy boy on her arm. She felt strong and confident. She wasn't going to let anything or anybody ruin her night. Then she heard his voice.

"You came," was all he said.

Diane turned around.

"Of course. It's not every day that one of your best friends invites you to spend Christmas in a castle."

God, he looked amazing. He was dressed in a tuxedo with a crisp white shirt and bow tie. The bow tie was slightly crooked and it took all of Diane's willpower not to move in to fix it. She would surely touch off his cheek which already had the shadow of the next shave coming on.

"You look incredible," he said.

Good. That was exactly the look she was going for. She wanted him to know what he was missing by messing around with mere girls who couldn't possibly give him what he wanted.

"Thank you. The place looks amazing. You must be very proud."

Jesus was by her side doing exactly what he was told to do. He looked sexy, smouldering and devoted. But Diane now needed to be alone with Oliver. She had to get this over with. She told Jesus to go into the banqueting hall and that she would be right in.

"You got your Hollywood A-listers," she said when Jesus had left.

"I told you before. When I heard Laurie was here a few months ago, of course the first thing I thought of was how great it would be if she and Kevin stayed here. It would put us on the map. But I didn't use you to try to get close to her. You've got to believe me. What I feel for you is more important than Ballygra."

307

Did he just say *feel?* What I feel for you? Not what I *felt* for you, past tense? Diane felt the hope rise inside her. But she couldn't do this to herself again. She had spent the last few months trying to get him out of her head and her heart.

She had taken on a humongous corporation to get the shop she wanted and by doing so she had single-handedly saved Sarah's business. She had opened La Choise 2 in Malahide. She was a fucking rock star. Now one little word from him was turning her world upside-down. She couldn't go there again.

"Well, I'm glad for you. And Richard of course. It really is an amazing place. Kevin and Laurie are talking about making a movie about Seamus and his magic potions. If that comes to fruition you'll have a lot of Hollywood stars staying with you in the future. Look, I'd better go on in to dinner. I don't want to leave Jesus on his own for too long."

"So Jesus Martinez, eh? You're dating him now?"

If only Oliver knew that she wouldn't date Jesus if he was the last man on earth. If only he knew that there was nobody she wanted to 'date' bar the man who was asking her the question.

"I'll tell you if you tell me who you're dating," she said playfully.

"I've no time for anything but work. All this work is making Oliver a dull boy, I can tell you."

Diane couldn't imagine Oliver being dull no matter what the circumstances. He was so full of energy and life that she could feel herself charging off his very presence. But she wasn't ready to accept any more lies.

"I don't believe you," she said bluntly.

"It's the truth. It's work, work, work. But I have nil interest in dating in any case."

"What about your little friend from London?" she blurted out.

"Who?"

Crap! Why didn't she keep her mouth shut? She had been handling their encounter so well. "Oh, nothing."

"Little friend? London? Who do you mean?"

"Oh, some girl you flew here from London. Long red hair. I saw the two of you wrapped around each other the day after we ... well, the day after we ... you know the day I'm talking about."

"I really don't know what you're talking about."

He didn't even have the decency to admit it, she thought. Not that it would have changed anything but at least she might have thought better of him.

"I'm sorry," she said. "I don't want to leave Jesus waiting."

She turned and made her way to the ballroom, leaving him standing there.

"Well?" asked Suze. "Jesus said you were talking to Oliver."

"Yes, we were talking. It was all going fine and then I told him I saw him with that girl. Why couldn't I just leave it alone? He'll know now that it bothers me. I wanted to come off so ultra-cool this evening but I just came across as a jealous ex."

Suze patted her hand and gave her sad smile.

The conversation around the table was all about babies and weddings. Diane tried her best to join in but her heart wasn't in it.

Their meal was served and Diane only played with the food on her plate.

"Are you going to be OK?" asked Suze.

Diane shrugged. She didn't know if she was going to be alright or not. The chances were she would eventually get over him. But there was no way she was going to get over him by spending Christmas in his castle, with the distinct possibility of bumping into him with "her". She suddenly knew what she had to do.

"I'm sorry, Suze, I have to go," she whispered. "Just tell everyone I've gone to the ladies' room. Nobody will notice for a while."

"Where are you going?" said Suze quietly.

"Home. I can't do it. I thought I could but it's just too hard. Don't say a word. Promise me."

Suze did promise. She would do anything for the woman who had done so much for her.

Chapter 43

Diane went back to her room and started to stuff her clothes back into her bags. She went to the bathroom and gathered all her belongings from there. Why did she have to bring her whole friggin' life with her everywhere she went, she thought, as she looked at the quantity of stuff on her bed. There was a knock at the door. She'd known Suze wouldn't let her go without at least trying to persuade her to stay.

"Look, I made my mind up, Suze," she said as she opened the door.

Except it wasn't Suze at the door.

"She's not my girlfriend," Oliver said.

"Whatever. It's none of my business. I don't care who she is to you."

She didn't want to hear his lies and excuses. She wanted to get into her car and get the hell out of there. She walked back into the room and continued to pack her bags.

"Her name is Jeri. She was our best waitress in London, and she agreed to come over and work at Ballygra. She's not that particularly young either. She's twenty-nine and has a master's degree in Hospitality Management. Her boyfriend is a horticulturist and is in charge of our gardens. I swear to you, Diane, there is nothing … there was nothing going on with Jeri and me."

He was standing beside her. She looked up at him and stared into his brown eyes. She wanted him to be telling the truth, but how would she know for sure?

"I don't … I thought … Mrs. Murphy said … and then I saw the two of you."

"Mrs. Murphy? Right! Well, it won't be the first time she's gotten the wrong end of the stick. She's the nosiest woman in Ballygra. She can't help herself. She's always gossiping about somebody. Bloody woman!"

"I don't know." It was all Diane could say. She didn't know what to do. She didn't dare believe him. She didn't want to risk getting her heart broken completely.

She had only limited powers of speech. She had a million questions waiting to be asked but none of them would form themselves into a coherent sentence.

"I'm sorry I didn't go after you that morning. I wanted to. So badly. But I had to go to the airport to pick Jeri up. And I thought you were going back to him. To Spain. I felt something happened between us but I wasn't sure if you felt it too. I was a fool. I should have hopped on a flight to Spain and begged you to come back with me. I should have done whatever it took to let you know how I felt because you are the most wonderful woman I have ever met. I haven't been able to get you out of my head."

Her responses still wouldn't come. She was looking into his eyes and she saw only truth. And love.

"When Laurie made the reservations, I was dreading seeing you with Serge. I wanted to be a thousand miles away from here but it's our busiest time. When Richard told me you arrived alone, I swear I couldn't believe it. I only hope that you're here alone because you're not with Serge anymore. And that you're not with Jesus either. Otherwise I'm making a total idiot of myself."

"Serge and I are finished. I couldn't pretend that you meant nothing to me even if I was never going to see you again," she said.

It felt good to be able to get her feelings out in the open. She had spent so long turning the beautiful thing they had together into something twisted and wrong. She let go of all the horrible things she thought about him and she let him take her in his arms.

"I'm sorry," he said. "I should never have let you go."

"It's OK. I used all my pent-up frustrations to kick some ass in Dublin. So some good came out of it."

"That's a beautiful dress," he said, slipping one thin strap off her shoulder.

"It would want to be. It cost a fortune. It's a silk chiffon and it marks really easily."

313

"Pity it's going to end up in a heap on the carpet then," he said slipping off the other strap.

The luxurious fabric slithered down her body and landed at her feet.

———

The next morning Diane opened her eyes and looked across at him. He was fast asleep. It hadn't been a dream as she had feared in that moment between sleep and wakefulness. He was beautiful to look at and she couldn't help touching his face. He woke up and smiled at her. Her heart melted and she knew she was doomed. Whatever it was that Laurie had been talking about – the love thing – she was in love with this man. She had never before felt so much in the right place. So present. So happy.

He sat up on one elbow and looked at her.

"Good morning, beautiful."

"Morning."

Diane lay back on the sumptuous bed, ready for another round of lovemaking.

"I have to get up and go on a shoot."

"What? You'd leave me, this, in bed, to go get your picture taken?" Diane said, indicating her naked self.

"It's a grouse shoot for the guests. It was a tradition that there was a shoot at Ballygra Castle every Christmas morning so we're reviving it. Blame Richard. I have to go because he couldn't shoot a gun if his life depended on it." Reluctantly he got out of bed.

Diane admired him as he picked up his clothes off the floor and put them back on. She didn't want him to go but there was no use arguing with him. His guests were all-important to him and the future of their luxury castle depended on everything being perfect.

"Do you want to come with me?" He took her hand and tried to drag her out of the sumptuous four-poster bed.

"*Eh.* Get out of this warm, comfortable bed to go out in the cold and snow? *Eh*, no. I'll stay here and sniff your pillow like a weirdo, thanks."

"I'll leave my boxers if you want to sniff those too."

"*Ew. Gross.* Get out of here, you filthy animal!"

"There's something else. It's awkward to say, but I don't think it's a good idea for the guests to see me coming in and out of your room. I don't want them to think I provide extra customer service to special guests."

Was she just a special guest? What was he saying? *Last night's lovemaking was great, but I can't be seen to treat you any differently to the other people staying in hotel?*

Diane got a sinking feeling.

"Now the party's over, is that what you're saying?" she said, throwing back the covers and standing naked in front of him.

"No, it isn't. I just think you should move your things into my apartment."

"What? Oh."

"The party's only starting. I have no intention of ever letting you go again. If that's alright with you ..." he said.

She let the words sink in. She wanted to make sure she didn't mishear or misunderstand. He wanted her. It wasn't the end, only the start of something wonderful.

"That's perfectly OK with me," she said, pulling him back down on the bed. The grouse and the guests would have to wait a few minutes more.

———

When Oliver left, Diane got dressed and made her way downstairs. She had packed her bags and a porter was going to take them to Oliver's private apartment. Suze, Sarah and Laurie were having brunch and she sat down at the empty seat at the table.

"So you got what you wanted for Christmas after all," said Suze, pouring a coffee for her.

"Several times," smiled Diane.

"You look disgustingly pleased with yourself," said Sarah.

"He asked me to move into his apartment. Just in case guests' tongues are wagging. It's probably not a big deal but it kind of feels like it."

"It is a big deal," said Laurie. "If he was only interested in shagging you, he'd be happy to have you holed up in your room, on tap for him. He cares about you, Diane. And I'm sorry for calling you those terrible names."

"Don't worry. I think calling me an emotionally stunted retard was just the kick up the arse I needed."

The others laughed at the thought of anyone calling

Diane an emotionally stunted anything and getting away with it.

"So, let me see that rock again," Diane said to Sarah. She took the beautiful solitaire and twisted it around her finger and made a wish. Her wish was to always have her friends and always to be as happy as she was right now. "It's beautiful. Tom has great taste. In engagement rings and future brides."

"He has, hasn't he?" said Sarah.

Her happiness was contagious and soon they were all trying on the ring. They even held it on a chain in front of Laurie's bump to see if they could determine the sex despite Laurie's insistence that she already knew it was a boy.

"You're very quiet, Suze," said Diane.

"Yeah. This is my first time not spending Christmas with Paul and Emma. I miss them."

"Aw. You poor thing. At least there's FaceTime?"

"Yes, but it's not the same."

"Of course not. They're having a good time though?"

"Yeah, they're sending me pictures. They look like they're on a photoshoot for *Hello Magazine* with their ski gear and sunglasses. Natasha's house in Val-d'Isere looks amazing. I don't know how the kids are going to go back to their student accommodation after this."

A kerfuffle in the lobby distracted Suze from her sadness. The usually unflappable receptionist was banging buttons on the phone on the front desk.

"What do you think is going on?" asked Suze.

317

"I haven't a clue. Maybe a guest has been taken ill," said Laurie.

They all felt a slight chill at the thought of somebody experiencing illness or worse on Christmas Day.

They went back to their conversation but couldn't shrug the uneasy feeling.

"Well, there ye are," said a voice behind them.

Diane bristled at the sound of Mrs. Murphy's West Cork lilt.

"'Tis lovely to see ye."

What the hell was she doing here, thought Diane.

"Mrs. Murphy! Happy Christmas!" said Laurie, hugging the old woman gently.

The others chimed in with their Christmas cheer but Diane couldn't bring herself to do it. The old biddy was the reason for her misery for the past three months. If she hadn't been such a bloody gossip, then she and Oliver could have been together all that time.

Mrs. Murphy sat down and, in a reversal of roles, Laurie poured a cup of tea for her.

"So? To what do we owe this pleasure?" asked Diane.

"Mrs. Flynn invited me," replied Mrs. Murphy snootily.

Diane looked quizzically at Laurie.

"Mrs. Murphy is coming back to LA with us. She's going to help me look after the baby," said Laurie.

Diane's mouth hung open and Sarah had to tell her to close it. She couldn't believe it. Why would anybody in their right mind voluntarily take it upon themselves to house Celia Murphy?

"I am. I'm going to Cali-for-ni-a. And I'm going to learn to Zumba," said Mrs. Murphy.

"That's wonderful," said Sarah. "What a great adventure."

Diane gave Sarah a dirty look.

"What? I think it's great," said Sarah.

Diane rolled her eyes. Laurie would be lucky if she didn't end up looking after the baby herself and looking after an old woman to boot. She worried that Laurie hadn't given it proper thought.

"I missed Mrs. Murphy when I got back to LA. It's going to be great to have a little piece of Ballygra with me in Hollywood."

Diane was about to say that if she wanted a piece of Ballygra, she could always take back a handful of soil. It would be far less maintenance. But it looked like the decision was made and Mrs. Murphy was heading stateside.

The commotion in the lobby was gaining momentum.

"What is going on out there?" said Suze.

"Someone's been shot," said Mrs. Murphy. "At the shoot."

"Shot?" said Laurie. "You mean with a gun?"

"*Ara*, sure what else? That's the problem with giving men guns. They think they're in a western."

They left her sitting there and ran to the reception desk.

"We actually don't have any information yet," lied the receptionist.

He had been given strict instructions not to release the name of the person who was shot and above all to keep an air of calm around the place.

They realised they weren't going to get any information from the well-trained staff member so they ran to the front of the hotel. There was a golf buggy and Diane told the others to hop on.

"We could run faster than this thing," argued Sarah.

"In these shoes?"

They all looked down at their footwear.

"You're right," she said and hopped on followed by Laurie and Suze.

"An ambulance is going that way, look!" said Sarah, pointing to the vehicle with its siren blaring.

Diane mounted steps and kerbs but managed to head in the general direction of the ambulance. Nobody could speak as they were all caught up in the horror of who might be lying dead on the cold ground. Laurie rubbed her little bump and prayed that Kevin was OK.

Sarah twisted her engagement ring on her finger and found she could hardly breathe with the anxiety. She couldn't bear it if Tom was hurt or, worse, dead. She wouldn't allow her mind to go to that dark place.

Suze worried for all of them. She didn't want any of her friends to suffer.

Diane didn't think. She drove. She weaved in and out of paths that were set out to be pleasure walks and she cursed how bloody slowly the cart went.

They saw the ambulance parked and Diane stopped the cart and told them all to get off. They ran towards the sirens and the large huddle of men. They each searched the crowd for the faces they so badly wanted to see.

Jesus was standing with Kevin. Joe and Paolo were close by too, holding each other. It was obviously bad by the look on the men's faces.

Sarah and Diane couldn't see the faces they loved. They ran through the crowd and pushed their way to the centre. Tom and Oliver were there. Oliver was lying motionless on the ground. Tom was kneeling down over him doing CPR.

Tom's jacket was under Oliver's head and some of the other men had put their jackets over him to try to keep him warm. Diane let out a pained cry. There was blood all over his chest. You could hardly tell that he had put on a white shirt that morning.

The beautiful man who had made love to her was lying there, not moving, wounded. She knelt down and was at eye level with Tom. He looked exhausted. He was keeping his rhythm and broke eye contact with her. He had a job to do.

The ambulance pulled up and the medics took over from Tom. Tom leaned back on his ankles and let his arms go limp. Diane was shoved out of the way by the medics and they started their work.

Sarah went to Tom and held him close to her. She was thankful that it wasn't him lying on the ground and she felt Diane's pain. Suze and Laurie had picked Diane up and they stood as Oliver was lifted onto a stretcher and put in the back of the ambulance.

"Hold on. I want to go with him," said Diane, jumping in.

Sarah jumped in too. She didn't want Diane to be on her own. She held Diane's hand all the way to the hospital and they watched as the medics worked on him.

"Only for that doctor at the scene, your husband wouldn't be alive right now," said the medic.

Diane didn't correct the guy's assumption that they were married.

"That doctor. He's my fiancé. He's wonderful," said Sarah.

The machines on board the ambulance beeped and lit up and Diane thought her nerves wouldn't survive the journey. She watched the machine that was helping him to breathe and she focused on that. Once the line was going up and down, he was alive. She didn't take her eyes off it. He was breathing. He was alive. That was all she needed to know for now.

They arrived at the hospital and Oliver was whizzed away by a team of doctors and nurses.

"We'll sit and wait," said Sarah, leading Diane to the waiting room.

She went to find out where they'd taken him and went back to Diane.

"He's gone to theatre. They wouldn't tell me anything cos we're not family."

"I don't even know if he has any family. This is crazy. I'm in love with a man and I know nothing about him. Oh God, Sarah. What if he doesn't make it? What if he dies?"

"Stop that. He's not going to die. He has too much to

live for. He has you. He has Ballygra. He has his whole life ahead of him. Imagine you and him together in the future. You're both happy. Focus on that. That's what Suze told me when we were on our way to Rosa in hospital. It works. Really it does. Happy thoughts."

Diane thought about waking up and looking at his beautiful face and when he opened his sparkly eyes. Even first thing in the morning, they sparkled. She thought about those eyes and leaned into the crook of Sarah's arm.

Chapter 44

"What happened? Who shot him?" asked Suze. They were all back inside the hotel lobby, drinking hot whiskies for the shock and the cold.

"Jesus did," said Joe.

Suze didn't want to hear that. Diane would somehow blame her. Jesus was being treated for shock by the local doctor and Suze hadn't seen him yet.

"How? I didn't think they were real bullets," said Suze.

"How would you shoot something without real bullets?" said Joe.

"I don't know," said Suze. "Should people not be trained in using weapons before they're allowed to pick up a gun?"

"Jesus was just sort of joking around," said Joe. "It was just a freak accident. He was re-enacting some scene from some video game for Kevin. Then Oliver walked into his line of fire and, *bang*, the shotgun went off."

"Do you think he'll be OK?" Laurie asked Tom.

"I don't know. His breathing was very shallow. I think we actually lost him at one stage, but I got his heartbeat back. It really depends on the guys in the ambulance."

Just then Jesus appeared. He looked like hell. He had a blanket wrapped around him to try to stop the shaking. Suze went to him and held him close. He started to cry and Suze took him upstairs to his room.

"Are you going to be OK?" asked Suze.

"I didn't mean it," sobbed Jesus.

"I know that. Everybody knows it."

"I was joking around. I was just fooling."

He started to cry again and Suze couldn't do anything except lie beside him and comfort him. He was like a child. A boy-child who confused real life with video games.

She waited until he was asleep and then got up and went downstairs to join the others.

"I'm going to the hospital. Kevin, will you keep an eye on Jesus please?. He's asleep but he's in a bad way. Somebody needs to stay with him."

"I'll go with you," said Laurie.

"I will as well," chimed in Mrs. Murphy.

Suze wasn't sure about that. Diane would be upset enough. But there was no telling Mrs. Murphy no to anything. She followed the women and got into the car.

They got to the hospital and found Diane and Sarah in the waiting room. Diane's eyes were red and swollen. They had been there for two hours and hadn't been told anything other than Oliver was still in surgery. Diane was so distressed that she didn't even seem bothered by Mrs. Murphy's presence.

"Sure they have to know something," said Mrs. Murphy for what seemed the hundredth time. She got up from her seat and left the waiting room.

"Sorry, she insisted on coming," said Suze.

Diane didn't seem to be aware of who was there.

Mrs. Murphy came back in and sat down.

"He's out of surgery. They got the most of the shell out of his chest. It missed his heart though. Did she say by a couple of inches? Do you know, I can't rightly remember what she said. Will I go and ask her again?"

"What? How do you know? They said they'd only give it to family!" said Diane, jumping up out of her seat.

"I told them I'm his mother. Sure a little white lie won't kill anybody."

Diane grabbed the old lady and ran back out the desk with Mrs. Murphy in tow.

"Can we see my, *em*, her son?" asked Diane.

"Name?" said the desk clerk.

"Diane Foster."

"The patient's name," the clerk said flatly.

"Oh yes, sorry. Oliver Butler."

The clerk clicked the mouse and read the screen.

"The patient is in the Intensive Care Unit. One visitor at a time. Are you related?" she asked Diane.

"I'm his ... fiancée" said Diane. She could see Mrs.

Murphy giving her a look. The cheek of her. She had just told the same clerk that she was Oliver's mother.

"That's fine. Take that lift to the third floor. There's a nurse's station there and they will show you where to go."

They hurried to the lift.

"Fiancée?" said Mrs. Murphy with arched eyebrows.

"Mammy?" replied Diane.

"It got you in, didn't it?"

The women rode the lift in silence. Diane didn't know what to expect when she got to the ICU. He had been so pale earlier and the amount of blood made her want to gag.

A kind nurse they met showed them to the ICU. They looked through the glass at him. He was hooked up to so many tubes and wires that Diane almost started to howl again.

"Don't be too traumatised by all the attachments," said the nurse. "A lot of them are for monitoring and not administering anything. The surgeon managed to get most of the pellets out and he repaired a tear near his heart muscle. His breathing is steady and his blood pressure is stable. He's as good as we could expect after being shot at point-blank range." She didn't say anything about him making a full recovery or even making any sort of recovery.

Diane felt a hand on hers and Mrs. Murphy rubbed her back.

"Go in and tell him you're here, girleen," she said, propelling Diane forward into the room.

The only sound was the hum of the machines and the

reassuring beep that told her he was still breathing. She wanted to touch him but it was out of the question. There wasn't a part of him that there wasn't a drip coming out of. He hadn't shaved that morning and his stubble looked rough against his smooth skin. She had delayed him. He would look clean shaven if she hadn't tempted him back into bed.

"Oliver," she started to say but a sob caught in her throat. She didn't want him to hear her crying. He'd want to hear her strong voice if he was going to recover. "It's me. I want you to know that I'm going to be here until you wake up. So whenever you're ready, I'm waiting for you. I love you."

She'd said the three little words. It didn't have any effect that she could tell. He still lay there motionless and the machines sounded louder still.

———

Suze, Sarah and Laurie went back to the hotel as only Oliver's "fiancée" and "mother" were allowed in to see him. When they pulled up outside the castle they were met by the sight of the gardaí trying to get Jesus into a squad car. He didn't even look at the women as they passed. Suze ran to him but a policeman told her to stay back. Laurie ran to Kevin who was trying to reason with the guards and trying to find out where they were taking him.

"They arrived five minutes ago and arrested him for dangerous and reckless behaviour with a firearm," he said.

"But it was an accident!" cried Suze.

"I'd better follow him to the station. You ladies wait here."

Suze wanted to go too but Laurie talked her down. They would end up waiting like spare parts in the Garda station too. Their presence wasn't wanted anywhere it seemed.

Chapter 45

Diane didn't leave Oliver's bedside. She held his hand and willed him to come around. Doctors and nurses drifted in and out, taking blood pressure, checking machines. They didn't say anything. Not saying anything was bad. And good, Diane argued with herself. She didn't want them to say that he wasn't going to make it. She couldn't bear that. He had to get better. He had to wake up.

"And who are you?"

Diane turned around to see a glamorous older woman looking her up and down.

"*Eh, em*, I'm Oliver's fiancée," she replied.

"Well, it seems I'm your mother-in-law-to-be in that case," said the woman.

Oliver's mother! *Fuck*, thought Diane.

"Although I had a job convincing the nurses of who I actually am. There seems to have been some other person claiming to be me. Really! Why would someone do something like that at a time like this?"

"*Eh*, I've no idea. Terrible," said Diane.

She decided that it wouldn't be a good time to come clean about not actually being engaged to her son.

"I'm Diane."

"Evelyn Butler."

The face was unlined and Diane wasn't sure it was down to good genes or a few needles full of botox.

"Richard told me what happened. Some crazy American with a gun shot him. How on earth could it have happened?"

"It was an accident. That's all I know."

"The doctor said he's stable."

"He is? That's good, isn't it?"

"Yes, I should say."

"He'll pull through?"

"He's tough, is my Ollie. Tough as nails. Of course he will."

They sat on either side of him, holding a hand each.

"So how did you two meet?"

"We met in Ballygra. In the local pub actually."

Diane remembered Oliver coming to the house the following day and wanting him to leave her alone. The situation was completely reversed now and she never wanted him to leave her.

"Have you known each other long? I'm very cross, you know. He told me that he'd tell me if he was about to get serious again. Especially after the last marriage debacle. They were totally unsuited. I told him at the wedding that it wouldn't last. But you know men. They never listen to anybody. They always know best."

They both heard a snort. Oliver started to cough but the tubes in his throat were threatening his breathing. Diane rang the buzzer beside his bed.

A crew of doctors and nurses almost knocked the women out of the way. They were forced out of the room while the medics crowded around his bed. Their view of Oliver was blocked. Diane was frozen to the spot and she felt Oliver's mum stiffen beside her. The curtains were drawn around his bed as the medics did their thing.

The two women stood by helplessly. Diane wanted to scream at the doctors and nurses to ask what the hell was going on. He was going to die and she couldn't stand it. She put her forehead on the glass and started to cry. She cried for the future she would have to live without him.

Then she thought of his mother standing beside her. She could see the worry in her beautiful old face. The poor woman was in serious danger of losing her son. It wasn't natural to watch your child die. It was another one of the reasons Diane didn't want to be a parent. She didn't want to be vulnerable to that kind of love and that level of pain.

It seemed like she was going to experience that pain anyhow. She doubled over and, only for Oliver's mother holding her, she would have ended up in a heap on the floor. Then she pulled herself together. If his mother could bear her pain stoically, then so could Diane.

An eternity passed before the curtains opened again. She wondered if they had pulled a sheet up over his face. Would she be allowed to lift it and look at him one last time?

One of the doctors moved aside and nobody moved into the space he had vacated. She saw him. He was awake. He was alive.

"Mr. Butler has been through a serious trauma and needs his rest. I'm afraid you won't be able to see him yet," said one of the doctors.

Diane and Oliver's mother sat in the corridor and waited for hours until eventually they were given the go-ahead to see him.

Diane went first. She tentatively approached the bed.

Oliver smiled up at her.

"How are you?" she asked. It was a stupid question. He had been shot at point-blank range in the chest.

"Horny," he said.

"Stop it! Your mother is right outside the door."

"You don't know why they think you're my fiancée, do you?" he asked mischievously.

Diane felt herself go bright red.

"It was Mrs. Murphy's idea," she started.

"Oh yeah?"

He wasn't going to make this easy for her.

"They wouldn't let us see you. Mrs. Murphy pretended

she was your mother. I had to be something too to get in. I didn't want to say wife in case they asked me to sign anything. I said fiancée."

"I'm glad you're here."

"I'm glad *you* are," she said, squeezing his hand.

"Oh, lord," he groaned, seeing his mother walk into the room.

"Well, really, Olly Bolly! Getting yourself shot – *tsk-tsk-tsk!*. I thought your father taught you all there was to know about guns," she said, air-kissing him on both cheeks.

"He did, Mother. But I didn't actually shoot myself. Somebody else did that," he said dryly.

"I jolly well hope he's arrested and charged with attempted murder," said Mrs. Butler.

"It was an accident. I saw his eyes when the gun went off. He didn't mean it. He's was just as shocked as I was to hear the bang."

Diane didn't know if she could be as generous to someone who almost killed her.

"Well, I'm so glad you're going to be alright but I'm very cross with you, Olly. You promised me you'd tell me if you met someone you were serious about marrying."

Diane was about to tell Mrs. Butler the truth but Oliver spoke.

"We were going to tell you, weren't we, darling?" he said, taking Diane's hand in his.

"*Er, em.* Yes," she said, looking at him.

"It all happened so quickly, isn't that right?"

"Yes. It was quick and well ...."

Oliver pulled her down to him and kissed her with more strength than he deserved to have after his ordeal.

"Well, alright, let's not get carried away, shall we?" his mother said. "Olly, you'll have to give Diane Grandma's ring. It's been in the family for generations, Diane. You're very naughty to ask a beautiful woman to marry you and not give her the ring, Ollie."

"It's up to Diane, Mother. She might not want to wear an old-fashioned ring. She might like to pick out something herself," said Oliver, buying Diane an out.

She loved him all the more for it.

"Nonsense. Of course she'll love it. Here, let her see for herself," said Mrs. Butler, rooting in her original Chanel handbag and taking out a black-velvet pouch.

"What the hell, Mother? Have you been carrying Grandma's ring around just on the off-chance that I would get engaged?"

"Don't be ridiculous, Olly. I carry all the Butler jewellery with me all the time. There's been so many break-ins lately."

"For the love of God. There's a greater chance of getting your bag snatched than getting broken into in Ballygra. You need to give me that jewellery to put in the hotel safe."

Diane stood by and watched the exchange. He was very sweet to his mother. That was a good sign, she thought.

He took the pouch from his mother and said: "Mother, would you mind giving us some privacy. Please?"

She left without demur, a faint smile on her face.

As the door closed, Oliver took Diane's hand.

"Diane, if I could get out of bed, I would get down on bended knee. But as that's not even a remote possibility, I'll just say: I wonder if you will do me the honour of being my wife?"

"You don't have to do this, you know. We could just tell your mum the real reason I lied."

"Don't you understand? I want to marry you. I think I've known it since the first time I met you in the pub in Ballygra. When you fell into my arms that night, I knew you were the one for me."

Diane's eyes started to water.

"Of course I'll marry you."

Oliver opened the little velvet pouch and took out the ring that had belonged to his grandmother and generations of Butler women before her.

Diane hoped it wasn't hideous. She had got off to a bad start with her future mother-in-law and didn't want to make matters worse by refusing to wear a family heirloom as an engagement ring. She needn't have worried. It was the furthest thing from hideous she had ever seen. The large emerald was surrounded by dozens of tiny diamonds. She put out her hand to his as Oliver slipped the stunning piece of jewellery onto her finger.

"It's beautiful!" she gasped.

"You're beautiful," he replied.

She bent to kiss him and noticed that the sparkle had returned to his eyes. She vowed to make sure he never lost that sparkle, ever again.

Chapter 46

Ballygra Castle was just as amazing in the summer as it was at Christmas. It was almost dusk and rows of candles lit Sarah's way to the registrar who stood under a flower-bedecked arch down by the shore. Joe stood by Sarah's side and she turned around when she heard him blowing his nose. Again.

"Joe, please. You have to stop sniffling. This is meant to be a happy time. You're going to set me off if you don't pull yourself together."

"OK, OK, I'm sorry," he said as he put away the silk handkerchief that had started out as a pocket square. "It's just that you look so beautiful," and he nearly started to cry again.

Sarah was wearing a gown from La Choise. As soon as Tom had proposed on Christmas Eve, Diane had informed her that she had seen the perfect wedding dress for her. And it was. As soon as Sarah saw it, she knew she wouldn't need to spend weeks or months trawling through wedding-dress shops. It was silk tulle with a big fluffy skirt that reminded her of all the beautiful confections that she and The Bakery had become famous for.

The quartet struck up and it was time for Sarah to make her way to Tom's side. She heard the sniffling again and decided to let Joe cry like a baby if that's what he needed to do. It was an emotional time for all of them.

May was walking ahead of them, keeping an eye on Rosa who was flinging rose petals rather than gently tossing them on the red carpet that ran between the lines of candles which were in glass lanterns. May was nervous about Rosa tripping and falling on top of one of the lanterns, and Sarah watched her take her little sister's hand to keep her steady on her feet and out of harm's way.

All of their friends and family were there to celebrate their marriage. Diane had taken her place back beside Oliver after making sure that the dress was sitting and fitting correctly. They made such a handsome couple. Oliver had made a full recovery from his ordeal and their insurance company had decided that there would be no more Christmas morning shoots at Ballygra.

The shooting turned out to be a blessing in disguise for Oliver and Richard. Footage of Jesus Martinez and Ballygra Castle had been beamed all around the globe. As a result of all of the media attention, the castle was booked out for months in advance.

Laurie and Kevin were there with Luna Stella Flynn, their

beautiful little girl, named for the moon and the stars. It had been a shock for them when Luna turned out to be, in fact, a girl. Diane had to bite her tongue so hard not to say *I Told You So*. Sarah was proud of Diane's restraint. They were all secretly delighted that Laurie was free to pick a name more befitting of a child of one of Hollywood's golden couples. Sarah could see Luna's sleeping head on Kevin's shoulder and was again full of happiness for them.

Suze was standing beside her friends. She didn't bring a plus one. She didn't have a special person in her life and she decided that she didn't need anybody to make her feel whole.

Tom turned around to watch Sarah walking up the aisle towards him. Towards becoming Mrs. Sarah Byrne O'Hara Harrison. It was a bit of a mouthful but Sarah insisted that the name represented who she was and who she was becoming. She had also decided that there would be no further additions to the name.

Rosa saw Tom first and made a beeline for him, shouting "*Daddy! Daddy!*" and flinging rose petals at him. "*Up, up!*" she cried. May led her away but she started to howl.

"You look amazing," said Tom, taking Sarah's hand from Joe's.

"You're not looking too shabby yourself," she said and she smiled. She thought she would surely burst with happiness.

Rosa's wailing had woken Luna who now wailed in unison with her. Tom walked over to May and picked Rosa up and then took May by the hand.

The new family stood hand in hand while Tom and Sarah were pronounced husband and wife.

———

"Are you sorry we didn't have all this?" Oliver whispered into Diane's ear.

"Are you mad? I'd hate all this fuss. I loved that it was just the two of us."

Diane and Oliver had gone to City Hall and had tied the knot without any fuss. Diane wore an off-white trouser suit that was part of a new collection she was stocking in La Choise. The only jewellery she wore was Oliver's grandmother's ring which she treasured and adored.

Oliver looked more handsome than she had ever seen him look before. Once he had removed the pieces of toilet paper where he had cut himself shaving that morning, he was to Diane the most gorgeous man in the world.

They promised to love and honour each other for as long as they both lived. Oliver had promised to do a few other things that were not for the ears of the registrar as they walked along Dame Street after the ceremony. She told him to stop but secretly she loved it. She couldn't wait to be alone with him. As they strolled along, Diane was shocked to realise that she had been there before. Walking hand in hand with Oliver was the happy place she went to when she worried in the ambulance that she was going to lose him.

Chapter 47

Suze was exhausted by the time she got back to Dublin. She loved Ballygra Castle but she was glad to be back in her own little house. She loved having the door open and hearing the waves lapping gently outside. She sat at the table and opened her laptop. She had tonnes of emails and she endeavoured to sort through them and see which ones she needed to prioritise.

She heard footsteps behind her.

"Hi."

"*Jesus fucking Christ!* You scared the crap out of me."

"Sorry. I thought you heard the door open," said Seán.

He looked tanned and rested and Suze couldn't believe how happy she was to see him. Despite the fact that he nearly gave her a heart attack.

"What are you doing here? I mean, I thought you were in Melbourne. I wasn't sure if you were ever coming back."

"I wasn't sure myself, to be honest."

"Oh. So are you here for work?" She hoped it wasn't just work that had brought him home.

"I came back for you."

"Oh."

"I know you don't owe me anything, Suze, but I had to give it one last go. I had to come back and tell you how I feel."

He looked at Suze and took encouragement from the fact that she was still listening and not running for the hills.

"I love you. I don't want to live without you."

Suze felt like all the pieces of her life suddenly fell into place. Seán was the missing piece. She had everything she wanted. She had two beautiful children who were on their way to becoming wonderful adults. She had a house she loved. A home that was given to her out of love. She had a job that she could never have dreamed about for most of her life. She was in a place emotionally where she felt that she thoroughly deserved all of it. Seán was the icing on the cake.

She missed him. *Him*. She missed the ease of him and his gentleness. His sense of fun and humour. She missed laughing her arse off in his kitchen in the middle of those sleepless nights.

And his physical presence. His strong arms. His handsome face. It hit her like a tonne of bricks how much she wanted him to kiss her.

"I'm sorry. I shouldn't have … I … should have called first."

"I'm glad you did."

Seán took her in his arms and kissed her long and hard.

"I've thought about nothing but kissing you since I left Australia," he said as they both came up for air.

"I don't want you to leave me again," Suze said as she took his hand and led him to her bed.

THE END